RAGE OF EAGLES

William W. Johnstone

Pinnacle Books
Kensington Publishing Corp.
http://www.williamjohnstone.com

PINNACLE BOOKS are published by

Kensington Publishing Corp.
850 Third Avenue
New York, NY 10022

Pinnacle and the P logo Reg. U.S. Pat. & TM Off.

First Printing: May, 1998
10 9 8 7 6 5 4 3 2 1

Printed in the United States of America

When you have nothing to say, say nothing.
Charles Caleb Colton

Prologue

Jamie and Kate MacCallister were together now, buried side by side on a ridge overlooking the huge valley they had settled and the town they had founded. It was up to their children now to carry on the MacCallister legacy—nine children, eight of them living through the harshness of the awakening land called the west.

A whole brood of blond-haired, blue-eyed kids who had produced another brood of blond-haired, blue-eyed kids. It was said in this part of Colorado that if one shook a tree, a MacCallister would more than likely fall out.

To say that Jamie Ian MacCallister was legend would be grossly understating history, although history, in its dry prose, never did justice to Jamie's exploits. Nor did history do justice to a MacCallister named Falcon. *Rage of Eagles* will attempt to set the record straight once and for all.

Some have written that Falcon MacCallister was a cold-blooded killer who terrorized the west, killing hundreds of men for sport after his wife's death in 1876. Actually, the number of men who fell under Falcon's guns was much lower than that, and there was no sport involved.

It is true that Falcon was a gunfighter, and it is also true that he was a skilled gambler, but it is not true that he was an outlaw and a highwayman. That is nonsense, for Falcon was a rich man at the time of his wife's death. He began riding what some call the hootowl trail through no fault of his own.

Falcon MacCallister was the spitting image of his father, Jamie. He stood six foot three and was heavy with muscle. Just like his father, Falcon literally did not know his own strength. And just like his father, Falcon was quick on the shoot. Jamie and Falcon were both known as bad men. In the west, being a bad man did not necessarily mean being a brigand. It just meant he was a bad man to crowd.

And Falcon was definitely a bad man to crowd.

The kids of Jamie and Kate MacCallister pretty much stayed close to home, except for Andrew and Rosanna, who became famous musicians and actors and toured the world. A MacCallister was the sheriff of the county, another was the mayor of the town. They all possessed huge holdings and were all successful ranchers and miners and businesspeople. The town had regular stagecoach runs and a fairly reliable telegraph wire. It was a peaceful town, with a large bank, a newspaper, good schools, and several churches.

Outlaws and riffraff knew better than to start trouble in MacCallister's Valley. But occasionally, one would drift in with news of interest to all and he would not be bothered as long as he did not start any trouble. The news usually was of Falcon MacCallister.

In the six months or so since Falcon buried his wife, Marie, and then went on the drift, alone with his grief, not much had been heard of him.

All that was about to change.

One

It was time to move on. He had waited long enough. Falcon had holed up for a month in a tiny cabin built into the side of a mountain. His grandfather had told his father about it and Jamie had told Falcon. He had received word that Nance Noonan had sent an army of men in pursuit of him after the shooting in Utah during which two of Nance's brothers had been killed after an altercation with Falcon. With an army chasing him, Falcon had wisely holed up. It was now summer in the high country, the sun hot upon the land, and Noonan's hands would be busy moving herds of cattle, getting them ready to drive to market. They would not have time to hunt for him . . . at least not for a while.

Falcon had grown a beard during the time he'd been holed up in the cabin. Now he carefully sculpted the beard and trimmed his hair. He inspected his face in the piece of broken mirror he'd found in the cabin: a little older, his eyes a little wiser as they reflected back at him. He turned away from the mirror and rolled up his blankets in his ground sheet, then carefully tidied up the cabin. Someone else might need a place to bed down and Falcon didn't want to leave the cabin looking as though a hog had taken up residence during the summer.

He slung his saddlebags over one shoulder, picked up his rifle, and closed the door behind him.

Falcon was slap out of supplies: no salt, no coffee, no flour, no beans, no smoking tobacco, nothing. It was past time to saddle up and move on.

Shortly after the shoot-out, he'd had traded horses with a man from Idaho Territory who had trailed a herd of horses down south and was heading home with a few of his hands. Falcon had told the man who he was and what had happened, not wishing the man to get shot by Noonan's hands or some damn bounty hunter for riding the wrong horse.

"Son," the rancher had said slowly. "I know Nance Noonan, and I don't like Nance Noonan. I knew your pa, and I liked and respected Jamie MacCallister. Anytime Noonan wants to lock horns with me, he can damn sure start gruntin' and snortin'. Now, sit down and eat."

Falcon picked out a good packhorse, then chose a huge chestnut gelding with mean yellow eyes. He was one of the biggest riding horses Falcon had ever seen.

"You sure you want that horse, boy?" the rancher asked. "He's a mean one. I've come damn close to shootin' him several times since I acted the fool and traded for him. Can't nobody ride him. He's done stove up three of my hands. He'll stomp you if he gets half a chance."

"He won't stomp me," Falcon replied.

An hour later, Falcon rode away on the big chestnut horse.

"Well, I'll just be damned!" the rancher said. "I always heard them MacCallisters had a way with horses."

The rancher had said the horse had no name, but everybody who had tried to ride him got throwed off and when they hit the ground they always said, "Oh, hell!"

"That's good enough," Falcon said.

"What's good enough, son?" the rancher had asked.

"Hell. That's what I'll call him. 'Cause that's where he just might be taking me."

Falcon had holed up in Wyoming, on the east side of the Wind River Range. He stayed on the east side as he headed north toward a town just beginning to blossom.

No one gave him a second look as he rode in; most were busy hammering and sawing and stretching canvas over hastily erected wooden frames to serve as makeshift roofs.

Falcon registered at a hotel that was so new it still smelled of fresh-cut lumber and there were little piles of sawdust in the corners of the room.

He hid a smile as he signed the book: *Val Mack*.

"Mr. Mack," the clerk said with a smile. "Welcome to our town. Here on business?"

"No. Just passing through."

"Going to be a fine place to settle down and start a business. Town's booming. Enjoy your stay, Mr. Mack."

"I'm sure I will."

The room was small, but clean, and the bed comfortable. The sheets appeared to be fresh. At least there were no bugs hopping around . . . that Falcon could see. He'd know for sure come the morning.

Falcon wadded up some dirty clothes and took them over to a laundry, then he walked over to the general store and bought new britches, shirt, socks, and underwear. He also bought a box of .44s.

At a bathhouse, he soaked and scrubbed until he was clean and free of fleas and dirt, then had the barber shape up his beard and trim his hair. He felt a hundred percent better as he located a café and walked over for a meal.

The stew was hot and there was plenty of it, and the apple pie was tasty. But the coffee was too weak for Falcon's liking. He walked back to the livery to check on his horses . . . mainly to see if Hell had killed anyone who got too close to him. The big chestnut had his nose stuck in a feed bag and was quiet, as was Falcon's sturdy packhorse.

"Be careful around the chestnut," Falcon warned the liveryman.

"I done figured that out, mister," the stableman told Falcon.

Falcon went in search of the marshal's office, found it, but the door was locked.

"Out of town, mister," a little boy playing in the dirt of the alley said. "Won't be back for a couple of days."

Falcon thanked him and walked on. One less obstacle he'd have to hurdle. Not that he was all that worried about what the local law might do. In the early days of the settling of the west, local lawmen took care of local business. What happened outside their jurisdiction was of little concern to many sheriffs and marshals unless the man in question caused trouble in their town or county.

Falcon strolled the town's business district, which did not take all that long ... up one side and down the other. He did not want to attract undue attention by wandering through the residential areas. His tour of the town complete, Falcon went back to the hotel, took a chair under the awning on the board-walk in front of the hotel, and lit a cigar.

A cowboy, by the look of his clothes, walked up and sat down in the chair beside Falcon. They were the only ones sitting on the hotel's boardwalk. The cowboy pulled out a sack of tobacco and rolled him a smoke. He licked and lit and said in a whisper, "Your pa befriended me a few years back, Falcon. He was a good man. I was bad down on my luck and headed down the wrong trail. He seen some good in me where nobody else could and straightened me out. You ride careful. Nance Noonan's got friends all over the damn place; any direction you want to ride for five hundred miles. What they're doin' is, they're all workin' to set up a cattle empire. I don't know if they'll be able to pull it off, but if they do, small ranchers won't have a chance. Rod Stegman married Nance Noonan's sister. He owns the .44 Brand. And Rod is one mean son of a bitch and his sons is all about half crazy. Same with his brothers, and they's about six or seven of them. They're all power-drunk. But the thing is, when one itches, they all scratch."

"And I cause them to itch," Falcon said.

"You shore do. In the worst way. Noonan and Stegman and some of the others has had riders out all summer lookin' for you. It's about to drive Nance even nuttier than he is already. They's federal warrants out for you, Falcon. Chet Noonan really was a deputy federal marshal. I don't know how he got that appointment, but he did."

"Probably his brother arranged it. How about the marshal here?"

"Oh, he's all right. For the time bein', that is. But he better watch his back. If he tries to buck the powers that be, some of Nance's cohorts will put a bullet in him and stick that badge on one of their own. It's gettin' really bad out here, Falcon. Worser than most folks realize."

"I've been thinking about heading back to Colorado."

"I don't know where to tell you to head. Ain't no place gonna be very safe for you as long as they's a single Noonan or Stegman alive. And maybe some of their friends. They're all a bunch of thieves and murderers."

"How'd you recognize me?"

The puncher chuckled. "Man, you and your pa look so much alike it's scary."

Falcon smiled. "We do resemble some."

The cowboy stood up and toed out his cigarette butt on the boardwalk. "Watch your back trail, Mr. Mack."

"I'll do it, friend. And thanks. Cowboy?"

The puncher cut his eyes.

"If you're ever in Valley, Colorado, look up any MacCallister and tell them about this meeting. They'll help you out. No questions asked."

The cowboy touched the brim of his hat with his fingertips and walked away.

Falcon walked over to the general store and bought supplies enough to last for several weeks. A different clerk waited on him this time. Falcon added several boxes of .44s to the list, then asked, "You got any dynamite?"

"Sure do."

Falcon bought half a case, caps, and fuses, and carried the supplies over to the livery, stowing them in the stall with Hell. No one would steal them from under the baleful gaze of the big chestnut . . . not if they valued their life.

Falcon went back to the hotel, ate an early supper, then went to bed. He was riding out of town before dawn the next morning, heading for the grasslands and cattle country.

* * *

He skirted a small settlement—which would be very nearly a ghost town in a few more years—giving it a wide berth, and kept riding, riding for days. He saw signs of Indians, but if they saw him—and they probably did—they decided to leave him alone. Then he remembered a trading post and cut toward it.

Falcon looked the place over carefully before riding on in. There were some saddled horses at the hitchrail that looked as though they'd been hard-ridden. He couldn't make out the brands and it wouldn't have made any difference if he could have read them. He was tired of riding around trouble. If there was trouble waiting for him at the trading post, so be it.

Falcon rode up and swung down at the rear of the building, now more of a huge general store than a trading post. He remembered the saloon section was at the west end of the long, low building, a partition separating the drinking area from the general merchandise part of the store. Falcon slipped the hammer thongs from his pistols as he walked around the building, entering the trading post from the front. He quickly stepped to one side, allowing his eyes time to adjust to the sudden dimness after hours of bright sunlight.

The interior of the place had been changed. There were now tables off to one side for eating. Falcon sat down at one, his back to a wall. He faced the closed door that led to the saloon. An Indian woman—he remembered the owner had married an Indian—walked over to the table and stared at him for a moment. Then her eyes filled with recollection. She cut them toward the saloon and Falcon nodded in understanding.

She smiled faintly and said, "Got stew. It's good."

"Bring me a plate. And a pot of coffee."

The stew was beef and potatoes, spiced with onions, and it was hot and good. The fresh baked bread was tasty and the coffee was good and strong. Falcon was working on his second plate of food when he heard horses outside, then a wagon rattle up. The Indian woman looked first at the front door, then at the closed door to the saloon, then at Falcon. She sighed audibly. Falcon made the sign for trouble and she nodded her head.

Falcon resumed his eating; the stew really was good and he was hungry.

The front door pushed open and a man who looked to be in his late fifties stepped inside, a woman of about the same age behind him. They were followed by another man of about the same age, then a young woman and a boy of about ten or so. Falcon could tell by their clothing and boots they weren't farmers. Small ranchers, he figured.

A man suddenly parted the curtains that led to the living quarters behind the counter and gave Falcon a very startled look.

So much for my growing a beard, Falcon thought. I might as well shave the damn thing off. Everybody I've run into has recognized me.

Falcon took a second look at the young woman. She was a beauty. Blond hair, pretty face, and a figure that would warrant a second look from a corpse. She was also dressed in men's britches, something that was rare in these days. The lad with the young woman was blond and the two bore a strong resemblance. The younger woman and the older woman also bore a resemblance and Falcon figured them for mother and daughter. The daughter must have married young, Falcon thought. She cut her eyes to Falcon and he smiled at her. He got a frown in return and feeling somewhat rebuked, went back to eating his stew.

"Mr. Bailey," the store owner said. "Mrs. Bailey. How y'all today?"

"Fine," the older man said. "We've come for our supplies."

The man with Bailey, whom Falcon figured to be the foreman, stepped to one side and faced the closed door leading to the saloon. Falcon noticed he was all ready to hook and draw.

Mother and daughter moved to the bolted cloth section of the store. The older man, Falcon figured the husband of the woman and the father of the younger woman, paused and gave Falcon a look. It was not an unfriendly gaze.

"Afternoon," Falcon said, tearing off a hunk of bread.

"Afternoon," the man replied. "Haven't seen you around here before."

"Just passing through."

"Maybe he's one of them hired guns of Gilman," the young boy blurted.

"Hush, Jimmy," the grandfather said. He lifted his eyes to Falcon. "He didn't mean nothin' by that remark, mister."

"I didn't take anything by it," Falcon said. "Who is Gilman?"

"The man who figures himself to be the he-coon of this area," the other man said. "Part of the cattlemen's alliance."

"Well, I don't know what that is either," Falcon replied. "I'm a long way from home ground."

That ended the chitchat and Falcon returned to his half-finished plate of stew and another cup of coffee. He was just sopping up the gravy with the last hunk of bread when the door to the saloon was flung open and several men stomped into the room. Falcon recognized one of them immediately. A bully and hired gun from down New Mexico way who was known as Red Broner. Falcon didn't know the other three but could tell they were of the same stripe as Red: hired guns who probably didn't know one end of a cow from the other. They had all been drinking and were now looking for trouble. Falcon sat motionless at the table, which was partly obscured by shadows in the dimly lit room. So far, the gunnies had not noticed him.

"Well, now," Red said, an ugly tone behind the words. "If it ain't the Bailey family done come to pay us all a visit. I figured you folks would have turned tail and run off by now."

"You figured wrong, Red," the foreman said, leaning against a counter.

Red cut his eyes. "Old man, you keep that mouth of yourn shut 'fore I shut it up permanent."

"Anytime you feel lucky, Red," the foreman said, straightening up, his right hand close to the butt of his pistol.

Bailey stepped between the two men, and cut his eyes to the foreman. "That'll do. We came in for supplies. Not trouble." He lowered his voice to a whisper and added, "I need you alive, Kip."

"All right, John," the foreman said in a low tone. "This time."

"I reckon two old men would near 'bouts make one whole man, don't you, Red?" another of the hired gunnies spoke.

"Now, that makes right smart sense to me," Red replied. "We could get shut of some pesky little trouble for the boss right here and now." He turned to face John Bailey. "How about that, Bailey? You think that's a right smart idea?"

"You leave my grandpa alone!" Jimmy yelled, running up and hitting Red in the belly with a small fist.

Red laughed and shoved the boy away.

Another of the hired gunnies laughed. "Hell, the boy's got more nerve than both them old men."

Jimmy lunged at Red and this time Red backhanded the boy, knocking him to the floor.

Before either the grandfather or the foreman could react, Falcon stood up. It was time for him to step in and get dealt some cards in this game. He knew that Red was pretty quick on the draw and doubted that either Bailey or Kip were really gunhands; just hard-working ranchers.

"Don't hit the boy," Falcon said.

All eyes turned toward Falcon, a tall figure standing in the shadows.

"This ain't none of your affair, mister," Red said. "Stay out of it."

"I'm making it my affair," Falcon told him.

"Do tell," another hired gun said. "And who might you be?"

"Val Mack," Falcon said. "If names make any difference."

"Well, Val Mack," Red spoke slowly, squinting his eyes, trying to get a better look at Falcon in the dimness of the large room. "You buyin' chips in a losin' hand here. You know who we ride for?"

"No, and I don't care."

"I'll take the drifter, Red," the fourth gunny spoke.

"He's all yourn, Green," Red said. "But he's got to be some sort of idgit for stickin' his nose in this."

Jimmy had retreated to the safety of his mother's arms. The

women stood off to one side, backed up against the front wall
of the building. The owner and his wife were behind the counter,
ready to hit the floor when the lead started flying.

"Your play, Green," Falcon spoke the words very softly.

Green smiled. His teeth were rotting and yellow. "OK, tinhorn. Now!" He grabbed for his pistol.

Two

Falcon shot Green in the chest before the so-called fast gun's hand could close around the butt of his .45. Green slammed back and sat down on the floor of the store.

"Jesus," breathed the foreman, Kip.

Falcon holstered his .44 and turned slightly, to face Red. "Looks like I won that hand, Red. Now, you big-mouth son of a bitch, it's your turn. You going to fold, call, or raise?"

Red suddenly looked a little sick around the mouth. He'd been around, he'd seen some fast gunhands, but he had never seen anything even come close to this tall stranger. Who the hell was this guy?

"Red," one of his men said. "Gilman needs to know about this. Let's ride."

"Good idea, Red," Falcon said. "You just tuck your tail 'tween your legs and slink on out of here. Run home to your master and whine. And take these rabid coyotes with you."

"He's crazy in the head, Red," another of the gunnies said. "Got to be. Let's get the hell gone from here. This guy's plumb loco."

"Drag Green out with you," Falcon told them.

"You're a dead man, Val Mack," Red said, his voice just a tad shaky.

"Shut up and get out of here!" Falcon replied.

"We're gone, Mack," a gunny said, bending down and grabbing Green by the armpits, dragging him toward the door. The other gunny grabbed Green's feet and he was toted out the front, slung over his saddle, and roped down.

But Red wouldn't leave it alone. He just had to run his mouth one more time.

"Val Mack ain't your real name, mister. What is it?"

"Well now, Red," Falcon said, "some folks say I'm part timber wolf, part grizzly bear, and part puma. I've been called lots of things in my life . . ." Falcon smiled, letting the lie grow bigger. ". . . but Val Mack is my real name. But you can just call me the better man."

That did it. Red flushed and said, "Why you dirty son of a bitch!" He jumped at Falcon.

Falcon reached up and jerked a bridle off a nail on a post. The bridle was fancy, with lots of silver work on it, and it was heavy. Falcon proceeded to beat the snot out of Red with the silver-inlaid bridle, the bit drawing blood each time Falcon swung. Falcon hit him in the face about a dozen times, until finally Red was begging for mercy.

"Ride, Red!" Falcon told him. "And you walk real light around me should we ever meet up again. Now, get out of here!"

Red crawled out of the store on all fours and managed to get into the saddle and gallop off. Falcon hung the bridle back on the nail and returned to his coffee. It had cooled until it was just right to drink without scalding his lips.

Falcon sat back down and rolled a cigarette and drank his coffee.

"Who are you, mister?" Mrs. Bailey blurted. "Red is supposed to be one of the fastest guns around."

Falcon ignored the question and said, "He's a yellow-bellied, back-shootin' tinhorn. Tell me, how many small ranchers are in this area?"

"Not near as many as there was a year ago," John Bailey replied. "I reckon there's 'bout eight of us left."

"This Gilman playing the game rough, eh?"

"There's been some night ridin' and house and barn burnin's," Kip said. "And some killin'."

"And Gilman then picks up the property for ten cents on the dollar or so?"

"You got it. Them that's left alive to sell, that is," John added.

The trading post owner's wife came out with a mop and a bucket and began mopping the floor where Green had bled and died.

"We'd better get the supplies and get on back to the ranch, John," his wife said.

"What? Oh. Yes. Of course. I'd forgotten why we came in."

Falcon knew there was a little two-bit town not far from here and wondered why Bailey didn't shop there. Probably because Gilman owns the town, he concluded. He tried to think of the name of the town. Wasn't much of a town, as he recalled. A big general store, a saloon, a livery, a barber shop/bathhouse—the owner serving as the town's barber, doctor, and undertaker—couple of other buildings.

Falcon drank his coffee and watched as the trading post owner began bringing out and stacking up bags and boxes and sacks of supplies.

"You want some friendly advice, Mr. Mack?" the rancher's wife broke the silence.

"Sure."

"You'd better not dally too long. Soon as Gilman's gunhands report what happened here, Miles will be riding to find you."

"That's good advice, Mr. Mack," Kip said. "He's got a rough bunch working for him."

"Oh, I like it around here," Falcon replied. "I just might stay for a few days."

The trading post owner gave him a quick glance and rolled his eyes. The expression said silently: *I hope to hell you don't do it here!*

Falcon looked at the little boy, standing wide-eyed, staring at him. He walked to the counter and got a fistful of peppermint candy and handed it to Jimmy. "Here you go, boy."

"Kind of you, Mr. Mack," the boy's mother said.

"The boy's seen some awful sights this day, ma'am."

"He's seen killin' before," John Bailey said. "That ain't nothin' we're proud of. Just statin' a fact."

Falcon nodded his head in understanding while Jimmy chomped away at the stick candy. Too many kids in the west had to grow up awfully fast; many of them doing a man's job by the time they reached Jimmy's age, never really enjoying any carefree times as a youth.

The Indian woman had cleaned up the spot where Red died and disappeared into the back of the store. The two ranch women were busy shopping. John Bailey looked at Falcon and jerked his head toward the outside. Falcon stepped outside with the ranch owner and foreman.

"You wouldn't be lookin' for a job, now, would you, Mr. Mack?" John asked.

Falcon smiled. Due in no small part to his own ambition and also to his father's inheritance, Falcon was probably one of the richest men in the west. Jamie MacCallister had left all his kids enormously wealthy. "Well, sir, not really. But I do know something about cattle and horses. You need a hand for a few weeks?"

"We sure do," John replied.

"I can stick around for a few weeks," Falcon said. "Let me settle up for my meal and I'll follow you out to your ranch."

"Not even goin' to ask what we pay?" Kip questioned.

"No. Three hots and a cot will do me for a few weeks."

"You're mighty easy to please, Mr. Mack," John said.

"Oh, I'm really a very easygoing fellow," Falcon replied with a smile.

"So's a grizzly," Kip said very drily. "Till you mess with it."

Falcon chuckled. "Oddly enough, that's what some folks used to say about my pa."

"He must have been an interestin' man," John said.

"Oh, I think you'd be safe in saying that. Yes, sir. A real interesting man."

John Bailey's ranch was not small by anyone's standards, and he was running a pretty good sized head. Problem was, as John had explained on the ride out, he couldn't get them to market 'cause he couldn't hire hands. . . . Miles Gilman had put out the word and that was that in this part of the country.

Falcon smiled when he first saw the brand: the Rockingchair. John watched the smile form on Falcon's lips and chuckled.

"You like that brand, Val?"

"I do. That'll be difficult to change into anything else."

"You seen the Gilman brand?" Kip asked.

"No."

"Striking snake. A really ugly brand."

"Another unusual one."

"It fits him just right," John said. "Miles is a human rattle-snake."

The ranch house came into view, and it was a nice, strongly built home, plain, but practical. The bunkhouse sat off to one side. There was smoke coming from the ranch house chimney.

"Cookie," Kip explained. "He's too crippled up to ride much, but he's a good cook. And he hates Miles Gilman."

"Too many broncs bust him up?"

"No," John said. "Miles Gilman crippled him with a shot-gun. Shot him in the legs. Cookie can get around, but he limps badly. And he's got a touch of old age comin' on him, too. But he's a damn good man. He wouldn't back up from a puma."

"You real particular about your hands, John?" Falcon asked.

The rancher gave him a quizzical look. "I don't follow you, Val."

"Well, I know some old boys who don't scare worth a damn. But they aren't really cowboys."

"Can they sit a horse?"

"They can ride anything with hair on it. Including a grizzly bear."

John gave him another funny look and nodded his head. "But they would ride for the brand?"

"One hundred and ten percent."

"How long would it take for you to get them here?"

"Where's the nearest telegraph office?"

"In town. But town is dangerous."

"What's the name of this town?"

"Gilman."

Falcon laughed. He should have guessed. "Oh . . . I can have them here in a couple of weeks. Give us a couple of weeks to round up the cattle, and we can have them on the trail to the railhead."

"How many of these men can you get?" Kip asked.

"Oh . . . six, maybe seven. But I have to warn you, they're not spring chickens. They'll be men mostly in their late fifties and early sixties. Maybe a couple older than that."

John gave him another very curious glance as they rode up to the ranch house. "You're sure they can stand up to a cattle drive, Val?"

"I'm sure."

"Well," the rancher said. "Hell, get them. I sure ain't got nothin' to lose."

"I'll ride into town first thing in the morning. I'll leave early and get there just as the telegraph office is opening."

"Son," John said, "that town is a death trap."

"We'll see," Falcon replied with a smile.

"I'll get you fresh blankets for your bunk," Angie said, smiling at Falcon.

Amazing how attitudes can change so quickly, Falcon thought, hiding his smile. Five hours ago she wouldn't give me the day of the month. "That's very nice of you, Miss Angie."

"Angie, please," she said, batting her eyes at him.

Falcon helped carry the supplies into the house, got his blankets, and by the time he returned, a man with a bad limp had taken his horses down to the corral and was waiting to howdy and shake with Falcon. He had not attempted to unsaddle Hell.

"I'm Cookie," he said, holding out a callused hand.

Falcon took the hand, hard as a rock, and shook it. "Val Mack."

"Uh-huh," the older man said, just as Falcon got the distinct impression that somewhere down the line he'd met the man. "You know what you're gettin' onto here, Val?"

"A peck of trouble, I reckon."

"More like a wagon load, Val. Come on, let's walk over to the bunkhouse and get you settled in."

The bunkhouse was well built and snug, the bunk comfortable and long enough for Falcon's tall frame. He'd been in some fancy hotels where his feet hung over the end of the bed.

Cookie limped back to the house and Falcon unpacked his gear and stowed it away. Then he went down to the barn and brushed his horses and forked hay to them. He had noticed that Cookie wore a pistol all the time, so Falcon checked his own six-shooters and his rifle. He made sure all the ammo loops in his cartridge belt were full, then sat outside the bunkhouse on a bench, smoking a cigarette.

Nice spread, Falcon thought. *John Bailey's done well for himself and his family.*

Then he wondered what had happened to the man who'd fathered Angie's child. Dead? Drifted away like some men do? Fine-looking woman like that, he rather doubted the husband drifting off. Course, he smiled, she might have a temper like a wolverine. That had caused many a man to haul his ashes.

Then Falcon gave some serious thought to the men he'd try, and the optimum word was *try,* to get hold of, come the morning. He would send a wire to some settled-down friends of his, and then they would attempt to get hold of the ol' war-hosses . . . somehow. Money to get them here as quickly as possible was no object, for Falcon had money in banks and with investment houses and attorneys all over the west, under various names. He had five thousand dollars with him, in a money belt and in his saddlebags (now hidden under a loose board in the bunkhouse, which was loose no longer), in gold and greenbacks.

But Gilman was small potatoes compared to Nance Noonan and his nutty brothers, and on his way to the cabin where he'd holed up, Falcon had learned there were ten Noonan boys. Well . . . there were eight left, since Falcon had dispatched Chet and Butch. And each of the brothers had five or six kids.

"Jesus," Falcon whispered to the breeze. "Nance has an army just with his brothers and their kids."

Plus, Falcon knew, with all hands combined, there were at least a hundred men at Nance's command . . . probably more.

Well, Falcon thought, his pa'd had about that many men chasing him on more than one occasion. Falcon smiled at that, knowing that he wasn't quite the hoss Jamie Ian MacCallister had been. Close, but not quite.

Hell, no man was.

Falcon rose from the bench and went to the washbasin to clean up for supper, scrubbing his face and neck and hands with strong soap and drying off with a towel from a peg. He ran his fingers through his thick hair and then looked at his reflection in the piece of mirror affixed to a post. In the mirror, he caught movement and turned. Kip was walking up behind him.

"Supper's nearabouts ready, Val. John wants you to come up to the house now for a drink 'fore we eat."

"I could stand a drink." Falcon stared at the foreman for a moment. "A question or two, Kip?"

"Ask away. You got the right now that you've throwed in with us."

"What happened to Angie's husband?"

"Name was Charles. He was a good boy. Him and Angie got married when she was sixteen and he was seventeen. Had Jimmy a year later. 'Bout two years ago, Gilman's oldest son, Lars, braced Charles in town one afternoon. Hell, Charles wasn't no gunhand. He was a pretty good shot, but no fast gun. He didn't want to fight Lars. But you know how it is out here. Lars called him some really vile names and Charles jerked iron. Lars is almighty quick. Remember that, Val. He's fast. Lars gut-shot him and left him in the street to die. Took the lad about forty-eight hours to die. Died hard, too. I 'spect you've seen men who was belly-shot."

"Yes. It isn't pleasant."

''No, it shore ain't. Well, after the family shook off the grief, the war was on. But John Bailey didn't start the second round neither. Gilman did. We had ten hands here then. Not countin' me nor John nor Cookie. One by one Gilman's men scared them off or killed them off. You ever heard of a man calls hisself Border?''

''Oh, yes. Supposed to be one of the fastest guns anywhere around.''

''He is. Lightnin' quick. A killer through and through. He's crazy, I think. He's been on Gilman's payroll for about a year now. He can usually be found at the Stampede Saloon in town, waitin' like a damn rattlesnake for someone to say somethin' to him so's he can call them out and either back them down and run them out of town or kill them.''

''Nice fellow.''

''Just peachy,'' Kip said sourly.

''You reckon he'll be there about dawn tomorrow?''

''He lives at the saloon. Got him a room on the second floor. Why?''

'' 'Cause I plan to be in town about dawn.''

Kip sighed. ''I feel obliged to ride in with you.''

''If you want to.''

''I'll meet you at the corral about four.''

''Suits me. Now let's go eat supper. I'm hungry.''

Three

The town of Gilman had grown since Falcon had last seen it. And Falcon did not recall it being named Gilman.

"It wasn't when we first come out here," Kip said. "Then Gilman became top dog and decided the town should have his name."

"The people didn't object?"

"Them that did have the courage to kick up a fuss soon changed their mind about it. Or left."

"Seems like to me the territorial governor would have something to say about this situation."

"He don't even know what's really goin' on. He did send a man in, but nobody in town would talk to him. 'Sides, Gilman ain't really doin' nothin' illegal . . . that can be proved, that is. It's our word against his. If one of us says he done something, he's got fifty people who says he didn't."

"Is there an attorney in town?"

"One. But he's in Gilman's pocket. Gilman gave him a small spread he took away from the Nettles family after Tom Nettles turned up dead one night."

"Dead? How? And what did the sheriff say about it?"

Kip smiled, rather sadly, Falcon thought. "Sheriff's two

days hard ride away, with two deputies to cover the entire county. 'Sides, Gilman's bought him off too. He's not goin' to do a damn thing.''

The men were resting their horses on a small rise overlooking the town. Just looking at the town, it seemed quite pleasant. A bank and a church had been built since Falcon had last seen the place, and a dozen or more other homes and businesses.

"Gilman owns the bank?" Falcon asked.

"Shore does. The man's got all bets covered."

"Not all."

"What do you mean?"

"I just bought into this card game, and I'm a damn good gambler."

"But you're playing against a marked deck, son."

Falcon smiled. "I've played against a few of those in my time, too, Kip."

Kip grunted and pointed. "If drunk cowboys or crazy Injuns, or vicey-versie, ain't tore down the wires, the telegraph office is wedged in 'tween the general store and the barber shop."

"Fine. Should be opening up about right now. Is there a café in town?"

"Rosie's Café." Again, he pointed. "There. That's the only spot in town that's neutral ground. Or supposed to be. It don't always work that way. But it's the only really nice café where a man can take his family for eighty miles any direction you want to ride."

"I'll meet you there in a few minutes. We'll have breakfast."

"I could use some food in my belly."

Falcon sent his wires, using a name the Cheyenne had given him long before he married Marie. He did not request a reply. If the mountain men got the word and could make it, they would be here. If not, well, they wouldn't.

"Funny name," the telegrapher said with a frown. "Injun name."

"That's right."

"These messages don't make no sense to me."

"They will to the people who get them." Falcon stood by the cage, waiting.

"I'll send them in due time."

"You'll send them now. And I read the code, and read it well." Falcon wasn't bluffing. He had learned it as a boy. He stood by the cage and read each tap until the last message was sent. Then he tossed money on the counter and left. With any kind of luck, he and Kip should have had their breakfast and been on their way long before the telegrapher could have gotten word to Gilman.

However, the gunfighter who called himself Border was another matter.

On the boardwalk, Falcon looked over at the Stampede Saloon. The doors behind the batwings were still closed, and the swamper had not yet begun his work for that morning.

Falcon walked over to Rosie's Café and pushed open the door. The place was already about half filled with men. Kip was sitting at a table in the corner. The buzz of conversation stopped when Falcon stepped in, the men looking him over. Falcon ignored them and walked over to the table where Kip was waiting and sat down.

Falcon waited until the waitress had brought them huge mugs of coffee and taken their orders before asking in a low tone, "Which side are these men on?"

"Some are solid with Gilman, others just members of the alliance. But that don't mean they even like or really believe in what Gilman is doin'. Just that they're afraid of him."

"So you don't really know which way they'll go if someone stood up to Gilman and forced his hand?"

"For most of them, that's true." He smiled. "They're givin' you the once-over, that's for sure. I 'spect the story 'bout the gunfight at the tradin' post and what you done to Red has spread all over the area."

Falcon took a sip of his coffee. It was fresh and hot and good. The odor of potatoes frying and bacon and eggs cooking filled the café.

"Damn!" Kip suddenly blurted in a low tone.

"What's wrong?"

"Here comes Border crossin' the street."

Falcon was sitting to Kip's left, his back to a wall in the

corner, and he lifted his eyes to the street. Falcon had seen the gunslick a couple of times in the past. Not a big man, but lightning quick with a Colt. Take his guns away from him and he wouldn't be much at all.

The waitress brought their orders, large plates that could almost be called platters filled with fried potatoes, a huge slice of ham, and three eggs. Half a loaf of fresh-baked bread and butter and jam on the side. She placed their orders before them and the men dug in. Both men heard the bell on the front door chime as it was opened. Neither of them looked up.

"Damn good grub, ain't it?" Kip asked around a mouthful of breakfast.

"Best I've had since supper last night," Falcon agreed with a smile, busy filling his own belly. He tore off a hunk of hot bread just as bootsteps sounded behind him. He still did not look up.

"You're sittin' at my table," a voice spoke.

"I didn't see your name on it, so pick another one," Falcon told the voice without looking around. He knew it was the gunhand, Border, looking for trouble.

"Get up!" Border commanded.

"Go to hell," Falcon calmly told him.

The café became hushed as a church as all conversation ceased. All eyes shifted toward the table in the corner.

"What did you say to me?" Border almost shouted the shocked words. Nobody spoke to him in such a manner.

"I said go to hell. Are you deaf as well as ugly?"

"Stand up!"

"When I finish my breakfast, little man," Falcon replied, smearing butter and jam on a hunk of bread. "Now go away, you're bothering me."

"Little man?" This time the words were shouted.

Falcon ignored him.

"Get up, you son of a bitch!" Border almost screamed the words.

Falcon told him to go commit an impossible act on his person. Kip almost choked on his breakfast. About half the ranchers and cowboys and local businessmen in the café could not hide their smiles.

Border dropped his left hand on Falcon's shoulder. Falcon knew the man's other hand was hovering near the butt of a gun. It was an old gunfighter's trick. Turn, and he was a dead man. Instead, Falcon reached up, grabbed hold of Border's index finger, and broke it.

The gunfighter screamed in pain and backed up. Falcon pushed back from the table and stood up. He set himself and hit Border a combination of punches: a left to the belly, then a right to the jaw. Border's boots flew out from under him and he landed butt first on a table, collapsing it.

Falcon was on him as fast as a striking snake. He jerked the man to his feet and began pounding him in the face. Before Border could even think about recovering, Falcon had flattened his nose and pulped his lips with hard fists. Then he picked up the gunfighter bodily and threw him through the café's front window. Border landed on the boardwalk and rolled off into the dirt and horseshit of the street.

Falcon calmly walked out the front door, jerked Border to his knees, and placed the man's hands on the edge of the boardwalk. Then he proceeded to stomp on Border's hands with the heel of his boot.

Everybody in the café cringed as Falcon's boots came down on Border's hands, breaking fingers and crushing knuckles. Border's days as a feared gunfighter and hired killer were over. If not forever, at least for a long time.

Falcon threw the man into a horse trough and walked back into Rosie's. He took his seat at the table, picked up his knife and fork, and resumed his eating.

Kip stared at him in amazement for a moment. Slowly the buzz of conversation began among the ranchers and hands and businessmen. Two men got up, paid their bill, and walked out the door. One of them hauled Border out of the horse trough and dragged him across the street toward what passed for the town's doctor.

"Jonas Chapman and Paul Major," Kip said, loud enough

for everyone in the room to hear. "Neither one of them can go to the privy without askin' permission from Gilman."

Some of the men in the room frowned, others smiled. One said, "So you scraped enough money together to hire one tough man, Kip. You still ain't gonna win in the long run."

"Maybe not, Ned," Kip replied. "But you and Gilman will know you been in a fight."

"I ain't never done you a hurt, Kip," Ned said.

"You ain't never done me and John no good neither."

Ned got up, his back stiff with anger, and stalked out of the café.

Another rancher looked at Falcon for a few seconds. "You got a name, mister?"

"Val Mack."

"Seems like me and you have crossed trails somewhere down the line. Your face is familar."

"Could be, I get around." Falcon sopped up the last of his eggs with a hunk of bread and chewed slowly.

"Riders comin' in," another man spoke. "It's Gilman's boys."

Falcon and Kip watched as Ned waved the riders to a dusty halt and spoke briefly, more than once pointing to the café.

"You boys better hit the back door," a woman spoke from the kitchen archway.

"I ain't never took no back door to avoid no man, Rosie," Kip said. "And I'm too damn old to start now."

Rosie immediately took down from the wall a small mirror and a painting of a mountain scene with a bear. She didn't want them pockmarked with bullet holes.

"Kip," another rancher spoke in a not unkindly voice, "you and Mr. Mack clear on out of here. When you're outnumbered five to one, that's just good sense, not cowardice."

Kip shook his head. "Those boys out yonder are trouble-huntin,' Jeff. And you know it. Better to face it here than out at the ranch where Martha, Angie, and the boy could catch a bullet."

"Any of those cowboys gunslicks?" Val asked in a whisper.

"None of 'em is known as such. But they're all drawin'

fightin' wages. I'd say they're all better than most with a six-shooter.''

"They've all had a hand in attacking and running off other small ranchers in the area?" Again, the question was whispered.

"Oh, yeah. I can state that for a pure-dee fact. All their names was told to me by one or the other of the families who was burnt out."

"Then that makes them no better than Gilman."

"That's the way I see it."

Falcon had spotted a Greener propped up in a corner behind the counter. A double-barreled sawed-off shotgun was a fearsome weapon, and would back down anyone if they had good sense.

"Get that Greener over there, Kip," Falcon whispered. "And a few extra shells. We'll meet them face to face on the boardwalk when they dismount. That way, we'll have the high ground."

"Good idea." Kip pushed back his chair and walked behind the counter, picking up the sawed-off shotgun and breaking it open. Both barrels were loaded. He grabbed a handful of shells from a box and stuck them in his jacket pocket just as Falcon was rising from the table and dropping a couple of coins for their breakfast.

The men looked at one another, smiled, and nodded, and then walked out of Rosie's Café to stand on the boardwalk. Before they reached the door, Falcon slipped his guns in and out of leather a couple of times to loosen them.

Two of the Snake riders had gone over to the doc's to check on Border. Eight had dismounted and were standing by the hitchrail.

"Claude," Kip said to an older man, "like the Injuns used to say, it's a good day for dyin'. If that's what you got in mind."

"We come into town for breakfast, Kip," Claude replied in an even voice. "Then we was headin' back to the ranch."

Kip smiled. "With bedrolls and your saddlebags packed heavy full of grub? I don't think so."

Claude returned the smile. "I keep forgettin' that you're an old Injun fighter, Kip. You don't miss much, do you?"

"Not a whole lot, Claude."

"How's Red?" Falcon asked innocently.

One of the Snake hands frowned. "He's abed. You whupped him pretty bad."

"He asked for it."

"That ain't the way we heard it."

"I'm telling you now."

The cowboy let it alone. He didn't want to call Falcon a liar, and had enough sense to know that was what Falcon had set him up for.

"What happens now, Kip?" Claude asked.

"Me and Val ride on out of town and back to the ranch."

"We ain't stoppin' you."

"Claude!" the shout came from the doctor's office. "Border's hands is all busted up. Fingers and knuckles broke. He's ruint."

Falcon smiled and cut his eyes to the rancher, Ned. Ned paled and backed away from the Snake hands at the hitchrails. He headed for the livery stable at a fast walk.

"Yellow-bellied coyote," Kip called after him.

Ned's back stiffened at that, but he did not stop walking nor turn around. A moment later, he was riding out of town at a trot.

"Kip," Claude said. "Some friendly advice?"

"Long as it's free."

Claude smiled. "We've known each other a long time, right?"

"That's right."

"Nance Noonan and Stegman is on the way here with some of their men. It's gonna get real nasty real quick."

"Showdown time, Claude?"

"Looks that way, Kip. You knew it had to come sooner or later."

Kip sighed audibly. "And they're pushin' herds from their spreads west of here." It was not put as a question.

"They need the grass, Kip."

"What about the rest of us?"

"You're history, I reckon."

"Not without a fight, we won't be."

Claude shrugged, being careful to move only his shoulders. Kip was no gunfighter, but he was a crack pistol shot, and Claude knew even with lead in him, the foreman could still kill one or two men as he was going down. And one of those he would kill would more than likely be him.

"It's progress, Kip," Claude said.

"It's nothin' but stealin', and you know it, Claude."

Claude again shrugged his indifference. "That ain't the way we see it."

Falcon had already picked out the two men he guessed would be the most dangerous when it came to a hook and draw. Those two were relaxed where the others were tense. Those two were watching him closely, the others were trying to watch the both of them on the boardwalk.

"Kip, this don't have to be," Claude said. "Gilman's made Bailey a good offer for the land. He can push his beeves a hundred miles south or east or north and start over. There don't have to no more killin'."

"The Rockingchair brand is here to stay, Claude. That's the way it's gonna be."

"Your funeral, Kip."

"Hell," one of the nervous Snake hands said, a shrillness to his voice. "Let's start the buryin' now."

He grabbed for his pistol.

Four

Falcon drew and fired before the cowboy could close his hand around the butt of his .45. He shot to wound, not to kill; the bullet slammed into the cowboy's shoulder and knocked him down. Before the startled Snake hands could blink, Falcon's left hand was filled with a .44 and Kip had jacked back the hammers on the double-barreled sawed-off and was ready to take out two or three riders.

"Hold it!" Claude shouted, his eyes on the Greener in Kip's hands, both muzzles pointed at him. Claude was just a little pale around the mouth, knowing that the shotgun would cut him in half. When he was reasonably sure Kip wasn't going to pull the trigger, he shifted his gaze to Falcon. "You ain't no gunslick I ever heard of, mister. Leas' not by the name you're usin'. But you're a gunhandler none the less. It must have cost John Bailey a pretty penny to bring you in. But you keep this in mind—as a matter of fact, you dwell on it considerable: For every gunslick John can buy, we can buy twenty." He unbuckled his gunbelt, let it dangle, and deliberately turned his back to Falcon and Kip. "All of you boys hang your gunbelts on your saddle horn. Then some of you get Gates over to the Doc." He hung his gunbelt on the apple and turned around. "It's over for this day. No more gunplay, Kip."

"Suits me," the Rockingchair foreman said.

"We're headin' over to the Stampede and we'll stay there till you and your gunfighter get gone."

"That'll be about forty-five minutes," Falcon said. He still had not holstered his .44s.

"Suits us," Claude said. "Let's go, boys."

The Snake hands walked across the wide street and into saloon.

"What the hell are we gonna do for the next forty-five minutes?" Kip asked.

"You go down to the livery and rent a wagon and a team," Falcon said, only then shoving his .44s back into leather. "Meet me in back of the general store. We're going to stock up on supplies."

"Ol' prune-face Dean and his buffalo-butted wife won't sell us nothin', Val."

Falcon laughed at Kip's description of the store owners. "I wouldn't bet on that, Kip. See you at the store."

Falcon walked over to the huge general store, just opening for the day, and stepped inside. The owner, Dean, looked up from a ledger and frowned. "We're not open," he said primly.

"Oh, yes, you are. Get a pad and pencil and take down this list I'm about to give you."

"I saw what happened a few minutes ago," Dean said. "I don't have to sell to Rockingchair trash. I'm under the protection of Miles Gilman."

Falcon slapped him off the stool. The store owner hit the floor just as his wife entered from the living quarters. She let out a pig squeal and exited much faster than she'd entered. Falcon noticed the floor shook every time one of her not-so-dainty tootsies impacted against the boards.

Falcon bought every round of .44, .45, and .44-.40 in the store. He bought every stick of dynamite, every cap and fuse. Then he stocked up on dried beans, potatoes, bacon, coffee, salt, flour, new blankets for the hands—if they showed up—and anything else he could think of that they might need. Then, with a smile, he bought a box of peppermint sticks and some horehound candy.

Guessing they might be hauling a heavy load, Kip had rented a freight wagon and four big pullers. The wagon was piled full when they pulled out.

"Charge this to Gilman," Falcon told the store owner. "In lieu of damages."

Dean was sputtering like a fish out of water as they headed for the ranch. He stood on the loading dock behind the store and sputtered and muttered oaths and dark threats ... but not too loudly. Kip was smiling as he drove the heavily loaded wagon back to the Rockinghorse spread, his horse tied behind.

After the supplies were off-loaded, the Bailey family listened to all that had transpired in town while Jimmy played outside and munched on hard candy.

After Falcon had finished, John poured another round of coffee for all and sat back down at the table beside his wife. "If Noonan and Stegman reach this country with their herds, we're finished. Together they're runnin' twenty-five or thirty thousand head—at least."

"We could stretch wire, John," Kip said.

John Bailey shook his head. "Wire won't stop that bunch, Kip."

"We've got some time to think about that," Falcon said. "It'll be two months or more before they get here. If they're even on the way."

"What do you mean, Val?" John asked.

"It might be a bluff. I think it is a bluff, for the most part. Noonan and Stegman need to get cows to market. They're no different than any other rancher: They need to sell some beeves. Oh, they might be moving some of the younger stuff up here. That makes sense to me. But not twenty-five or thirty thousand head. Not all the way from their spreads in southern Wyoming."

John and his foreman were silent for a moment. The ticking of the grandfather clock was the only sound in the pleasant and comfortable home. Kip broke the silence. "Spreads they killed small ranchers to get. But I think you're right, Val."

John nodded his head in agreement. "I'll go along with it.

And you're right about them needin' the money. Maybe not as bad as we do, but the word I get is that they need to sell some cattle.'' He met Falcon's eyes. ''I can pay fightin' wages for a few months, Val. After that, I'm broke.''

''Don't worry about that, John.''

The rancher grunted. ''Well, if I don't worry about it, who will?''

Falcon smiled. ''Just don't worry about money. I know a few people out here who would be glad to give you a loan.''

''You know a few more than I do then.''

Falcon laughed softly, pushed his chair back, and rose to his boots. ''I'm going to take a ride around your range, John. Get to know it and look over the cattle. Maybe start heading a few toward that box you showed me. I'll be back in a couple of days.''

After Falcon had closed the door behind him, Martha said, ''I wonder who that man really is?''

Kip shook his head. ''I've seen him somewheres. I know I have. I just can't put a name to the face. I know it ain't Val Mack.''

''He's got some education and plenty of manners,'' Angie said. ''He had some good raising. He's a gentleman.''

''I agree,'' her mother said.

''A gentleman he may be,'' Kip said. ''But he's the fastest gun I've ever seen. And he can be mean as a puma when he puts his mind to it.''

''You think Border's out of the game?'' John asked.

''Oh, yeah. Val ruined his hands.''

''But he'll still be able to use a rifle.''

''In time. But not no time soon.''

''Gilman will just bring in more gunfighters,'' Martha said.

John patted his wife's hand. ''I'm afraid you're right about that.''

Angie was standing by a front window. ''There he goes. Heading off toward the north. Riding like he doesn't have a care in the world.''

''Shore wish I could place that feller,'' Kip mused.

* * *

"Who the hell is this Val Mack?" Gilman shouted at Claude.

The foreman shook his head. "I don't know, Miles. I never heard of no gunfighter named Val Mack."

"He's comin' on like a one-man wreckin' crew," the rancher groused. "And I want him stopped. Damn, Claude. He's just one man. Send some of the boys after him."

"Well, there's a crowd of 'em itchin' to go, for a fact."

"Cut 'em loose."

"Against just this Val Mack?"

Miles looked at his foreman for a few seconds. "Take him out first, then we'll move against the Rockinghorse in force."

"What about these telegrams he sent?"

"It's gibberish." He waved copies of the wires Claude had given him. "I can't make any sense out of it. It's about a puma and a wildcat and a mustang and other silly stuff. I think it's some sort of trick just to throw us off."

"I'll get the boys supplied up and moving."

"Good. Let's get ourselves shut of this damn Val Mack and get back to business."

After his forehand had left the main house, Miles Gilman sat in his study and pondered the situation. But he didn't give Val Mack much more than a couple of minutes' thought. Just another two-bit gunhand, he figured. Hell, he had twenty on his payroll. This Val Mack just got lucky, that's all. But it was too bad about Border.

Miles had to have the Rockinghorse range, and that was all there was to it. Miles was overgrazing his grass and John Bailey had the best grass and water anywhere around. How the old coot had managed to hang on this long was a mystery.

But he couldn't be allowed to hang on much longer. Not with Stegman and Noonan coming up with a herd of young stuff.

John Bailey had to be moved. Or buried. And that was that. And if his family got in the way and got hurt or killed? Well . . . too bad.

* * *

In Colorado, northern California, and New Mexico, attorneys read the wires from Falcon MacCallister and laughed, all of them wondering what in the world Falcon was up to. Within the hour, the attorneys had dispatched riders in all directions to find the men Falcon wanted. The riders carried money to outfit the men and get them on stagecoaches and trains. But why in the world Falcon MacCallister, a very wealthy man, wanted these disreputable old farts was a mystery.

The attorneys had already sent investigators into the town of Noon and were working to clear Falcon's name and have the federal warrants against him dropped. That would be done. It was just a matter of time. The legal process worked, but it was oftentimes very slow, the slowness something men of the west did not seem to understand.

The attorneys also wrote out bank drafts and got them moving toward Falcon, aka Val Mack.

The attorneys who handled some of Falcon MacCallister's considerable wealth, and who were located around the west, all chuckled, knowing that whatever Falcon was doing, there would be a considerable amount of excitement related to it. The man seemed to draw trouble quicker than a lightning rod.

Falcon knew he was being followed an hour after leaving the ranch. The man was pretty good, but Falcon was one hundred percent his father's son, and *nobody* was a better tracker than Jamie MacCallister.

Falcon had ridden through this country many times, but it had been a while, and his memory was busy trying to remember all the ins and outs.

After a few minutes, Falcon came to a spot he recalled. There was a tiny creek that flowed just behind a huge upthrusting of rock, if his memory served him correct. He quickly swung in behind the rocks and ran back to deliberately cover his trail as clumsily as possible. Then, staying on rocky ground, Falcon got his rifle and ran to a smaller outcropping of rocks about forty feet away and directly across from the rocks that lay in front of the creek.

He made himself as comfortable as possible and waited.

The minutes ticked past and the sun grew hotter. The soft murmuring of the cold waters of the tiny spring-fed creek grew mighty appealing to Falcon. His mouth felt as though it were filled with cotton.

"Gettin' thirsty, boy?" The voice and question came from behind him.

Falcon's hands tightened on his rifle and he waited for the shock of the bullet.

Five

The bullet never came. Instead, a low chuckling reached Falcon's ears.

Falcon smiled as he recognized the quiet laughter. He turned and looked at the source.

"Big Bob Marsh," Falcon said, exhaling anxiety-filled air from his lungs.

"In the flesh and as handsome to the ladies as ever," the man said, stepping closer.

Falcon stood up and the men shook hands.

"What in the world . . . ?"

Big Bob waved him silent. "I was about a hundred miles north of that pissant town in Utah when you put lead into Chet and Butch Noonan. If two ever deserved killin', them two did. But I knowed Nance would send men out lookin' for you. I thought and thought 'bout where you might go to hole up. Felt you wouldn't go back to Colorado; you wouldn't want to bring trouble to your kin. Then I 'membered that old cabin built into the mountain. Went there. But by the time I reached the cabin, you'd done hauled it outta there. Been trackin' you ever since."

"Now you found me, and a peck of trouble, too."

"Hell, boy, I ain't never shied away from trouble in my life."

Falcon stepped back and looked hard at Big Bob. Falcon figured the man to be about sixty years old. But still in fine physical shape. A huge man, standing several inches taller than Falcon, and Falcon was no little man. Big Bob had come out west when he was just a boy, and Falcon's dad had talked often about the man. Big Bob was one of those larger-than-life legends of the mountains.

"You want a job, Bob?"

The man shrugged massive shoulders. "I might do a dab of work for a month or so. What you got in mind?"

"Let's fix some coffee and jaw about it."

"Long as I can fix the mud. I recall yours is too damn weak for this child."

Falcon built a small fire and coffee was soon on. Falcon talked while he worked. Finally, after a cup of coffee strong enough to melt an anvil, Big Bob Marsh grinned. "Oh, that shines, boy. It purely does. Hell, yes, I'll stick around. I hate a bully like this Gilman. When you reckon the others will drag their asses in?"

"Couple of weeks, maybe sooner. Depends on how close they are and how soon they get the word."

"Be good to see some of them ol' boys. I ain't seen Wildcat Wheeless in ten years or so. I thought Jack Stump was long dead. Good to hear he's alive and kickin.' You shore Mustang is still breathin'?"

"Positive."

"Well, I'll be damned. Ain't seen him since . . . oh, I reckon it was '62 or thereabouts. But I seen Puma Parley 'bout two years ago." Bob shook his shaggy head. "He had just lost his old cat and was trainin' 'nother one. Big cat, too. I purely hope he leaves that son of a bitch to home. Home bein' that cave he lives in. Beats me how a man can live with a damn mountain lion."

Falcon smiled. But like Bob, he hoped Puma would leave his snarling pet at home. Mountain lions made him nervous. "What's this cat's name?"

"Jenny. Just as gentle as a baby with Puma. Kept lookin' at me like I was supper. Made me plumb edgy. You tryin' to get hold of anybody else?"

"Dan Carson."

"Las' I heard he was hangin' 'round Denver. And that was just two, three months ago. Some woman had just about dabbed a loop on him and he was tryin' to figure out a way to get shut of her. This ought to do it."

"I don't know whether the world is ready for six or seven of you old coots all together in one spot," Falcon said with a grin.

"Whaw!" Big Bob snorted. "We'll shore enough kick up a fuss, now, let me tell you."

"Bob, in all seriousness, have you ever worked as a cowboy?"

"Shore! I can rope, brand, herd . . . you name it, I've done it. So have the others. Don't you worry none. Me and the boys will get them critters to a railhead. Or die tryin'." Then he sobered. "But I'll add this: 'Fore all of us die tryin', there'll be blood on the moon, boy. Bet on that."

"I sure wouldn't bet against you, Bob."

Big Bob Marsh grinned, exposing a pretty good set of choppers for his age and the time. "Let's finish up this coffee and head on to the ranch, boy. I want to meet the folks I'll be working for and stow my possibles."

John, Martha, Angie, Jimmy, Cookie, and the foreman, Kip, stood in a group and stared for a moment at Big Bob Marsh. He was the biggest man any of them had ever seen: six feet, seven inches tall and weighing about two hundred and ninety pounds, all bone and gristle and muscle.

Finally, John found his voice. "Bob," he said, walking up and holding out his hand, "welcome to the Rockingchair."

Bob's hand swallowed the rancher's. "Thankee, Mr. Bailey. You can be shore I'll give you a day's work for a day's pay. I don't believe in slackin' none."

"I'm sure you will, Bob," the rancher said, looking up into

50   *William W. Johnstone*

the broad and whiskered face. "I'm payin' fightin' wages: sixty a month and found."

"Whew! Them's good wages. If the grub's as good as the pay, I found me a home for a time."

John smiled. "We've got the best cook in this part of Wyoming."

Kip stepped up and howdied and shook. "Come on, Bob. Let's get you settled in."

After the foreman and Bob had walked off, Jimmy asked, "Is that man a giant?"

After a good laugh, John tousled his grandson's hair and looked at Falcon. "How'd you find him so quick?"

"I didn't. He found me. We just crossed trails a few miles north of here. Bob was just wandering. He's known me since I was just a tadpole. He and my father were good friends."

"Someday you'll have to tell us about your father," Angie said, smiling at Falcon.

"Someday I will, Angie. My dad was quite a character."

"Brothers and sisters, Val?" Martha asked.

"A whole bunch of them, Mrs. Bailey. It's a long story." He touched the brim of his hat with his fingertips. "Now if you all will excuse me, I want to get Bob settled in and pick out some horses for him to ride. It takes a big horse for him."

As Falcon walked away toward the bunkhouse, Angie said, "I am determined to learn the truth about that man."

John took off his hat and mopped his forehead with a bandanna. "He'll tell us when he's good and ready, daughter. And maybe he never will."

Martha smiled and took her daughter's hand. "Let's go bake some pies for supper."

"Now, that just might do it," John said with a laugh.

There were a few moments of silent shock and then some mild panic at the Bank of Gilman as the bank president read the wire just received from a very prestigious bank in San Francisco. A line of credit had been set up for one Val Mack in the sum of twenty-five thousand dollars, the money guaranteed by the bank in San Francisco.

Within minutes, the bank president was in his buggy, heading for the Striking Snake ranch.

"Twenty-five thousand dollars!" Miles Gilman screamed. "Where the hell does a saddle-bum gunfighter get that much money?"

"I ain't never even seen that much money all in a bunch," Claude spoke the words wistfully.

"Damn few people have," Miles told him, settling down somewhat. He waved the wired message. "What the hell is goin' on around here?"

"I think we best do some checkin' on this Val Mack," Claude said. "Take a look down his back trail real close."

Miles thought about that for a time, then shook his head. "Time we arranged for all that and got it done, it would be too late. Stegman and Noonan is movin' herds from their range down south right now. It's gonna take some time 'fore they get here. But I don't want this Val Mack to be around when they do. Cut the boys loose, Claude."

"Consider it done, Miles."

"You noticed, I reckon, this place is built like a fort?" Big Bob said to Falcon. "Main house, bunkhouse, even the barn."

"Ten years ago there was a lot of Indian trouble here. Many of the settlers didn't last long. Men like John Bailey dug in and stayed. They built to last."

The men were sitting on a bench outside the bunkhouse, smoking and jawing while they waited for the call to come to supper at the main house. While there was just the two of them, they would eat with the Bailey family. When, or if, the others showed up, the hands would eat separately, their meals prepared by Cookie in the kitchen adjoining the bunkhouse.

"Sooner or later, boy," Bob said, "you gonna have to tell these good folks who you are."

"I know. Sooner or later."

"That Angie gal, she's got her cap set for you."

Falcon sighed. "I haven't been able to think of another woman since Marie was killed. Too soon, Bob."

"I understand, boy. I felt the same way when Crow Woman was killed back in '51. I tracked them damn men for five years. But I finally got 'em all."

"What happened to your kids, Bob?"

"Fever got one. I heard the other was killed at the Little Bighorn. Me and him never was close."

"How long after Crow Woman was killed 'fore you could take more than a passing interest in another woman?"

Big Bob Marsh was silent for half a minute. "Long time, boy. I reckon that was the only woman I ever loved. You might be the same way." Then he smiled. "But that don't mean that ever' now and then you can't get an itch that only a woman can scratch."

Falcon laughed, then sobered. "I haven't even had one of them since Marie was killed."

"You will, boy. You will. Give it time. You're still followin' a trail called grief. But it will fork one of these days. Believe me."

"Yo, boys!" John Bailey called from the front porch. "Supper's on the table. Got steaks and taters and gravy and hot bread and fresh-baked apple pie."

Big Bob slapped Falcon on the leg and Falcon wondered if he could even stand up after the blow. "Let's eat, boy!" the big man thundered.

"I don't know if I can even walk," Falcon muttered, standing up. He bent over to rub his leg just as someone on the ridges around the ranch complex squeezed the trigger. The bullet tore a hole in the outer wall of the bunkhouse, missing Falcon by only a few inches.

Five seconds later, Falcon and Big Bob Marsh were inside the thick walls of the bunkhouse, rifles in their hands.

"Now this really pisses me off," Big Bob grumbled.

"Getting shot at?"

"No. Startin' a war 'fore I have time to eat my supper!"

Six

"Stay in the house!" Falcon shouted through an open bunk-house window. "The rifleman is on the ridge behind you."

"Either of you men hit?" Kip shouted.

"No. We're all right."

"Keep the supper hot," Big Bob roared, lifting his rifle and banging off several fast shots toward the ridge.

"Will do," Kip yelled.

Several minutes passed with no more shots from the ridge. Bob took his hat and stuck it on the end of a broom handle. He slowly edged it past an open window. Nothing. "Either they ain't fallin' for that old trick, or they're gone."

"I think they're gone. That shot was meant for me. They missed. They'll try again."

"Damn sure wasn't no warnin' shot. If you hadn't a bent over, right now we'd all be arrangin' mourners and horn tooters for your plantin'."

"You're such a cheerful man, Bob."

"I know it," the big man said with a straight face. "It's one of my finer qualities."

Falcon shook his head and slowly opened the door to the bunkhouse. No shots split the warm late-afternoon air. Falcon took a deep breath, then sprinted toward the barn, no gunfire nipping at his heels. He quickly threw a saddle on a horse, opened the big rear doors, and left the barn at a gallop. He stayed low in the saddle, bent over the horse's neck, and headed for the ridge above the house. When he reached the crest of the ridge, he found exactly what he thought he'd find: nothing but a few tracks.

Dismounting, Falcon carefully scouted the area. He found one cartridge casing and lots of bootprints. He found where the gunman had picketed his horse, and hoofprints leading off toward the north. There were no distinguishing marks on either the bootprints or the horse's shoes.

Falcon rode slowly back to the barn and stabled the horse, then walked to the bunkhouse.

Big Bob took one look at his face and said, "Nothing?"

Falcon held out the brass casing. "Just this."

Bob grunted. "Too bad it wasn't a .32-.20. That would have made it easier to find the owner."

"Well, there's one thing for certain."

"Whoever it was will try again."

"You got it. Come on, let's eat."

"I'm shore ready for that."

But Falcon wasn't sure the Bailey family and Kip were ready for the big man's appetite. Falcon remembered how Big Bob could stow away the food and he had to fight to keep from laughing at the expressions on the others' faces as Big Bob ate enough supper for five people. There wasn't a scrap left on the table when Bob finished his third piece of pie and drank his fifth or sixth cup of coffee . . . Falcon had lost count.

"That there is the finest grub this child ever et," Bob proclaimed, wiping his mouth on a checkered napkin. Then he let out a thunderous belch and said, " 'Scuse me."

Everybody at the table sat in shock for a few seconds, then, as if one, burst out laughing while Big Bob grinned.

"Good thing you hauled in those other supplies, Val," John Bailey said, wiping his eyes with his napkin. "If all the others you contacted do show up, food's goin' to be a problem."

"Yes, but that will probably be the last time I can pull that stunt. That's why I laid in such a supply of dried beans and the like. I don't figure we'll run short on beef."

"Oh, them other boys will be here, John Bailey," Big Bob said. "You can count on that. Let's just say they owe, uh, Val, here a favor or two."

"You know the others, Bob?" Kip asked.

"Been knowin' 'em all 'bout forty years. They're good boys, too. Ain't no back-up in none of 'em."

"I'm looking forward to meeting your friends, Bob," Martha said.

Falcon smiled at just the thought of that day.

Big Bob and Falcon stayed on Rockingchair range for the next week, familiarizing themselves with the land and checking on John's herds. The cattle were in fine shape, fat and ready for the drive to market. There were a number of Snake-branded cattle among the Rockingchair herds, as well as several other brands.

"They all belong to members of the cattlemen's alliance," Kip said. "They claim all this land for their own."

"Even though John and his family have legally filed on it and proved it up?" Falcon asked.

"That don't make no difference to those bastards," Kip said. "They want all of Wyoming for their own. No farmers or small ranchers allowed."

"Then the federal government is going to have to step in and do something."

"Not damn likely," the foreman replied. "The cattlemen's alliance has too much stroke with the politicians for that to happen. Lots of money bein' passed under the table. Over in Johnson County it's gettin' real bad."

"I heared 'bout that place," Big Bob said. "They're hangin' people and shootin' others. Night riders callin' farmers rustlers and takin' the law into their own hands."

"That's right," Kip said. "And it's gonna get that way here, too, 'fore it's all over."

"What are they waiting on to start it here?" Falcon asked.

"Nance Noonan and Rod Stegman and their army of gun-slingers. Soon as they arrive, all hell's gonna break loose. They're fixin' to claim everything from the Johnson County line west."

"How far west?" Big Bob asked.

"Far as the law will allow 'em. Probably over to Dakota."

"That's hundreds of thousands of acres."

"You bet it is, Val. And if they get their way, there ain't gonna be a small rancher or farmer left alive to talk about it."

Kip busied himself rolling a cigarette and Big Bob and Falcon exchanged glances, followed by tight, mean smiles. The slight curving of the lips silently stating that the grand plans of the cattlemen's alliance just might be subject to change.

"Let's cut out the Snake brands and start them movin' toward their own range," Kip said. "I'm agin it, but them's John's orders. He likes to play it straight and on the up and up."

"Good way for them to call us rustlers if any Snake riders come up on us," Falcon stated.

"I know it. But John don't want no other brands mixed in with ours."

Falcon checked his guns and Big Bob did the same. Falcon asked, "Where is John this morning?"

"Him and little Jimmy is ridin' the east range. It's fairly safe there. By that I mean there ain't been no trouble so far over there. That's just a tad too many miles away from the Snake riders' home base."

"That's where most of the remaining smaller ranchers and farmers are located?"

"You got it. The Rockingchair is sort of the line 'tween the Snake range and what's left of the small ranchers and farmers. If we was to pull out, it would be a slaughter."

"So if they can't run you out, they'll have to kill you all," Falcon stated.

"That's it. Gilman and them in the alliance ain't got no other choice in the matter."

"They'd kill the boy, too?" Big Bob asked, open disgust in his voice.

"Sure. They've killed several boys younger than Jimmy.

They've killed whole families by burnin' their houses down around them whilst the night riders laid down gunfire to keep them from runnin' outside.''

"Real nice folks, these rich cattle barons," Big Bob muttered.

"Yeah," Kip said, as he pinched out the end of his cigarette and touched spurs to his horse's sides. "Regular salt of the earth. And that's 'xactly where I'd like to put them."

"Maybe we'll get lucky today," Big Bob said. "And run into a passer of them."

Falcon's thoughts were of the times his town in the valley had been hit by brigands, and of the dead women and kids . . . and of his mother, Kate. His face was tight with fury when he said, "I think I'd like that, too, Bob. I really would."

"I wouldn't mind it a bit myself," Kip said. "I was tellin' John this mornin' that it was high time for us to start drawin' some decent cards in this game."

"What'd he say 'bout that?" Bob asked.

"Oddly 'nough, not much. Usually, he's the peacemaker, but ever since that rifleman on the ridge the other day, John's changed some. I think he knows now that the time for talkin' is over. I think he knows it's gun time."

They were moving the cattle along at a walk. Even though they were someone else's cows, and that someone a sworn enemy, they didn't want to run any pounds off of them. That was typical of many ranchers in the west.

When the sun was center-sky, they stopped to noon. They ate sandwiches Cookie had fixed for them before dawn, and Falcon made a small hat-sized fire to boil coffee. Just as Falcon was adding cold water to settle the grounds, Bob lifted his shaggy head and said, "Riders comin'. Sounds like a bunch of 'em."

"We're still on Rockingchair range, aren't we?" Falcon asked.

"It's debatable," Kip replied. "I say yes, the Snake people say no."

The three of them loosened their pistols in leather and waited. They had been pushing about forty head of Snake-branded cattle along, and they all felt they knew what the Snake trouble-hunters would say when they rode up.

"Eight of 'em," Bob announced.

"That'll give 'em courage," Kip replied. "Agin three of us."

Without looking up, Falcon asked, "Can you recognize any of them, Kip?"

"Not yet. Is that coffee ready?"

"Just about."

"Smells good," Big Bob said. "I'd favor a cup of coffee 'fore the shootin' starts. But," he added mournfully, after glancing at the fast-approaching Snake riders, "looks like I'll have to wait. Story of my life."

"You're breaking my heart, Bob," Falcon said.

"I know it. I can get right pittyful at times, can't I?"

The Snake riders reined up a few hundred yards away from the Rockingchair men. They stared at the cattle for a moment, then pulled rifles from saddle scabbards. They began walking their horses slowly toward the smell of coffee.

"I don't know a single one of them," Kip said softly. "Must be those new hands Gilman hired. I heard people in Rosie's talkin' 'bout them. Hired guns from Texas and New Mexico."

Falcon stared at the slow-approaching riders. "They're about to start earning their pay."

The Snake bunch stopped their horses about twenty-five feet away from the three Rockingchair riders. "Well now," a stocky, flat-faced man said. "Looks like we done found us some rustlers. The boss said he'd been losin' beeves out here."

"We're pushin' those cattle back to Snake range," Kip told him. "If you had any sense you'da circled 'round and seen that by lookin' at the tracks 'fore you came ridin' in here and runnin' that mouth."

One of the hired guns laughed. "I reckon he done told you how the cow ate the cabbage, Monroe. I think that old-timer just called you a dummy."

"Yeah, Monroe," another Snake hand said. "You gonna take that lip offen that old coot?"

With a flush rising from neck to cheeks, Monroe looked

square at Kip and said, "I think I'll hang you first, you old bastard."

"You got it to do, boy," Kip calmly told him.

Kip, Big Bob, and Falcon had spread out, twelve to fifteen feet between them. All three of them were wearing two pistols; Kip and Big Bob had the second pistol tucked behind their gunbelts, Falcon wearing a two-gun rig, the left side .44 worn on a slant, butt forward.

"Drop them guns, boys," one of the Snake hands told the trio. "We caught you cold rustlin', so there's no use arguin' 'bout it." He grinned and tossed a running iron down to the ground, the rustler's best friend landing with a plop and a spurt of dust close to the fire. "There's the proof." He laughed and the others joined in.

"Don't git dirt in the coffee," Kip warned. "I got my mouth all fixed for a cup."

"You'll never get a chance to drink another cup, you old fart," the Snake hand said.

"To be no more than a couple of years away from your mommy's titty, you're 'bout a mouthy son of a bitch, ain't you?" Big Bob said.

The Snake hand who had just flapped his lips cursed and lifted his rifle. A second later the Snake-branded cattle were off and running, the sudden sounds of gunfire spooking them from their quiet grazing into a stampede.

Seven

Falcon blew the flat-faced one out of the saddle. Bob's pistol barked and the mouthy puncher went ass over elbows backward, hitting the ground and not moving. Kip's six-shooter roared and a third Snake gunhand's butt left the saddle.

Falcon, Kip, and Big Bob each hammered out three more shots and two Snake punchers were mortally hit and two wounded. Kip had a burn on the outside of his right leg from a rifle bullet, Bob had a crease on his left arm, and Falcon's hat was blown off his head. But the Rockingchair riders were still standing and the Snake riders had three dead and several wounded. Those Snake riders still in the saddle dropped their rifles, managed to get their rearing, frightened horses calmed down, and raised their hands in the air, the two of them bleeding from minor wounds.

"You boys shuck them gunbelts," Kip ordered. "Now!"

Falcon and Bob were busy ripping the gunbelts off the dead and the wounded and gathering up rifles. They hoisted the dead belly-down across saddles and helped the wounded get back on the hurricane decks of their still spooked horses.

"You boys can round up your own damn cattle," Kip told the Snake riders. "Just clear out and do it right now."

Ten seconds later, the Snake riders were gone, taking their dead with them.

Falcon found his hat and looked sadly at the huge holes in the crown, front, and back.

"It'll help keep your head cool in the heat," Bob told him, squatting down and pouring a cup of coffee.

"We were damn lucky, boys," Kip said, leaning over and dabbing at the slight wound on his leg with a bandanna. "By all rights, we should be eatin' dirt about now."

"It ain't my time yet," Big Bob said, slurping at his coffee. "A gypsy woman tole me oncet that I was gonna die in bed, an old man, surrounded by six beautiful young women, all moanin' and sobbin' and carryin' on 'bout my passin'."

"And you believed her?" Falcon asked, still irritated about his hat.

"Hell, no! But it's a beautiful thought, ain't it? You boys sit and have some of this coffee. Hits the spot after that little fracas."

"Rider comin'," Kip announced, looking toward the east. "Now who could that be?"

"It's Angie," Falcon said, standing up and squinting.

"Alone?" Kip blurted. "Out here?" He shook his head. "That girl's always been headstrong . . . ."

Angie galloped up and swung down. Bob's mouth fell open and he gaped at her. She was wearing men's britches and had been riding astride.

Kip just shook his head at the unseemly sight.

Falcon stood and let his eyes take in her figure in the tight-fitting men's pants. The young woman filled them out admirably.

"I was riding and I heard shots," Angie said.

"Girl," Kip admonished her, "you been told and told 'bout ridin' alone. They's still Injuns out here, not to mention Snake riders who would shoot you on sight. Or worse," he added.

"Now I've been told again," Angie responded. "Anyway, I'm here. You want me to ride back alone?"

"No!" the foreman said firmly. "Girl," he said patiently,

"your pa bought you a sidesaddle rig. It ain't proper for you to be wearin' men's britches and ridin' astride."

"Oh, pish-posh!" Angie said. "I hate that uncomfortable thing. Why . . ." She paused. "You men are wounded!"

"Nothin' serious, Miss Angie," Bob said, pouring her a tin cup of coffee. "Grab you a piece of ground and rest a spell. Then we'll head on back."

Kip was walking around in tight little circles, muttering to himself about a woman's place and indecent behavior . . . among other things about women in general.

"Oh, settle down, Uncle Kip," Angie said. She had told Falcon that Kip wasn't really her uncle, but that he had been with her father since before she was born and he was accepted as a member of the family.

"Let's get back to the ranch," Falcon suggested. "I don't like the idea of Martha being alone."

Kip smiled at that. "Don't you worry none about Martha, Val. Or this gal here, for that matter." He cut his eyes to Angie. "They've both fought off Injun attacks more times than you can count. And they're both crack shots with a rifle and pretty fair shots with a pistol. Any Snake rider who comes within shootin' range of Martha is gonna be in real trouble. Believe it. But we do need to get back, I reckon. Miles Gilman ain't gonna like what we just done to his hired guns."

The owner of the Snake ranch sat in his study and listened as his foreman, Claude, told him about the shooting. He didn't get mad, not at first. He just had a slight sick feeling in the pit of his stomach. Ever since this Val Mack had met up with some of his men at the old trading post, Miles had felt somewhat disturbed about the situation. Now there was another man riding for the Rockingchair who was quick on the shoot. An older man, but slick with a gun nonetheless.

"All right, Claude," Miles said, in a surprisingly calm tone of voice. "Thanks. Get them wounded into town to the doc's and I'll see about buryin' the others."

"All right, Boss." The longtime friend and foreman hesitated. "You all right, Miles?"

"What? Oh. Yeah, I'm fine." Miles sighed. "Claude, Dexter described the other feller with Val and Kip. You got any idea who this older man is?"

Claude fiddled with his hat for a few seconds. Opened his mouth a couple of times. Closed it without speaking.

"Come on, Claude," Miles urged. "You're holdin' back on me."

"Well, from his description, my guess is that it just might be Big Bob Marsh."

That brought Miles straight up in his chair. "The army scout? The bounty hunter?"

"Yeah. And a hell of a lot more than that. Big Bob's been prowlin' the high country for forty-five years. Ever since he was about twelve or thirteen years old. He's friends with ol' Preacher and Smoke Jensen too. Big Bob Marsh is one mean son of a bitch, Miles. If he was to put the call out, this country would be swarmin' with what's left of the mountain men. And them old bastards don't know the meanin' of the words *fear* or *back-up*."

Miles's oldest son, Lars, had entered the study and was standing quietly, listening. Now he snorted contemptuously. "Crap! A pack of old turds who need help gettin' on a bronc. I can't believe you'd be afraid of a pack of old men."

Miles lifted wiser eyes to his son. "Boy, them men opened up this country. They might not have been the first white men here, but they wasn't far behind. Them ol' boys is wang-leather tough and mean as a grizzly. Back in '61 or '62, when I was down in Colorado, I seen a mountain man name of Jack Stump kill five men 'fore any of 'em knew what was happenin' to them. I seen another mountain man name of Dick Wheeless, goes by the handle of Wildcat, cut three men twicest his size all to bloody pieces. Dick's about five feet, five inches tall and don't weigh a hundred and twenty pounds, but every pound is mad-dog mean. Don't you never tangle with no mountain man, and I don't give a damn how old he is."

Lars mouthed a few very ugly words, all of them tinged with

disgust and sarcasm—but none of them directed at his father—and left the room.

Embarrassed, Claude waited until the angry flush had left Miles's face. "Damn hotheaded kid," Miles muttered.

"His brothers ain't far behind him in that department, Miles," Claude took a chance by saying.

"I know, Claude. Bein' raised without a ma might have something to do with that."

Miles Gilman's wife had taken off for parts unknown after their last child, Terri, was born. Miles had tried to raise four boys and one girl.

Unsuccessfully, for the most part.

Dan Carson and Jack Stump rode in together. Both of them were men of about sixty years, and both of them in excellent physical shape for their age and the time. Both had come west as boys just moving into their teen years and had stayed to become legends.

Unlike Big Bob Marsh, both Dan and Stumpy—as he was called—were not physically overpowering men. But there was a lasting toughness and capability about both that invisibly marked them as men to ride the river with . . . and as men that it would be best not to crowd.

Falcon left them to settle in the bunkhouse, and for Big Bob to explain the situation to them, and walked over to the ranch house. Kip saw him heading toward the house and joined him in the short walk.

"I'd hate to mess with either one of them ol' boys," the foreman said.

"They won't take much pushing, for a fact, Kip. My father had a lot of respect for them."

"Your pa a mountain man, Falcon?" the foremen gently prodded.

Falcon smiled. "Not really. But my grandfather sure was."

"Ah. That explains a whole lot. So your family's been long in the west?"

Falcon never lost his slight smile, knowing that whatever he said would get immediately to John Bailey and family. "My grandfather came to the high lonesome before the turn of the century, I think. And when my father came out here he took to the mountains like he was born there."

"A lot of men do," the foreman agreed, and asked no more questions about Falcon's family.

Seated around the big table in the huge kitchen and dining area, Falcon laid a thousand dollars in gold coin and greenbacks on the table. John Bailey's eyes bugged out for a moment as he stared at the hard cash. A thousand dollars was two and a half years' work for the average cowboy.

"That'll help with the wages for the men coming in," Falcon said. "And to feed these randy yahoos. 'Cause until you've seen mountain men eat, you have missed a sight."

"How can I repay you?" the rancher asked.

"Don't worry about it. I have ample funds, believe me. And by the way, I 'spect there are telegrams for me in town right about now stating very clearly that I am now the sole and legal owner of twenty sections of land north and south of the Rockingchair range."

John and Kip's eyes bugged out again. Kip stuttered, "But . . . how?"

"Miles claimed it, but he didn't bother to clear the titles through the bank or the land office. I bought up the mortgages and paid the taxes. It's all free and clear."

The Bailey family and Kip sat around the table and stared at Falcon. Falcon smiled and took a sip of his coffee, which had now cooled enough to drink. Finally, John asked in a very quiet voice, "You going to start your own spread, Val?"

"No. But you can use part of it if you like. I thought I might sell or lease a few sections to farmers. But for most of it, I'm going to let Big Bob and Jack and Dan and the others have use of it when they finish working here. Believe it or not, a couple of them are pretty good farmers."

"And with that bunch on the land, the cattle barons will think a long time before attacking them," Kip said.

"Exactly," Falcon replied.

"Who are you, Val?" Martha gently asked.

Falcon shrugged his shoulders. "Just a drifting gambler, Martha." Not really a lie. "A man who enjoys getting away from a deck of cards every now and then and doing some hard physical work." Falcon pushed back his chair and stood up. "Well, the others will be here within the week. I'm going to ride over to the trading post in the morning and order about four wagons of supplies. Stumpy or Dan will probably ride with me. Anything special you ladies would like?"

"Can't think of a thing," Martha said.

"Then I'll surprise you," Falcon said. "I'd better go check on the boys. See you all at suppertime."

Kip and the Bailey family sat in silence for several moments after Falcon had left the house. John finally sighed and finished his coffee. Martha got up and refilled her husband's cup and Kip's. John said, "Man talks about thousands of dollars the way we'd talk about pennies and nickels." He looked at the stack of greenbacks and gold coins on the table.

Martha said, "He's no dandy dude from back east, that's for sure."

"No, mother," John agreed. "You're right about that. He's a western man, through and through. He knows cattle, knows horses, knows guns."

"And I guess he knows cards," Angie said.

"I'd hate to face him across a poker table, for sure," her father said.

"His grandpa was a mountain man," Kip said. "He told me that not thirty minutes ago. But Val's pa come out later. I didn't want to push no further."

Martha shrugged her slender shoulders. "Well, whoever he is, he's a godsend. He'll tell us who he really is when he's good and ready."

John smiled. "I'll just bet ol' prune-face Willard at the bank is beside himself."

Kip chuckled. "And you can bet on something else, too: Whatever Willard knows, Miles Gilman knows it within the hour."

"True," John said, stirring his coffee. He looked at his daughter, who was smiling. "Something funny, girl?"

"I was just wondering what Miles's reaction will be when he finds out about Val buying all those sections of land. His attorneys surely went through the state office to do that."

"I hadn't thought of that," her father said. "But you're right. It might be days or even weeks before news of that reaches Gilman."

"Don't bet on it, John," his wife gently contradicted, "considering all the men at the capital who are taking money from the cattlemen's alliance."

John patted his wife's hand. "Right again, mother." He smiled at her. "As usual. Whichever way the wind blows, it's gonna be interestin' around here from now on."

Eight

Falcon saddled up and was gone before dawn, Jack Stump riding along with him. The men had fixed a pot of coffee at the bunkhouse and eaten a couple of cold biscuits before setting out.

Stumpy was a man who usually had little to say, only occasionally engaging in idle chitchat. He was not a dour man, just a man who kept his thoughts to himself. He was a man who enjoyed solitude. But he could be a very dangerous man when crowded. He was no quick-draw gunfighter, but he almost always made his first shot count. Falcon didn't really know how old Stumpy was, guessing him to be in his early sixties. He rode a Palouse, a tough-bred mountain horse that could go all day and still have some bottom left.

"Dan shore was glad to get shut of that woman." Stumpy surprised Falcon by opening a conversation. "She had gettin' hitched up permanent on her mind."

Falcon smiled.

"Woman had three of the most worthless growed up kids a man could ever see. I met the whole kit and caboodle of 'em 'fore we rode up here. Sorry bunch."

And that was the extent of the conversation until the men reached the trading post.

As they topped the ridge overlooking the creek and the store, Jack grunted. "Looks like we're gonna run into a crowd."

There were a dozen horses at the hitchrails, and the horses appeared to have been hard-ridden. When the pair of Rocking-chair men drew closer and could make out the brands, they were unfamiliar to them.

All but one.

Stumpy smiled. "That's Dick Wheeless's mustang in the corral. I was with him when he caught it a couple of years ago. I don't know them other brands."

"You can bet they're not drifting cowboys just passing through," Falcon said.

"I already gleamed that, Falcon."

Falcon laughed at the expression on Stumpy's face and swung around to the rear of the old trading post. Stumpy walked over to Dick's horse and tried to stroke the animal's nose. The mustang tried to bite him.

"Son of a bitch!" Stumpy jerked his hand back and cussed the once wild horse. "Got the same disposition as Wildcat— lousy!"

The mustang peeled back his lips and showed Stumpy his teeth.

Walking back to Falcon, Stumpy said, "I told Wildcat when he caught that damn horse the best thing he could do was shoot it. But no, he said he just had to have it 'cause it was purty. Goddamn worthless hammerhead."

"Dick or the horse?"

Stumpy grinned. "Both of 'em."

Falcon pushed open the rear door of the old store and stepped in, quickly moving to one side to allow his eyes time to adjust from the bright outside light. Stumpy stepped in and moved to the other side. The men stood there for a moment, listening to the rough language and hard laughter coming from the saloon side of the store.

They walked through the storeroom and entered behind the

store. The owner looked up from the counter and nodded his head, then cut his eyes to the closed door leading to the saloon. Falcon nodded his understanding and looked over at the half dozen tables. A small man was seated at a far table, his back to a wall. He grinned at Falcon.

"Howdy, you young squirt," Dick "Wildcat" Wheeless said. "Who's that damned ugly old reprobate trailin' you?"

"Go to hell, you midget," Stumpy said, in the form of a greeting between two old friends.

"Been there. Didn't like it. Too damn hot." He waved a fork at his platter of food. "Steaks is good. Sit and eat."

"I reckon I could eat a mouthful of food," Stumpy said.

"Considerin' the size of your mouth, that's 'bout enough grub to half fill a hungry alligator."

"I really don't know why I put up with this half-pint," Stumpy said, walking over to the table. "He ain't never got a kind word for anybody."

"Do too," Wildcat said. "I like the company you're ridin' with. But I'm sure he makes you ride fifty feet behind him, considerin' the fact that you probably ain't had a bath in six months."

Falcon smiled at the insults that were flying between the two old friends and began speaking in low tones to the store owner. The man nodded his head and looked over the sheet of paper Falcon handed him.

The deal settled and a pickup date for the supplies agreed on, Falcon walked over to the table and sat down with the two men, who were still busy insulting one another. A younger woman, a half-breed that Falcon figured was the daughter of the couple who ran the store, brought over a pot of coffee and two mugs. She returned a few minutes later with two plates of food and left without changing expression or speaking a word.

"Woman ain't half bad to look at," Wildcat remarked. "But she sure talks a lot, don't she?" Without waiting for a reply, he said, "You ought to see 'bout cuddlin' up with her, Stumpy. Man of your advanced age needs a good woman to take care of him durin' his declinin' years."

Stumpy spent the next several minutes calling Wildcat every

vile name he could think of, then added, "I'll be ridin' the high country when it comes time for you to use a ladder to get in your wheelchair, you half-baked buffalo turd."

"Tsk, tsk," Wildcat said. "Such language in a public place."

Falcon shut his mind to their insults, for he knew it would go on for hours, and kept one eye on the door to the saloon while he ate. Wildcat hadn't been kidding about the steaks being good. They were delicious. The meat was smothered in gravy, the fried potatoes tasty with spices, and the bread hot.

Falcon ate slowly, but steadily, for he knew that when the door to the other side of the store opened, odds were good that there would be trouble.

The owner of the store walked over, glanced toward the saloon, and said in a low tone, "Hired guns. They drifted in about an hour ago. They bought several bottles and told me to get out of the room."

"They ask anything else?" Wildcat queried.

"The shortest way to the Snake ranch."

Falcon had looked around and spotted a rack of Greeners on the wall: mean-looking sawed-off shotguns. "How come you have so many shotguns?"

"I ordered them for the stage line that used to run past here. They went out of business before I could get paid for them. You want them? I'll make you a real good deal."

"I'll take three of them now and put the others in with my order when it comes."

"Comin' right up."

"And all the boxes of buckshot you have."

"That's three cases!"

"Well, give us a handful each and put the others with the order."

"I like a shotgun," Wildcat said. "Buckshot don't leave no room for doubt."

"Wonder if the store owner can loan us a hammer and some nails?" Stumpy asked.

Falcon looked at him. "Why?"

"To nail Wildcat's boots to the floor. If short-stuff has to shoot one of them Greeners, the kick is gonna knock him clear over into the next county.''

The insulting between the two old friends started anew.

When the door to the saloon area finally open, the sawed-offs had been inspected and loaded up and were laying on the table, the noon dishes cleared away. Only a pot of coffee and three mugs remained on the table with the Greeners.

The hired guns took a glance at Falcon and his friends, then grabbed a harder look as they spotted the shotguns on the table. One of them beat it back into the saloon. Soon the mercantile side of the store was filled with men, most of them wearing two guns, some of them even having a third six-shooter tucked down behind their belts.

The hired guns mumbled and whispered among themselves for a moment before one of them stepped forward.

''Damn, he shore ain't much to look at,'' Stumpy muttered.

''What'd you say, grandpa?'' the gunny asked in a too-loud voice. ''If you was talkin' 'bout me, speak up, you old fart.''

''If he don't watch his mouth, he ain't gonna have time to get much uglier, either,'' Wildcat opined in low tones.

''Now the dwarf is whisperin', Bonnie,'' one of the gunnies said, then took a slug of whiskey straight from the bottle.

''Bonnie?'' Wildcat said, then laughed. ''Your name is Bonnie? Does your mommy know you're runnin' with such a rough crowd, my dear?''

Falcon could not contain his laughter at that.

''Now the big ugly one thinks it's funny,'' another hired gun said.

''Are you makin' fun of my name, you old goat?'' the man named Bonnie shouted.

Wildcat smiled at him.

''Let's put it this way,'' Stumpy said, ''anybody who would hire on with Miles Gilman and his bunch is low enough to crawl under a rattler's belly.''

The hired guns were standing shoulder to shoulder, all crowded up in one part of the large room, and Falcon could tell several of the older gunnies realized they were in a lousy position to start any gunplay. They started spreading out.

"Stand still," Falcon said. "Or I'm going to think you boys are about to start something that's going to get a lot of you hurt."

One of the older hands told Falcon to go commit an impossible act upon a certain part of his anatomy.

"My goodness!" Wildcat said, staring at the gunhand. "I'm deeply offended by your vulgar language."

"Yeah, me too," Stumpy said.

Several of the newly hired mercenaries had confused expressions on their faces. They couldn't figure what the three men at the table were up to. All three of them were sitting there making jokes.

"You boys don't really want to sign on with the Snake, do you?" Falcon asked.

"Why not?" a man asked.

"It might be real bad for your health, that's why."

"Yeah, it's plumb unhealthy over on the Snake range," Stumpy said.

"How's that?"

"Folks keep getting shot," Falcon told him.

"The Snake didn't hire us," another hired gun blurted. "We was hired by the Double N."

Wildcat cut his eyes to Falcon.

"Noonan and his people," Falcon explained, for Wildcat did not yet know the entire story. Falcon had only touched on the high points when he could get a word in during the insults being hurled back and forth between the two men.

"Ah," Wildcat said. "The plot thickens."

"Do what?" Stumpy asked.

"I heard that in a play oncet. I liked the sound of it." He glared at Stumpy. "You uneducated heathen," he added.

"Who the hell is Plot?" Stumpy asked. "Is he part of the cattlemen's alliance?"

"I'll explain later," Falcon told him.

"Don't you call me no heathen, you popcorn fart," Stumpy told Wildcat. "I read books."

"Hey!" Bonnie shouted. "You want to talk to us?"

"Not really," Stumpy said, momentarily returning his gaze to the gunmen.

The store owner, his wife, and his daughter were behind the counter, ready to hit the floor when the shooting started.

"You wouldn't know what a book was if one fell off the shelf and hit you on the head," Wildcat told his friend.

"Them three ain't got good sense," one of the older hired guns said. "I think they're loco in the head." He moved sideways toward the door, keeping his hands away from his guns. "I'm outta here."

"I'm with you," another said.

Ten left in the room, facing the three men at the table. Several of the ten looked as though they wanted to let the whole matter drop. But the younger guns weren't having any of that.

"Have to be Rockingchair hands," Bonnie said.

"Well, I'll just be go to hell," Stumpy said. "The kid figured it out."

"Took him long enough," Wildcat said. "I was beginnin' to wonder if Miss Bonnie was touched in the head."

"Miss Bonnie!" the gunhand yelled, his hands hovering over the pearl-handled butts of his pistols.

Two of the men hired on at the Snake for fighting wages began backing away, both of them holding their hands in front of them, signaling that they were out of it. They were old hands at hiring out their guns, and they realized there was something wrong with this picture. The three men at the table were too calm. That meant, to any experienced hand, the three of them had been down this road before . . . and lived to tell about it.

The two men walked out the door and mounted up and rode away. Both of them were breathing easier as they put distance between the old trading post and themselves. There would be another day, maybe. And just maybe the two men would forget the fighting wages and just punch cows. Let somebody else get shot full of bloody holes.

"Well," Falcon said, after drinking the last of his coffee. "I think the time for talking is over."

"Yep," Stumpy agreed. "We done listened to the band, now it's time to pay up or leave the dance hall."

"The only way you three is leavin' is for somebody to carry you out," Bonnie made his brag.

"Then go for your iron, boy," Wildcat slapped him with a verbal glove, "or shut your damn mouth."

Bonnie reached for his guns.

Nine

Falcon and Stumpy threw themselves backward to the floor, Greeners in their hands, just as Bonnie pulled iron and fired. They eared back the hammers and let the shotguns roar. Wildcat had ducked under the table in a move that caught the hired guns by surprise, and added his shotgun music to the deadly symphony of buckshot. The low-ceiled room was filled with arid gunsmoke and the roar of gunfire. The wall separating the store from the saloon was splattered with blood when the howling of lead faded away.

The shotguns had put every hired gun on the floor. Three were dead, nearly cut in half by the sawed-off shotguns. Two were wounded, and the others had all the fight ripped from them.

"No more!" one shouted. "We yield. No more shooting."

Falcon stood up, his eyes burning from the thick gunsmoke and his hands filled with .44s. "Get up!" he commanded. "Leave your guns on the floor and put your hands in the air."

Those who were unhurt, just scared crapless, crawled to their knees, hands high over their heads.

Bonnie was on the floor, shot in both legs. He was moaning about dying.

"Shut up," one of his pals told him in a shaky voice. "You ain't hurt bad."

"Oh, Christ," another of those unhurt said. "Look at Manley's head. It's blowed 'most clear off!" Then he threw up on the floor.

"Get their guns," Falcon told the store owner.

The trading post owner gathered up all the guns, being careful to avoid stepping in the gore, then quickly backed away.

"You boys take a message to Miles Gilman," Falcon told the survivors of the shoot-out. "Tell him we can either live in peace and get along, or we can have the damnedest war he ever saw. It's all up to him. Now clear out of here. And leave the dead men's horses."

Those few left alive helped the wounded to their boots, left the dead behind them, and scrambled for the door, and were in the saddle and gone half a minute later.

"You bury them and you can have their horses and guns and money," Falcon told the post owner.

"Deal, if you'll help me drag 'em out of here."

"Done. You going to get in trouble with Gilman for this?"

The post owner grinned. "Not damn likely. The cavalry leaves patrol remounts here and this is a stage stop. Gilman leaves me the hell alone."

"Good enough. Let's get the bodies out of here."

The hired guns had managed to bang off only four shots, hitting nothing but a side wall of the old trading post.

Falcon bought several bolts of cloth for the ladies, some candy for Jimmy, and the three of them headed back to the ranch.

Miles Gilman was in a blue funk. The news of someone buying twenty sections of land, north and south of the Rockingchair range, had just reached him, and he had gone into a towering rage. To make matters even worse, he had no idea who had bought it, for it had all been done by a bunch of lawyers in San Francisco and Denver. And now the hired mercenaries sent by Noonan had come staggering in, shot all to pieces at the trading post by Val Mack and two old geezers.

"Jesus Christ!" Miles screamed. "What in the hell is going on around here?"

Whatever it is, Claude his foreman silently and sourly mused, *it's probably gonna get worse.*

Martha and Angie oohed and aahed over the bolts of cloth, Jimmy chomped on the few pieces of candy his mother would let him have, and John, Kip, and Cookie listened to Falcon tell about what had taken place at the old trading place. During the telling, Jimmy sneaked a few more pieces of candy out of the jar and took off for the bunkhouse. The boy loved to listen to the wild tales of the older men.

"He'll just send ten or twenty or fifty more gunhands, Val," John said, after Falcon had finished and was drinking his coffee. "Do you and the rest of the boys plan on killin' them all?"

Falcon secretly smiled. His dad sure wiped out a gang after they attacked his town and killed Falcon's mother. "I don't think it will come to that, John."

"You don't know Miles Gilman, Val," John said grimly.

Puma Parley and Mustang rode in together a few days later and the outfit was complete. No one knew Mustang's real name and he wasn't about to give it up.

"That is, if he even remembers what it is," Big Bob commented.

Average age of the Rockingchair hands: sixty.

"What a crew," John remarked one morning. "I can truthfully say I don't think I have ever seen anythin' like 'em."

"Nobody else has either," Falcon replied with a laugh. He had noticed that Big Bob Marsh would occasionally take a long slow look all around him. He finally walked over to the big man and asked what in the world he was looking for.

"That damn beast of Puma's."

"He left it back in the cave."

"So he says," Big Bob said with a grimace. "But Puma has been known to tell a lie ever' now and then. Jenny's sneaky;

sneakiest varmint I ever did see. Just like his old cat was. I'll bet you a month's pay she's around here close.''

''Well, we'll know for sure if she pulls down a steer.''

Big Bob shook his head. ''She wouldn't do that unless she was desperate. I know it sounds far-fetched, but she was trained to leave cattle alone . . . usually. Some people claim that pumas is the dumbest animals on earth. Well, I reckon some is and some ain't. Jenny is one of them who ain't. That's a damn smart cat.''

Mustang was a man of average height and weight. But like all men of the mountains, he was all wang-leather and rawhide tough. Puma stood just a shade under six feet and was still a very powerful man. Any man who had a cupful of experience under his belt could, or should, be able to take one look at these men and know it would be best to give them a wide berth.

And Cookie found out that first evening they were all together about a mountain man's appetite: the average mountain man could put a grizzly to shame when it came to eating.

''Good thing you ordered them other wagons of food,'' Cookie told Falcon after the evening meal that first day. ''You should have told the post owner to fill the same order ever' month.''

Falcon laughed and said, ''I did!''

Falcon spent the next three days prowling the thousands of acres of Rockingchair range, looking for cattle. What he found did not surprise him.

''Somebody's rustled about half your herd, John,'' he reported back to the Rockingchair owner. ''No point in rounding them up for a drive. It wouldn't be worth it.''

John Bailey sat down heavily at the kitchen table and rubbed his face with his callused hands. ''Then I'm finished,'' he said wearily.

''Not at all,'' Falcon contradicted the rancher. ''We'll just get them back for you, or make Miles pay for them. You'll have to delay the drive until next year, but you'll have your cattle back.''

John lifted tired eyes to Falcon. ''You and six old men are goin' to do that?''

''Me and six mountain men,'' Falcon corrected.

* * *

The next morning, Falcon and six mountain men were up and riding toward Snake range before dawn. They each carried grub enough for two days and their pockets were stuffed with cartridges and their belt loops full.

Within an hour of crossing onto Snake range, they found a small herd of Rockingchair-branded cattle and started them moving back toward their own grass. The next hour they came up on a herd of Snake cattle with a lot of Rockingchair beeves all mixed in, and began cutting out those that did not belong to Miles Gilman. Two Snake punchers soon rode up and stared for a moment.

"What the hell do you people think you're doin'?" one finally demanded.

"Taking back our cattle," Falcon told him. "Get used to it. Because before it's all over, we'll cover every inch of Snake range."

"The hell you say!" the other Snake rider blurted.

"That's right. And when you people get your roundup completed, we'll be there to check brands."

"I don't think so, mister."

"I do." Falcon turned his horse to face the puncher. "You want to argue about it right now?"

The puncher thought about that for a few seconds, then shook his head. He was one of the few Snake riders left who was not drawing fighting wages. He rode for the brand, but had no desire to get himself killed. He had heard the stories about this Val Mack.

"I reckon not," the puncher finally said.

"Good," Falcon replied. "You and your partner can start these cattle moving toward their own range. That'll save us some time."

"You want us to do . . . what?" the other Snake hand asked.

"Get these cattle moving. They don't belong to you and I just might get it in my head to hang you both for rustling."

Big Bob Marsh and Stumpy started forming hangman nooses.

"Now wait just a damn minute!" one of the Snake punchers hollered. "We didn't rustle these cattle."

"Looks pretty bad to me," Puma said. "I just can't abide a thief."

"We ain't thieves!"

"Well, you work for a murdering thief," Falcon told him.

"And that's all we do," the second puncher said. "We ain't drawin' fightin' wages."

"You still work for a skunk," Dan Carson said.

"We got to work, mister."

"That's a fact. A man that don't work is a bum. But I'll bet there are other ranchers around who need hands."

Both punchers sighed.

"That's the truth, Dan," Falcon said. "I heard Tom Gorman over on the Double Triangle was paying top wages for good hands. Why don't you boys head over there and tell him I sent you. After you push these cows back onto Rockingchair grass, that is."

"We do that, and our lives won't be worth spit," the other puncher said.

"They will be if you stay out of town," Falcon corrected. "Just think, come the fall you boys can have about a hundred and fifty dollars saved up. Then you can do what you want to do. And boys, this situation around here will all be cleared up come the fall. You can bet on that."

The two cowboys exchanged glances, one asking, "How about our gear back at the bunkhouse?"

"What'd you have there?"

"Britches, shirts, socks, bedrolls, winter coats, gloves."

Falcon took a notepad out of his saddlebags and scribbled a short note, signing it Val Mack. He handed the note to the punchers. "You take this over to the old trading post and get outfitted new what you left behind. It's on me."

"Say now!" one of the punchers said. "That shines, mister. Thanks. Tom Gorman just got himself some hands."

"You'll sleep a lot better now that you're away from Miles Gilman."

Both cowboys smiled. "You're probably right about that."

"Any others over at the Snake who might be persuaded to leave?"

"Three that I can think of. We'll probably run into them 'fore long."

"Same deal for them."

"We'll tell them. Whether they take your deal or not is up to them. We'll get these cows back to the Rockingchair."

One of the punchers hesitated and said, "Val, you watch out for Lars Gilman. He's lookin' to make a name for himself. And he's fast, real fast."

"And about half nuts," his partner added.

"Thanks for the word. I won't forget it."

"See you boys around," Mustang said cheerfully.

"Nice fellers," Big Bob said.

"They are now," Wildcat added.

The men spend the rest of the day on Snake range and by the middle of the afternoon, had found about seventy-five more Rockingchair cows. They decided to call it quits for the day and push the small herd back to home range. They had seen no more Snake riders.

"We was lucky this day," Big Bob said. "But you can bet that from now on, this range will be swarming with Snake riders."

Falcon smiled. "So tomorrow, we'll work the far north sections for a couple of days. Then move to the extreme southern part of Snake range. There is no way we'll ever recover all of John's cattle, but if we can get several hundred, I'll be happy."

"I haven't spotted no altered brands," Stumpy said. "I think the Rockingchair brand is damn near impossible to cover."

"It would be difficult," Falcon agreed.

John and Kip were waiting at the corral when the riders returned. John smiled at Falcon and said, "I had an interestin' visit from a couple of, uh, former Snake riders this day."

"Did you now?"

"Yes. They brought back about thirty head of cattle. They were on their way to work for Tom Gorman."

"We talked to them boys for a few minutes and they had a change of heart 'bout workin' for Miles Gilman," Bob said. "We could tell right off they was troubled 'bout it."

"Do tell?" Kip said.

"Yep," Stumpy replied. "They seemed real happy 'bout leavin' Gilman."

"I just bet they were. "You boys decided not to spend the night on Snake range, hey?"

"We couldn't find no comfortable spot to bed down," Bob told him with a straight face. " 'Sides, we miss Cookie's grub."

"I see," John said.

"Anything exciting happen here while we were gone?" Falcon asked.

"Quiet as a church," the rancher replied. "Well, I been doin' some thinkin'. I probably don't have to remind you, but the weekend is comin' up."

"Do tell?" Stumpy said.

John smiled. "You boys wouldn't be thinkin' 'bout headin' into town to blow off a little steam, would you?"

"The town of Gilman is really jumpin' on a Saturday night, hey?" Puma asked.

"It can get right crowded when it fills up with Snake riders," Kip said.

"Tell the truth," Dan Carson said, standing with the other men, "I have been lookin' forward to a bottle and a friendly card game. We been on the move since we heard from, uh, Val, here and we just ain't had much time for relaxation. A night on the town would be sorta nice."

Both John and Kip noticed the slight hesitation when mentioning Val's name, but neither man said anything about it.

"I thought you boys might want to slick up and go in," John said.

"How about you and your family, Boss?" Big Bob asked.

John smiled and shook his head. "Can't risk it. Gilman's tried to burn us out twice. But with five good shots here, he won't dare attack the house."

"You want us all to stay?" Falcon asked. "After what happened this day, Gilman might throw caution to the wind and attack."

"No. You boys head on in and whoop it up. But you know, of course, that you're going to run into Snake riders."

Puma Parley smiled. "Countin' on that, Boss. Countin' on it."

Ten

Tom Gorman of the Double Triangle rode over the next day and thanked Val personally for sending him the two ex–Snake riders.

"I think they're basically good boys," Val said. "But keep them close to the bunkhouse for as long as you can. Some of the hired guns of Gilman will surely be carrying a grudge for them."

"Don't you worry about that. My wife's been cookin' up a storm since they arrived. All those boys are thinkin' 'bout doin' is eatin'."

Saturday afternoon, Falcon and the crew began slicking up for their visit into town. They all took turns in a horse trough bathing and washing the cooties out of their hair. Then Cookie volunteered to give them all a haircut. They shaved and brushed and curried and combed and primped and blacked their boots and put on their best.

"I swear," Big Bob said, turning slowly so all could get a look at him. "I shore am a handsome feller."

"You resemble a moose to me," Dick "Wildcat" Wheeless said.

"You mean I sorta remind you of that last squaw you took up with?" Bob came right back.

Laughing, the men saddled up and headed for town. To a man they knew they were riding into trouble, and to a man they didn't care ... indeed, they were looking forward to it.

About four miles from the Rockingchair ranch, the men came up on a wagon, a man and a woman on the seat, several kids in the back, two riders flanking the wagon.

"Howdy," Falcon called cheerfully, reining Hell back to a walk.

"Afternoon," the man called, after giving the riders a once over.

The outriders nodded at Falcon and the others, their eyes flicking over the various brands, for the men weren't riding Rockingchair stock.

"Joe Gray," the man said. "I own the spread just east of Bailey."

"John speaks highly of you," Falcon replied. "I'm Val Mack." He introduced the others and the man and woman and outriders all visibly relaxed.

"Y'all headin' into town for a bit of shoppin'?" Big Bob asked.

" 'Fraid so," Joe said. "Got to visit the doc and the apothecary. We usually trade at the old post, but this time we got to go to town."

"We haven't been to town in near'bouts a year," his wife added. "Not since it got too dangerous for us."

"Because of Miles Gilman and his bunch of trash, ma'am?" Stumpy asked.

"Yes," the woman replied. "And my name is Sarah." She smiled and introduced the others.

One of the outriders was their son, Jack—Falcon guessed him to be about seventeen—and the kids in the wagon were Lou Ann, fifteen, a very comely lass, and two boys, ages ten and eight.

"Well, if you folks don't mind," Falcon said, "we'll just ride along with you and see that you're not troubled by any of the Snake riders."

"I can handle myself," Jack said.

The older outrider grimaced at that remark, but said nothing.

"I'm sure you can, boy," Puma said. "But it never hurts to have backup, do it?"

"I reckon not," the teenager said. The young man was wearing a six-gun, low and tied down.

Falcon had carefully dressed in his only good clothes: a dark suit with a white shirt and a black string tie. He was wearing a long duster to keep his clothing relatively clean, and his twin guns were covered by the duster.

"Heard what you boys done for Tom Gorman," Joe said. "Kind of you. You see anyone else wants a job punchin' cows, send them over to the Four Star."

"We'll do that, Joe. How many hands do you need?"

"Three more would do it for me."

The older man's name was Sal, and he was the foreman at the Four Star. He'd been with Joe Gray and family for years. Sal dropped back from the right side of the wagon and rode over to Falcon, walking his horse along beside him.

"Jack's a hothead," Sal said softly. "He's a damn good son, loves his ma and pa, but he's got a quick temper and thinks he's better with a pistol than he really is."

"I got that impression, Sal."

"The job of bird-doggin' him whilst we're in town falls to me." He cut his eyes to Falcon. "He's gunnin' for Lars Gilman."

"That isn't good. Lars is almighty quick, so I hear."

"That ain't all he is. He's twisted real bad. All them boys of Miles's ain't normal in the head. They've all raped girls around the area. I hear tell that Miles don't believe none of it. Thinks it's all madeup. But it ain't madeup. It's true."

"The boys get that side from their father?"

Sal slowly nodded his head. "That's the word I get. Miles likes to get rough with women."

"The more I hear about Miles, the less I like him."

"There ain't a whole lot to like, for a fact."

"How does the town doctor stand in this fracas?"

"You mean what passes for a doc? Oh, he's all right . . .

when he's sober. And he really ain't a bad doc. Had a couple of years of medical school back east somewhere. Boston, I think. He's dug a lot of lead out of a lot of men.'' Sal chuckled for a moment. ''I heard what you done to ol' turd-face at the general store. I'd like to have seen that, for a fact.''

''He wasn't too happy.''

''I just bet he wasn't.''

''You can't buy supplies there?''

''Not a pound of coffee nor a peck of taters. Mainly it's his moose-butted wife who sucks up to Miles. They've got a worthless boy who gets all weak-kneed every time he gets around Miles's daughter. They think there might be a marriage someday.''

''Any chance of that?''

''None. That vile-tempered, rattlesnake-tongued female don't even know he's alive.''

Falcon smiled at Sal's description of Miles's daughter. ''I gather you don't like the girl?''

''I don't even think her daddy likes her much. Terri's a mean, spiteful heifer. She's just as twisted as her brothers. Whole entire family's nuts. Only one who ever had any sense was Miles's wife. She pulled out right after Terri was born and nobody's seen hide nor hair of her since.'' He eyeballed the crew who rode up with Falcon and shook his head. ''I don't recall ever seein' a meaner-lookin' bunch than this one. Mountain men, right?''

''Yes. I've known them all since I was just a little bitty boy. They're a good crew, long as nobody crowds them.''

Sal took another look. The mountain men were all wearing two guns and he suspected they probably had a third or maybe even a fourth pistol tucked away on their person somewhere.

''Town just might get real interestin' 'fore this day's done.''

''Oh, I think you can count on that, Sal.''

Sal grinned. ''I think I'll encourage the boss and his lady to take a room at the hotel for this night. Have a meal at Rosie's.'' Then he shook his head. ''No. I'd do that if it wasn't for young Jack. I don't want him to get killed.''

"You know the way it is out here, Sal. Boy straps on a gun, he becomes a man."

"Both his pa and me has tried to tell him that. But it's like talkin' to a fence post."

"Seventeen is a tough age, all right." Falcon remembered all too well his own youth. He looked up at the sky. Dark storm clouds were rolling in and gathering thick and ominous. "They might be forced to spend the night in town. We all might. It's about to come a real frog-strangler."

"Well, the ranch house is covered. The cook and the one hand we got left could hold off a small army. We sure could use a couple more hands, though."

"I'll ask around."

The town of Gilman came into view and the group stopped on the crest of the short ridge that overlooked the buildings set on either side of the wide main street. There were only a few horses at the hitchrails and the corral was empty.

"The Snake riders haven't made it in yet," Joe called, lifting the reins.

"But they will," his wife said.

"I hope so," Jack said.

"You keep your distance when they do," his father warned him. "And if you run into a pack of 'em, keep your hand away from that gun. You hear me?"

Jack did not acknowledge his father's words. He sat in his saddle, a sullen look clouding his young features.

"I ought to take that damn gun away from you," his father said.

"Nobody takes my gun," the young man replied. "Not you, not nobody."

At that, Falcon exchanged glances with his men. No getting around it: If any Snake riders showed up, there would be trouble. Young Jack Gray was primed and cocked and sitting on ready.

Joe clucked to the team and the parade rolled into town. Joe pulled around to the rear of the doc's offices, and Falcon and his men stabled their horses at the livery. Big Bob and the others shied away from hotels, preferring to sleep on the hay in the loft of the livery. Falcon walked over to the hotel and got him a room.

In his room, he removed his duster and brushed off his suit, then checked his guns. The men had not seen his guns. He was wearing pearl-handled, nickel-plated twin .44s. The guns had been specially made for him several years back.

Falcon walked over to the general store and the shopkeeper and his wife almost fainted when he strolled in, but they both kept any sharpness from their tongues as he picked out a new hat and paid for it in hard money. Falcon went over to the livery and stowed his old bullet-torn hat; he would wear it for everyday use.

His crew were over at the Stampede, having a bottle and arranging for a romp in the bed with some of the soiled doves. Then they would all go to Rosie's for a huge supper and then back over to the saloon for more drinking and card playing.

Joe Gray and family were still over at the doctor's office. Sal was leaning against a post in front of the office.

Falcon glanced over at the bank. It was closed. Then he heard the sound of horses. He looked up toward the end of the street. The hired guns from the Snake had arrived.

Eleven

Falcon looked over at Sal and caught the man's eye. Sal shrugged his shoulders before turning and walking into the doctor's office. Falcon stepped back into the shadows of the awning and counted a dozen Snake riders riding into town. Some tied their mounts to hitchrails, a few rode down to the livery. Before he could step out of the shadows, a half dozen more riders came racing into town, riding too fast. Anyone caught out in the street would have been trampled. Falcon frowned at the careless and arrogant riding. The men whooped and hollered and cussed without regard for any womenfolk who might have been on the boardwalks as they tied up at the hitchrails in front of the Stampede.

Falcon studied the brand for a moment. *N/N*, and the end of each N had a fancy curlicue, making it almost impossible for anyone to change it to a Box X.

Falcon carefully rolled a cigarette and licked and lit. He waited. He knew the Noonan riders could not have possibly pushed a herd up to this part of the country this quickly. That would have been impossible. Nance was sending some of his men in to beef up Gilman's boys.

Before he could ponder on the situation any further, more

riders came galloping into town with the same carelessness and arrogance shown by the Noonan riders. This bunch rode horses carrying the .44 brand: Rod Stegman's boys. The man who married Nance Noonan's sister; a man whose holdings were nearly as vast as his brother-in-law's; and, from what Falcon had been able to find out, just as ruthless as Nance.

Falcon stepped out of the shadows and walked over to the stage company's office. The noon stage had come and gone and Falcon was interested in seeing if he'd received any postings from his attorneys. He had ... several letters, all addressed to Val Mack, and all from various attorneys in San Francisco, Denver, and St. Louis.

One of the letters advised him that any and all warrants against Falcon MacCallister had been withdrawn. But Falcon knew that while that was wonderful, legally speaking, there were still hundreds of wanted posters with his name on them tacked up and posted all over the west, and they would stay up for a long time to come. There would be a dozen or more bounty hunters looking to collect the reward on his head.

They would not know the reward had been withdrawn.

One of the other letters was from his sister, Joleen, down in Valley, Colorado, bringing him up to date on anything and everything that was happening and had happened since Falcon left the town their father and mother had settled shortly after the fall of the Alamo down in Texas.

The third letter was from an attorney in St. Louis advising Falcon that he was several hundred thousand dollars richer (at least on paper) due to the rising value of stock in the railroads. Falcon smiled at the irony of it all: One of the richest men in the west was working as a ranch hand for a few dollars a month and found.

Falcon tucked the letters into a breast pocket of his suit coat and stepped out into the street, crossing over to the Stampede Saloon. He pushed open the batwings and stepped inside, standing for a moment to let his eyes adjust to the sudden darkening.

His men were sitting at a far table, playing cards and sharing a bottle, but actually drinking very little.

Falcon walked up to the long bar and ordered a drink, conscious of many eyes on him. He ignored the open stares, concentrating on his shot glass. Trouble would start soon enough, he felt. No need for him to hasten it.

All that changed when a local sidled up to his side and whispered, "You see that big feller at the end of the bar, mister?"

"Yes," Falcon returned the whisper.

"He's been braggin' for several days. Ever' time he comes into town. He claims to be one of the men who killed Jamie MacCallister."

Falcon felt a coldness wash over him. He lifted his eyes and stared down the bar at the man pointed out to him. A big burly fellow, with swarthy looks and a scar on one side of his face.

"What's his name?" Falcon asked the local.

"I heard him called *Rud* a time or two."

Falcon motioned for the bartender and told him to give the citizen a drink. The drink poured, Falcon said, "You'd better drink that and then get out of the way."

"Yes, sir. Thank you." The citizen gulped down the bourbon and walked off to a far corner of the huge first floor of the Stampede Saloon.

Falcon brushed back his coat, exposing both .44s, and stepped away from the bar, down to the end. "I hear tell there's a man here claims to have killed Jamie MacCallister," he spoke in a loud voice.

Sal and Joe Gray and his son Jack were standing on the boardwalk outside the saloon, looking through the windows.

"I killed Jamie MacCallister," the swarthy man said, stepping away from the bar. "It was a fair fight."

"You're a liar. Way I heard it, Jamie MacCallister was shot in the back. Twice, with a rifle."

"No man calls me a liar, mister."

"I just did," Falcon said. "I knew Jamie MacCallister. No two-bit loudmouth like you would have had the courage to stand up and hook and draw against a man like him. So that makes you a liar and a back-shooting murderer."

"I was there, mister. I faced MacCallister and shot him dead. So you can take your mouth and go to hell, or drag iron."

"Make your play, back-shooter."

Rud cursed and went for his gun and Falcon drilled him just as his hand touched the butt of his .45. The bullet slammed into the center of the man's chest and knocked him back against the bar. He slowly sank to the floor, dead.

Falcon holstered his .44 and stepped back to his position at the bar, signaling for the barkeep to pour him another drink.

"Jesus Christ," Sal breathed. "I never saw a man that fast."

Young Jack was standing with his mouth open, speechless.

The mountain men smiled and returned to their card game. None of the other hired guns standing at the long bar seemed at all anxious to pick up the fight.

"Well, hell!" the bartender shouted. "Somebody haul the body out of here. We can't have a body sittin' on the floor. That's bad for business."

Two Snake riders grabbed Rud by the arms and feet and toted him out and over to the undertaker's down the street.

"Val Mack," Falcon heard someone say in a hoarse whisper.

Falcon drank his whiskey and left the saloon. He nodded at Sal and Joe and Young Jack and walked across the street to take a seat in front of the hotel. In only a couple of minutes, his crew walked out, booze and women forgotten for the time being. The six of them spread out all up and down the main street, taking chairs in front of establishments or sitting on the edge of the boardwalk. They all knew that after the hired guns in the Stampede knocked back a few more drinks and worked up their courage, they would be ready for trouble.

It was just a matter of time before the streets of the small town would become a battleground.

"Why don't you take your men and leave?" The question came from Falcon's right side. "How many more must die from your guns?"

Falcon had seen the man walk up, all dressed in a black suit with a white collar. Reverend Watkins, the town's preacher.

Falcon cut his eyes to the man. "Just ride away and let the evil continue?"

"There are different kinds of evil, sir."

"Double-talk, Preacher. Words won't stop men like Miles

Gilman and Stegman and Noonan and all the others in the cattlemen's alliance.''

"And bullets will?''

"They seem to have a permanent effect if placed in the right spot,'' Falcon said drily.

"Who was that man who was just killed?''

"His name was Rud.''

"That's all? Just Rud?''

"That's all I know.''

"And you killed him?''

"Yes, I did.''

"I'll pray for you both.''

"I'm sure I need some prayer, Preacher. Now you better get off the street before the lead really starts flying.''

"More people are going to die this day?''

"You can count on that, Preacher.''

Thunder rumbled in the distance. The dark clouds were still gathering, turning the midafternoon dark and ominous. But still the rain held off.

Falcon dug in his coat pocket and handed the preacher some money. "For the collection plate in the morning.''

Watkins looked at the money. "Blood money from a hired gun? You think that will appease God?''

Falcon chuckled. "I'm no hired gun, Preacher. I've never hired my guns out to any man. You want this money, or not?''

"That's a lot of money. Who are you to come riding in here with your pockets filled with gold and greenbacks?''

"Maybe I'm an avenging angel.''

"Ahh . . . you're a Saint, then?''

"No. I'm not Mormon, Preacher.''

"God doesn't send mercenaries.''

"And what was Michael, Preacher, if not God's warrior?''

Watkins was silent for a moment. "You've had some religious training, that's evident.''

"Up to a point. I do read the Bible occasionally.''

The Preacher took the money and tucked it away in the breast pocket of his suit coat.

"Why don't you go over to the doc's office and see about

Mrs. Gray and her children, Preacher? I'm sure you could be a comfort to them.''

"You're a strange man, gunfighter.''

Falcon smiled. "I've been called worse.''

"I will pray for your soul.''

Falcon watched as several men pushed open the batwings to the saloon with a bang. "Get off the street, Preacher. Right now!''

Watkins hurried away, quickly crossing the dust and ruts of the road to the doctor's office.

The guns of the cattlemen's alliance spread out under the awning over the boardwalk in front of the saloon. Falcon knew they were sizing up the situation and not really liking it. More men pushed open the batwings and crowded the boardwalk, spreading out left and right.

Sal, Joe Gray, and young Jack had moved away from the saloon, down to the general store. The door to the general store was now closed, the shades pulled down tight over the front windows. The storekeeper and his wife had probably retreated to the rear rooms, getting as far away as possible from any stray bullets.

There was no resident foot traffic on either side of the street. The town's hundred or so citizens had gone home and closed the doors behind them.

Lightning licked the dark sky, thunder bumped the clouds, and a few fat drops of rain fell plopping to the dust of the street. But the main force of the storm was not yet ready to roar in.

Falcon stood up and brushed his coat back.

A couple of the hired guns left the boardwalk and led the horses away to the livery. The street was now empty.

Falcon waited for the other side to start the dance. He cut his eyes left and right. His men had left their chairs and perches on the boardwalk to stand in doorways and alleys.

Still, the hired guns of the cattlemen's alliance hesitated in hauling iron and letting the bullets fly.

The piano player in the Stampede Saloon had ceased his banging of the ivory. The sighing of the wind before the storm was the only sound as it whistled through the street and the alleyways.

"All right!" a man's voice cut the silence. "Snake riders get your horses. We're out of here. You Rockingchair and Four Star men just stand easy. We're pulling out."

Two minutes later, Miles Gilman's men had cleared the town and were heading back to friendlier range.

"Since we're bunkin' at Snake, I reckon we'll head on back, too," a bearded man called to Falcon. "That suit you, Val Mack?"

"Suits me," Falcon called. "We just came into town for a good time."

"Rud didn't have no good time."

"Rud was a liar and a back-shooter."

"Maybe so. We're gone. Let's ride, boys."

The riders for the alliance pulled out. The piano player at the Stampede began tickling the ivory. The shades at various businesses were raised and the front doors opened, welcoming trade from everybody except from the Four Star and Rockingchair crews.

Falcon walked over to Stumpy. "You think they're circling around, Stumpy?"

"Yeah, I do. I figure about two hours. They'll slip back into town and get into positions to ambush us, one by one. Just about at dark."

"That's the way I figure it. Let's see if we can't turn this thing around to our advantage."

"I'll tell the boys."

Falcon walked across the street to Joe Gray. "I think they're circling around. If you're going to stay in town, I suggest you get your family situated in the rear of the hotel and tell them to stay put."

Joe nodded his agreement. "I'll register them now. The doc's just about done lookin' over the kids."

"Anything serious?"

"Childhood sniffles, that's all. Some castor oil will get them goin' again."

"It always did me. If ma could catch me and hold me long enough to pour it down my throat, that is," Falcon said with a smile.

Twelve

About an hour after the hired guns rode out, the clouds began spilling over, dumping torrents of rain on the small town. The downpour lasted about fifteen minutes, then eased off to a softer steady rain.

Sarah Gray and her younger children were safely tucked away in a far room of the hotel, while Falcon sat with his men and with Sal, Joe, and Jack in the saloon. Young Jack had his lip all poked out because he could not have whiskey. He had to be content with a glass of sarsaparilla, and was none too happy about it.

"I reckon 'bout one more drink and we'd all best be thinkin' 'bout gettin' into position," Puma said, pouring another shot glass full to the brim.

"They'll be soaked clear through and madder than all get out," Mustang said with a chuckle.

"And them that brought slickers will be sweatin' like hogs in 'em," Big Bob added, a mean twinkle in his eyes.

Wildcat Wheeless cut his eyes to the outside. "Good night for what we have to do."

Falcon knocked back the last of his drink and pushed his chair back. He stood up. "Might as well get to it." He looked down at the foreman of the Four Star. "Sal, you and Jack take the hotel lobby, if you don't mind. Joe, the upstairs. OK?"

"Suits me," Sal said, pushing back his chair and getting to his boots.

Joe stood up. "Sounds good. I'll be on the upstairs overhang with a rifle. Let's go, boys."

When those three had exited the saloon, Dan Carson said, "I'm glad to see that squirt gone. The kid is too hotheaded for me. That was good thinkin'. Sal will keep him in line and behind cover."

"It's quit rainin'," Stumpy said. "But it's gonna be muddy and sloppy out there. We should be able to hear at least some of them when they make their move."

"I'll be in the alley between the saloon and the ladies' shop," Falcon said. "Luck to you all."

Falcon looked up at the sky. The storm was far from over, but for now the sky was only drizzling rain, the clouds producing a fine mist. Falcon pulled both guns from leather and waited at the rear of the alley. By now, his men would have spread out all over the town, waiting for the attack.

Falcon's eyes had adjusted to the darkness and he caught a dark blot of movement, the shadow darting from the two-hole outhouse behind the saloon to the single privy behind the dress shop. The shadow was carrying what appeared to be a rifle. Falcon did not fire. The movement might have been a local citizen with a cane, although Falcon doubted that.

Gunfire shattered the night, coming from down by the livery, followed by a harsh scream of pain. The man Falcon had been following stepped out from behind the privy and raised his rifle. He was wearing a hat with a tall crown. None of Falcon's people owned a hat like that. Falcon drilled Tall Hat in the shoulder and the man screamed and dropped his rifle, one hand clutching his bullet-torn shoulder. He staggered back behind the outhouse, out of Falcon's line of sight.

Falcon shifted positions in the alley, moving to the other side and crouching down to present a small target. Two fast shots cut the night, the muzzle of the pistol flashing a tail of fire behind the slug. The bullet slammed into the side of the building where Falcon had been standing.

Falcon fired twice, both .44 slugs hitting their mark. Falcon watched the outline of the gunman as he fell to the wet ground and was still.

From over the first floor of the hotel, Joe Gray's rifle barked several times. A man fell off the boardwalk at the mouth of the alley, behind Falcon, the fallen man's pistols clattering down the steps, suddenly loosened from numbed fingers.

Falcon quickly reloaded and, staying in a crouch, moved back to his original position, kneeling down, one knee sinking into the wet ground.

Across the street, hard gunfire ripped and roared. Falcon could not tell if it was coming from his people or some of the hired guns. A few seconds later, that was settled, as a man staggered off the boardwalk, both hands holding his belly. He lurched to the middle of the street and collapsed facedown in the mud.

From the other end of the street, pistol fire lashed, followed by a yelp of pain and a lot of cussing. Falcon did not recognize the profane voice.

Falcon smiled, thinking that the hired guns did not realize that with his men, they were up against of crew of highly experienced Indian fighters: men who had lived their entire adult lives on the razor-sharp cutting edge of danger, where one careless move could mean death. Men such as Puma and Wildcat and Big Bob and the others were as calm as a stump in a fight, making no moves they hadn't proven out over years of harsh living in the wilderness.

From the lobby of the hotel, pistols barked half a dozen times. Then, silence slowly enveloped the small town and settled in for a few moments. The Four Star and Rockingchair men waited, guns ready.

"Let's ride!" came a shout. Falcon could not tell where it was coming from. "This ain't no good."

Falcon waited, suspecting a trick. A few seconds later, his suspicions proved accurate as he heard a sound behind him. He was facing the street, so his white shirt, soiled and wet as it was, could not be seen. His black suit and black hat blended in with the night. He waited without turning around. The sound of footsteps grew closer.

Falcon threw himself to one side and the gunman behind fired, the slugs ripping into the side of the dress shop. Falcon fired just as he hit the ground full length. The impact threw his aim off, and he missed. He fired again and this time his aim was true. The man doubled over and then staggered from the alley.

All over the town, gunfire was tearing the night apart as the hired guns' trick backfired on them and Falcon's crew poured on the lead.

This time when someone shouted to pull out, it was no trick. The sounds of running boots slopping through the mud faded as the hired guns exited the town. In a couple of minutes, the sounds of horses galloping away into the night reached Falcon, then faded into silence.

"Anybody get hit?" Falcon called.

No one had gotten a scratch during the nighttime shoot-out in the town of Gilman.

"Lucky," Mustang said, strolling up the boardwalk toward Falcon. "But we sure put some hurt on them gunslicks."

"Help me!" a man called from the alley that ran between the hotel and a small leather shop. "I'm hard hit."

"Me, too," another man called weakly, his voice just carrying up the street.

"I'll see to this one," Puma called from the livery. "But he's gut-shot and there ain't much anyone can do for him."

"Oh, Lord!" the belly-shot man wailed.

"You a little late callin' on Him, son," Puma said.

The wounded man cussed him.

"Shame on you," Puma said. "You 'bout to meet your Maker with swear words in your mouth."

All over the small town, wounded men were crying out for someone to help them.

"I'll get the doc," Wildcat called from across the street.

"Better get him to call for a carpenter, too," Dan Carson yelled. "We've got some dead."

"Oh, Lord!" the gut-shot gunny yelled. "I ain't ready to die."

"Hardly anyone is, boy," Puma told him. "Leastwise I ain't never found nobody who was all that anxious."

Reverend Watkins walked up the street, Bible in hand. He knelt down beside a fallen .44 rider. "Would you like me to pray for you, son?"

"I want a doctor, you psalm-singin' son of a bitch!"

"I'll pray for you anyway."

The town's doctor was working on one man who was sprawled on the boardwalk. A local was holding a lantern. The doctor stood up and shook his head, then moved on to another man. "Get the rest over to my office," he said to no one in particular. "Come on. Help me get them out of the weather and the mud."

"Come on," Falcon said to his men. "Let's lend a hand."

"Yeah," Wildcat said. "Then we can get back to the serious business of drinkin'."

The cattlemen's alliance lost six men that stormy night, and the doctor treated six others for wounds ranging from minor to serious. Two of those seriously wounded would probably not make it.

Falcon gathered up all the pistols and rifles of the dead and wounded and stowed them in the back of Joe Gray's wagon. "Keep those for me, Joe. I've got a hunch they'll be put to good use later on."

The sky dumped rain on the land for most of the night, and the next morning the violent storm had rumbled on past and the sky was blue and the sun shining. Joe and his foreman and family headed back to the Four Star, Falcon and his crew headed back to Rockingchair range.

"Joe's a good man," John Bailey told Falcon, after Falcon related all that had taken place in the town. "He won't run and he won't back up. But his son . . . ?" The rancher shook his head and fell silent. He lit his pipe and puffed, filling the room with fragrant smoke. "Jack is determined to tie up with Lars

Gilman, and when he does, he'll lose. Lars is just too good a hand with a pistol."

"I suppose he'll brace me one of these days," Falcon mused.

"You can bet on it, son. If you're ever in town at the same time, Lars will call you out. You can get ready for that." He puffed for a moment, then asked, "What's on tap for tomorrow?"

"Rounding up more of your cattle."

"Any activity on those twenty sections of land that were just sold?" Miles Gilman asked his foreman.

"Couple of farmers have moved in, just north and south of the Rockingchair range," Claude informed his boss. "The boys report that Joe Gray visited each family and armed them to the teeth with the guns taken after that shoot-out in town."

"That damn Val Mack is behind all this," Miles spoke through gritted teeth. "John Bailey doesn't have enough cash or sense to pull off something like this." He looked at his foreman. "Will these sodbusters fight, you think?"

"Right down to the last drop of blood, Miles. I done some checkin' on them. Both men are veterans of the civil war. One fought for the north, the other for the south. And they won't hesitate to pull a trigger."

"Well, leave them alone for the time being. It's too late for them to get a crop in anyway. Soon as Nance and his boys get here, we'll settle this thing."

Claude wasn't too sure about that last statement, but he kept his thoughts to himself. His last two cowboys—those men not drawing fighting wages—had pulled out and gone to work for the Four Star. The men he had left, hired guns, were for the most part a lazy, surly bunch. They had been hired for their skills with a gun, not for their experience with cattle. But so far, Claude thought sourly, they sure as hell hadn't showed him much when it came to gunplay.

"When is Nance supposed to get here?" Claude asked.

"Trailin' a herd, so who knows? That bunch of so-called

gunhands who blew in here said he told them to tell me he'd been delayed.''

"So-called, is right," Claude muttered.

Miles heard him and smiled. "They're really not much, are they?"

"Well . . ." Claude scratched his head. "Truthfully, Miles, they're probably better than average. It's just that the men they're up against is old experienced hands, and they don't waste lead."

"Nance is bringin' his main guns with him. I think things will change when they arrive."

Claude almost said they damn sure couldn't get much worse, but he held his tongue, figuring Miles didn't need any smart-aleck comments like that at this time.

"Claude, you and the boys keep an eye on Lars, will you? He's makin' noises about huntin' up this Val Mack and drawin' down on him. Lars is fast; he could probably take this Mack person. But a lot of things can go wrong in a gunfight. Just . . . keep an eye on him for me, will you?"

"We'll watch him, Miles."

"Hotheaded kid," Miles said. "And his sister ain't makin' things any easier for him. She keeps eggin' him on."

Claude knew some things about Terri he could tell Miles, too, but he knew better than to bring up anything bad about Terri, for she was the apple of her daddy's eye. Miles went into a rage at the slightest hint of impropriety on Terri's part. Her father thought his little darling was still as sweet and innocent and virginal as the day she was born. Claude suppressed a sigh: if Miles only knew the truth.

Miles inaccurately read the expression on Claude's face. "It'll all work out, Claude. You worry too much about this Val Mack and them old men with him. If we have to wait until Nance gets here with his boys to settle this Val Mack's hash, so what? All Nance is gonna do is complain, that's all."

Claude didn't immediately reply. He stood and fiddled with his hat. The foreman didn't like to discuss Terri, for he knew the truth about that wild little heifer.

"Anything else, Claude?" Miles asked.

"Uh . . . no, I reckon that's it, Miles. I best be gettin' back to work."

"Claude?"

"Yeah, Miles?"

"You and the boys find any Rockingchair riders on our range, kill them on the spot. Understood?"

"Consider it done, Miles."

Falcon and Puma were working the northeasternmost corner of Snake range. They were riding cautiously, and not just because they might run into Snake riders. For even though it had been a year since Custer and his men were slaughtered by the Indians, and an all-out campaign by the Army to end the Indian wars was proving successful, there were still roaming bands of warriors looking to lift some hair. The west was settling down as more and more settlers were coming in and building homes and towns and churches and schools, but it would be a good twenty-five more years before the law of the gun and the smell of gunsmoke would start to fade.

The two men had found only a few head of Rockingchair cattle, and they had headed them back toward their own range. But five or ten or fifteen head a day adds up over a period of time.

The two men rode deeper into Snake range. They found five more head of Rockingchair cows and got them walking and grazing back east.

"That's ten head for the day," Puma said. "Want to try for more?"

"I guess we'd better head on back, Puma. It'll be late afternoon time we get back as it is."

"I was hopin' you'd say that. Miss Martha and Miss Angie was goin' to spend the afternoon makin' bear sign and my mouth's been salivatin' something fierce just thinkin' about it."

Falcon smiled. Just the smell of doughnuts cooking could bring cowboys riding in from fifty miles in any direction.

"Well," Falcon said, straightening in the saddle, "I hope

the boys leave you some, Puma. 'Cause I don't think we're going to make it back in time for supper.''

Puma jerked his head up, his eyes sweeping the landscape. He twisted in the saddle, looking all around him. ''Damn!'' he muttered.

There were riders all around them, four and five to a bunch. And the way the riders were positioned, escape for the Rocking-chair men was impossible.

''I'm thinkin' 'bout that cluster of rocks just up ahead,'' Puma said. ''With that cold little bubblin' spring smack-dab in the middle.''

''I was thinking the same thing.''

''We got ammunition aplenty and cold biscuits and beef left.''

''You ready?''

''Now!'' Puma yelled.

Both horses jumped forward, heading for the rocks at a full gallop.

Thirteen

Bullets whined all around the two men as they made their run toward the rocks, some of the bullets coming so close Falcon and Puma could feel the heat. They reached the rocks and threw themselves from the saddle, grabbing their rifles and getting into position. The horses walked toward the spring and drank deeply, then stood with heads down. It had been a long day and the animals were tired.

Falcon and Puma settled in for a siege. They had food and water and each carried several boxes of cartridges in their saddlebags, plus their belt loops were full. They could hold out for a long time.

The Snake riders had dismounted and taken cover wherever they could find it all around the upthrusting of rocks. There were several in an old buffalo wallow, several more behind natural depressions in the earth. Others were on the far side of the shallow creek behind the rocks. Left and right of the rocks, Snake riders had disappeared into the tall grass.

It was midsummer in Wyoming, and the sun was high and hot.

"Gonna be a lot tougher on them ol' boys out yonder than

it is on us," Puma remarked. "We got a little shade and lots of cold water. They got the sun and that's it."

Puma wasn't expecting a reply and Falcon didn't offer one. He took a sip of water from his canteen and then rolled himself a cigarette. A couple of exploring shots hammered at the rocks. Falcon and Puma did not return the fire. There was nothing to shoot at.

It was going to be a waiting game.

"Falcon?" Puma asked.

Falcon cut his eyes.

"This may seem like a stupid question, but I ain't kept up with the news lately. Who is president of the U-nited States?"

"Grant, isn't it?"

"Damned if I know. Last time I heard, it was Johnson."

A couple of rifle shots interrupted their political conversation.

"No. Grant got elected in '68, then got elected again. I guess we have a new president now. Why? You thinking of writing Washington and asking for help?"

Puma chuckled and took a bite from his plug of chewing tobacco. He chewed for a moment, then hollered: "Hey, you boys out yonder! Anybody know who the president of the U-nited States is?"

Several heartbeats thudded silently by. Then, from the tall grass, a voice called: "It's Ulysses S. Grant!"

"It ain't done it," another voice called. "We got us a new one. It's Hayes."

"Who the hell is Hayes?" another Snake rider shouted.

"Hayes?" Puma asked Falcon.

"That's right. I recall reading about that. Rutherford B. Hayes."

"I sure am behind the times," Puma remarked. "Thank you!" he shouted.

"You're welcome," a Snake rider called.

Then there was no more conversation as both sides fell silent. The sun beat down and the trapped and their attackers sweated under its glare.

"Oh, my," Puma called, after a trip to the spring and a long drink of the cold pure water. "This here spring water is sure tasty. Anytime you boys want a drink, just come on down and hep yourselves.''

"Very funny,'' a Snake rider called, a definite edge to his voice.

"I thought it was right neighborly of me,'' Puma returned the shout. "I just hate to see a man goin' thirsty when they's water aplenty.''

One Snake rider got a tad careless and exposed part of a leg. Falcon broke it with a bullet and the man began yelling in pain.

"We got to get him to a doctor!'' a Snake rider yelled.

"Why, sure, boys,'' Puma yelled. "Three, four of you just amble on over to him and tote that sufferin' feller off into town. I 'spect that bullet's still in the leg, and it might get infected. We wouldn't want that.''

"Why don't you boys surrender?'' another Snake rider yelled. "You ain't got a chance.''

"Why don't you go to hell?'' Puma replied.

"You're trapped. We'll get you sooner or later.''

Any other time, those words might have been true, but not this afternoon. If they weren't back by dusk, the rest of the crew would come looking, for Puma wasn't about to miss chowing down on a couple dozen bear sign.

Falcon watched as Puma carefully lifted his rifle and sighted. He had spotted something that was out of place. After a moment he squeezed the trigger, and a man suddenly rose up out of the grass, grabbing at his shoulder. Puma put a round in the man's leg for insurance, and the already wounded man's leg buckled under him and he fell to the ground, out of sight of those in the rocks, and started hollering.

"There's two that need to go see a doctor,'' Puma shouted. "You best get them into town 'fore they croak on you. They'd never forgive you if that happened.''

"Of course you'll let us gather up the wounded and ride out without openin' fire?'' the question was shouted from the buffalo wallow.

"Why, sure we will,'' Puma yelled, enough sarcasm in his words to fill a coffeepot. "Go right ahead, boys.''

"You can all ride out," Falcon shouted. "Gather up your wounded and ride out. We won't fire."

"You go to hell!" came the reply.

"Suit yourselves," Falcon yelled, and settled back in a more comfortable position among the rocks.

Over the next hour, a few shots and several dozen insults were tossed out from both sides. The Snake riders' horses, although ground-reined, had wandered off a few yards during grazing. The Snake riders' could not reach them without exposing themselves. Both sides were, in effect, trapped.

"This ain't worth a damn," one disgusted Snake hired gun called to another.

"Sure ain't, Ted," his partner agreed. "I'm hungry, I'm thirsty, and I'm sweatin' like a hog."

"Me too. Seems like we've trapped them and they've trapped us. And if they ain't back to the Rockingchair by dark, some people's gonna come lookin'."

"You can bet on that."

Ted called across the grass: "What do you think, Greely?"

"What d' you mean?"

"This situation. It ain't no good."

"You got a better idea?"

"I do," a .44 hand called. "Leave."

"I'm for that," an N/N rider called. "We can't even see where them two are up in them rocks. This ain't gettin' us nothin' but picked off, one by one."

"We go back now," another entered the debate under the blazing sun, "and some of us are gonna lose our jobs. Gilman will be madder than hell."

"I wasn't lookin' for a job when this one come along," still another spoke up.

"Me neither," his partner said. "I've had a bad feelin' about this country ever since that damn Val Mack come ridin' in. Then he brung in all them old mountain men and things ain't been doin' nothin' but gettin' worser."

"If they'll let me, I'm ridin' out of here," still another rider tossed out. "If Gilman wants to fire me, that's OK with me."

This mixed bunch of Snake, .44, and N/N riders had no boss

riding with them. Their only orders from Claude had been to find Rockingchair hands and kill them if possible. On this day, that was proving a very difficult task.

"You in the rocks!" a .44 rider shouted. "You let us ride out?"

"If you all go in a bunch," Falcon called.

"We'll all leave."

"Get your horses, then get your wounded, and ride out then. We'll hold our fire."

No one had been killed that day, and the men who had been shot, while their wounds were serious, would live. The Snake, N/N, and .44 hands rode west, and Falcon and Puma headed east, toward Rockingchair grass, pushing their small herd of cattle ahead of them.

"You boys were lucky," John Bailey said. "They jumped the gun, that's all. Showed their hand in the worst possible place, for them. I know those rocks and that spring. You could have held out there for a long time."

Puma grunted his agreement. He couldn't speak; his mouth was stuffed full of bear sign, which he was washing down with great gulps of coffee.

"Me and Miles held off Injuns there all one day and night," Kip said.

"You and Miles?" Falcon asked, surprise in the question.

"Oh, yeah. We used to be friends. All of us used to socialize. Till Miles started gettin' greedy and wantin' more and more land. Miles's foreman Claude and me was pals for years. Till he turned just as mean as Miles."

"We all went through the bad times together," John said. "Drought, Injuns, terrible winters. That's why this whole situation leaves such a bad taste in our mouths."

"Miles's wife saw it coming before any of us," Martha said, placing another hugely piled platter of doughnuts on the table in front of the men. "She warned me that Miles was changing. And she was right."

"In one way," Puma finally spoke up, taking a rest between

doughnuts. "What happened this day ain't gonna be good for us. Them ol' boys that pulled out, some of them anyways, is gonna lose their jobs. And they're gonna be replaced with hardcases. This will probably be the last time any agreement will ever be reached 'tween any of us."

"You're right about that, Puma," Kip said. "From now on, you boys stay on Rockingchair range. You've brought back a lot more head than any of us ever expected you to find, and that will have to do us."

"Kip's right and that's settled," John said. "The young stuff have to be branded anyway. We'll have work aplenty right here close to home."

"Well, in a few days the additional supplies will be coming in over at the post and they have to be picked up. We're going to have to patch up some wagons to haul it all back here. That'll take a day or two. We've got enough work to last us for a time."

"I reckon we can call this the quiet time before the storm," John said.

"Oh, it's going to bust loose," Falcon agreed. "We haven't seen anything yet."

"Have any of you ever heard of a gunfighter people have nicknamed the Silver Dollar Kid?" Kip asked.

Puma shook his head. "That's a new one on me."

"I have. I've seen him," Falcon said. "He's crazy. He's just a kid, only about twenty or so, but he's killed a lot of men. Has silver dollars on his vest and gunbelt and holster. He's vicious. Why, John?"

"Nance Noonan is rumored to have hired him and about a dozen more just as bad to clean out the farmers and small ranchers in this area. Friend of mine from up in Montana came through here while you boys was in town. He was on his way down south of here to buy a herd of horses. Told me about this Silver Dollar Kid. Said wherever he goes, people die."

"That's the truth, and he's quick, for a fact," Falcon conceded. "But like so many fast guns, he doesn't really have good control. You can count on him missing his first shot fifty percent of the time." Falcon sighed as he reached for his hat.

"I wondered when Nance or Rod or Miles would start bringing in the real shooters. Now we know."

"These boys won't be makin' no stupid mistakes, neither," Puma added. "And they won't be playin' by no rules 'ceptin' their own. I 'spect we'd all better ride in pairs from now on. And Miss Angie doesn't dare leave the compound without an escort."

"You're mighty right about that, Puma," Kip said. "John, you're gonna have to put your boot down about this."

"I will. And I think Angie will understand the seriousness of the situation."

"She better," Martha said grimly. "Or I'll step in and put *my* foot down."

"Oh, Lord have mercy on us all!" her husband said, rolling his eyes.

Martha took a fake swing at him and he laughed and ducked. Falcon and Puma took that time to exit the main house, after Puma had filled up his hat with bear sign.

"Gettin' serious now, ol' son," Puma said, during the walk to the bunkhouse.

"It is for a fact."

"You seen this Silver Dollar Kid work?"

"Once. He's quick."

"Better than you?"

"He's just as fast as I am, Puma. But he counts on speed rather than accuracy."

"And he's crazy?"

"Nuttier than a tree filled with squirrels. Laughs uncontrollably. Giggles like a girl. Very touchy; takes offense at anything. You never know what's going to set him off."

"And he likes to kill?"

"He lives for it. I think he's twisted, if you know what I mean."

"One of those."

Puma frowned. "I don't even like to be around that type. Gives me the goose bumps."

"Stay away from the Kid, Puma. Pass the word to the others."

"I'll be sure do that, son. But you know he's been hired to kill you?"

"Probably. But that's been tried before."

The men paused at the bunkhouse door. "You comin' in now?" Puma asked.

"No yet. I think I'll take a walk around for a bit. I'm a little restless."

"Want some company?"

"No."

"I know that feelin'. Night, boy."

"Night, Puma."

Falcon circled the house, then walked down to the corral. The horses were restless, moving. They sensed something amiss. But what was it? The Baileys didn't have a dog. Night riders had killed Jimmy's little dog before Falcon had appeared on the scene. That irritated Falcon, for he liked dogs and didn't have much use for men who killed them just for the hell of it. Another mark against Miles Gilman and the men who rode for him.

Kip had told him it was Lars who'd shot the dog. Falcon would settle Lars's hash one of these days—he was sure of that. But he wanted to do it with his fists, not with guns. What Lars needed was a good old-fashioned ass-kicking.

Falcon walked down to the henhouse. Maybe a varmint had gotten in there. But no, the hens were settled in their nests.

That left the barn. Falcon circled wide around and came up at the rear of the barn. Hell was raising it in his stall. Falcon smiled. Someone was in the barn. But it would be the last barn they ever entered if whoever it was made the mistake of getting into the stall with Hell. Hell was one of the meanest horses Falcon had ever seen . . . other than some of the ones his pa used to ride.

Falcon pushed open the door and stepped inside, pistol in his hand.

A shadow stood up and said, "Don't shoot. I'm friendly. It's about time we met, Falcon MacCallister."

Fourteen

"I can just make out your hands," Falcon warned. "Move your arms and you're a dead man."

The man in the shadows chuckled. "Relax, Falcon. I'm a United States deputy federal marshal."

"Name?"

"I'd best keep that a secret for the time being. I was sent into this area to find and arrest you. But I never did believe what those warrants said happened over in Utah. I tried to pet that horse or yours. Bastard tried to bite me."

"It's a wonder you still have a hand."

"You want to put up the gun, now?"

"No. Not yet. Tell me more."

"Can't say as I blame you. All right. Long before the warrant on you was lifted, I started smelling the stink of all the rotten goings-on in this part of Wyoming. But I can't do very much about it right now."

"Why?"

"It's all political, Falcon. Big money at work here, and big money puts politicians deep into those monied pockets."

"Does it reach all the way to the president of the United States?"

"If it does, it will never be proven."

"Nice system we have in place."

"Believe me, Falcon, as time progresses and the nation grows, it will get much worse."

"Hopefully, we won't be around to witness that."

"I share your sentiments."

Falcon holstered his pistol and started to move toward the man standing in the shadows. The federal marshal held up one hand in warning.

"Don't, Falcon. What you don't know can't be tortured out of you."

Falcon stopped. "The cattlemen's alliance has done that to people?"

"Oh yes. Rape, torture, murder, extortion . . . you name it, they've had their greedy hands in it."

"And the government can't do anything to stop it?"

"Certain elected and appointed people in the government *won't* do anything to stop it."

"So the small ranchers and the farmers in this area are on their own, right?"

"That's pretty much the way it is now, and pretty much the way it's going for be for some time."

"Until . . . what changes?"

"Back east, the public doesn't know what is really happening out here. To them, this is still wild and woolly country, untamed. Savage Indians, wild cowboys who settle every issue with a gun. People don't carry guns back east, Falcon. They have policemen and courts and judges; that's how they settle disputes, not with gunplay. But they need beef back east, and the big ranchers can supply that beef. And the big ranchers have a huge voice back east when it comes to the press. The public is getting only one side of the story, and they will continue getting only one side of the story."

"So everything is stacked against the little man."

"Unfortunately, yes."

"No immediate relief in sight?"

"None whatsoever. And I doubt there will be any help for years. The sheriffs in every county in the northern part of this state are bought and paid for by the cattlemen's cartel. You'll get absolutely no help from them.''

"Why are you telling me this?"

"I can't come close to making the odds even for you and the people you're trying to help, but I can at least warn you what you're up against.''

"But no help for us from the government?"

"None. It's going to have to get a hell of a lot worse before the government will be forced to step in. And that will probably come about by an outraged public all over America.''

"I know that many small ranchers and farmers in the area have written letters to the government.''

"They never got past some obscure clerk in a dusty office.''

"I do appreciate you telling me this.''

"It's about all I can do. I'll be around, but for the most part, my hands are tied.''

Falcon stepped to one side and the shadowy figure walked past him and out the rear door of the barn without another word being exchanged between the two men.

Falcon stood in the silence and listened for the sound of a horse. He heard nothing. The federal marshal must have left his horse some distance away.

Falcon walked over to Hell and stroked the animal's nose. The big horse nickered softly. Anyone else who had tried to touch Hell would have immediately been minus several fingers.

"Interesting little talk I just had, ol' boy," Falcon whispered. "But it damn sure pointed out plain and clear the direction the little man has to take against the cattlemen's alliance.''

Falcon lit a lantern and inspected the still damp earth just outside the rear barn door. There were his own bootprints, and the prints of a person walking away from the area. Those prints had a clearly visible V-shaped cut in the right boot heel.

Falcon squatted there for a few moments. He wouldn't tell John Bailey about the federal marshal. No point in further depressing the rancher; the situation was bad enough as it was without adding to it.

All Falcon could do was wait for the cattlemen's alliance to make the next move.

* * *

Falcon told no one about his meeting with the federal marshal. All the hands stayed close for the next several days, for there was plenty to keep them busy. In the middle of the week, Falcon, Wildcat, and Stumpy hitched up teams to three wagons and pulled out early for the old trading post. Falcon had ordered enough supplies to last, hopefully, until the end of the summer. He had also ordered enough ammunition to start a major war.

A drifting cowboy had stopped at the Rockingchair the day before and told his story about approaching the Snake ranch to see about work. He had known nothing of the trouble in this part of Northern Wyoming. He said he had never seen so many hired guns in all his life. He said a man would be hard-pressed to find a real cowboy in the whole bunch. Falcon told him about a small rancher over east of the Rockingchair who needed a hand and the man thanked him and headed that way.

"So the hardcases have arrived," Stumpy said, during a rest break at a shallow running creek.

"Looks that way. Some of them."

"Least he didn't didn't say nothin' 'bout no kid with silver dollars on his vest and gunbelt."

Falcon smiled. "Don't worry about the kid, Stumpy. I haven't lost any sleep over him."

Stumpy cut his eyes to Falcon. "You that sure you can take him?"

"I've seen the kid do his stuff. He's a showboat. Most of the time he has to work himself up to gunplay. I don't think he's ever faced anyone who was really good with a gun."

"Max Wells," the older man corrected.

"Max was drunk. That's the way I heard it."

"Maybe so."

"Max was also gettin' on in years and he'd 'llowed hisself to get fat," Wildcat said. "And careless. Thought his reputation could get him out of any trouble. He was wrong."

"You was there?" Stumpy asked. "I didn't know that."

"I was there. Little town in Arizona. Max's best days was long behind him and he'd taken the job as marshal just to have somethin' to do. Max hadn't pulled iron on nobody in five, six years. The kid comes sashayin' into town, makin' his brags. Backed Max into a corner and forced him to draw. But as drunk as he was, Max still cleared leather 'fore the kid plugged him.''

"My pa knew Max Wells," Falcon said. "Rode with him a time or two. Said he was a good man as long as he stayed off the bottle.''

"That was his undoin', all right," Wildcat agreed. "I believe he'd a taken the kid sober.''

"We'll never know," Falcon said, standing up from his squat by the creek. "But if he braces me, I'll kill him. I got no use for people like the kid. All right, boys, let's push on. We're going to have a slow pull back to the ranch.''

"I never seen so many supplies in all my borned days," the trading post owner allowed. "I had to store some of them in the barn. I don't think them three wagons you brung will hold 'em all.''

"Then we'll come back another day for what's left," Falcon told him. "Soon as we finish this coffee, let's get them loaded up and get out of here before trouble shows up.''

"You expectin' trouble?" the post owner asked.

"The way this country is filling up with hired guns?" Falcon put it as a question.

"Good point," the man agreed. "Say, you heard anythin' 'bout the Silver Dollar Kid comin' in?''

Falcon sighed. He was already getting weary about hearing the name of that crazy killer. "I heard Nance Noonan hired him. Don't know if he's here yet or not.''

"I heard he's faster than Billy the Kid.''

"Billy isn't fast," Falcon corrected. "He's just about half nuts, that's all.''

"You've seen Billy the Kid?''

"I've seen him. He didn't impress me.''

"Well, I'll be damned! Have some more coffee and I'll help you get loaded. Tell me about Billy the Kid.''

"Not that much to tell. If he ever had a stand-up face-off in the street with anybody who was any good, I haven't heard about it."

"Who's the best?" the trading post owner asked.

"John Wesley Hardin," Falcon said without hesitation. "The Texas gunfighter. But there's probably dozens out there just as good or better. They just haven't gone around looking for a name. John Wesley and Wild Bill Hickok faced each other a few years back. Neither of them would draw."

"Hickok's dead, ain't he?"

"So I hear. Somebody name of Jack McCall shot him in the back over in Deadwood."

"They hang him?"

"Not yet. I heard the first jury found him not guilty. Judge called for another trial. That jury found him guilty and sentenced him to hang."

"Hickok was holdin' aces and eights," Wildcat said. "McCall slipped up behind him and shot him in the back of the head. Hickok never made a sound, way I heard it. He just straightened up for a few seconds, then fell over dead."

"How come he shot him?" the trading post owner asked.

"Don't no one really know."

"I heard one story about the man claiming Hickok cheated him at cards," Falcon said. "Then he changed that to claim that Wild Bill had killed his brother."

"Had he?"

Falcon shook his head. "No trace of a brother was ever found."

"When's he gonna swing?" Stumpy asked.

"Soon, probably." He sat his coffee mug down on the counter. "Well, let's get to work, boys." He smiled. "We've only got about three tons of supplies to load." He looked at the post owner. "And don't forget those shotguns and cases of shells."

"They're packed and ready to go."

The men worked for over an hour, not working in a hurry, but getting a lot done and packing the boxes and crates and barrels of supplies carefully for the long pull back to the ranch.

They paused and looked up as the post owner came rushing

out onto the loading dock after a trip back inside. "Trouble, boys. Snake riders comin' in."

"How many?" Falcon asked.

" 'Bout ten or so. They don't never ride nowheres 'ceptin' in a big bunch."

"Somethin' tells me we're gonna be late gettin' back to the ranch," Wildcat said, straightening up and mopping his sweaty face.

"Well, hell," Stumpy said. "I want a beer anyways. It's time to take a break."

"Lars is with 'em," the post owner added softly. "And he's primed and cocked for trouble."

"This should be very interesting, then," Falcon said, stepping onto the loading dock. "Let's go meet Mr. Lars Gilman. It'll be my pleasure."

Fifteen

Falcon, Stumpy, and Wildcat entered the post from the rear at the same time the Snake riders were coming in the front door. They reached the steps of the saloon at the same time. For a few seconds, it looked as though trouble would start right there while they were all jammed up, neither side willing to give an inch to clear the steps. The men stood and glared at one another for half a minute.

Finally, Wildcat took off his hat and with a sweeping gesture and a bow, said, "Oh, after you boys, please."

"I'll be damned!" a Snake rider said. "You go first."

"Oh, no," Wildcat said. "I insist."

"Hell, no!"

"Well, I want a beer," Stumpy broke the impasse. "I'll go first."

Stumpy shoved his way through the knot of men and a few Snake riders followed. Then Falcon and Wildcat, followed by the rest of the Snake bunch and the post owner, who was wearing a very worried expression.

Falcon, Stumpy, and Wildcat ordered beer. The Snake bunch ordered whiskey, then took their bottles and shot glasses to the tables and sat down. Stumpy and Wildcat positioned themselves at opposite ends of the plank bar. That left Falcon and Lars standing near the center the bar.

Falcon sipped his beer and ignored the young man. Falcon figured it would take at least a couple of shots of Who Hit John for Lars to get his courage worked up.

Several minutes ticked by, with no one saying a word. The Snake men glared at Stumpy and Wildcat. Stumpy and Wildcat grinned back at them and deliberately slurped their beer as loud as possible, followed by loud smacking noises and belches.

"That's disgusting!" Lars finally said, glaring at Wildcat. "Why don't you go outside and sit with the hogs?"

"If you don't like it in here, you can always leave," Wildcat told him.

Falcon hid his smile. Just as Stumpy and Wildcat had done, Falcon had taken an instant dislike to Lars Gilman, accurately sensing that the young man was spoiled and arrogant and very much accustomed to getting his own way whenever he chose . . . no matter what the cost.

The Snake riders seated at the tables were edgy, not liking this situation. They were experienced gunhands, and knew if trouble started inside the saloon, neither side would emerge victorious. The two older men at the ends of the long bar had the better positions, for they were standing. And while they would surely go down, before they did they would put a lot of lead into the men seated. The Snake riders had seen right off that the two older men were each wearing two guns: one in leather, the other tucked down behind their gunbelts. The Snake riders also knew how dangerous these older men were, for they were the last of a breed known as mountain men, and there was no back-up in them.

"I guess you think these old men belchin' and carryin' on in public is funny," Lars said, cutting his eyes to Falcon.

"It doesn't bother me, sonny boy," Falcon replied, holding his beer mug in his left hand.

Lars tossed back another shot of whiskey and set the glass down with a bang. "Well, it bothers me."

"I suppose you just might be a little bit more delicate than the rest of us," Falcon said. "Your sense of propriety's much more easily bruised."

Lars turned at the bar to face Falcon. "Huh?"

"That means you a pretty little flower, boy," Wildcat said. "Maybe a petunia."

"Now, you just wait a damn minute here!" Lars flared, his face reddening.

"Or maybe he's a black-eyed Susan," Stumpy remarked. "Or a pretty little buttercup."

A couple of the Snake riders ducked their heads and hid their smiles.

"Tell me, Mars," Falcon said. "You shot any dogs belonging to little boys lately?"

"My name is Lars, damnit! Not Mars!"

"Oh, excuse me. Well, have you?"

"I don't know what you're talkin' about."

"You're a liar, Gars," Falcon said softly. Falcon cut his eyes. Stumpy had left the room and he wondered why.

Lars turned slowly to face Falcon. "No man calls me a liar!" Lars's face was beet red with anger.

"I just did, sonny boy. You killed Jimmy Bailey's little dog for no reason. And I'll tell you what you're going to do about it."

"What *I'm* goin' to do?"

"That's right, Jars. What *you're* going to do. You're going to find Jimmy a puppy and bring it over to him and deliver it personally. That's what you're going to do."

"When Hell freezes over!"

"Oh, I think it's going to be before then."

Stumpy walked back into the saloon carrying one of the sawed-off shotguns. He took his position at the bar and broke open the Greener, loading up both barrels and snapping it closed. Then he smiled at the Snake riders.

One of the Snake hired guns sighed. A sawed-off shotgun at this range could kill or seriously wound half a dozen men.

Young Lars was on his own for this go-around.

Lars looked at the smiling Stumpy and the very lethal shotgun and turned a little green around the mouth, realizing that any move his men might make on his behalf could well result in their death.

"Don't you think that would be a nice gesture on your part, Bars?" Falcon asked.

"You go right straight to hell, mister!"

Falcon smiled and took off his gunbelt, laying it on the bar. He faced Lars. "Now then, you spoiled brat. Either tuck your tail between your legs and ride out of here, or stand up on your hind legs and fight."

Lars knew he had to fight. He had absolutely no choice in the matter. If he didn't, no matter how much his father paid the men and told them to take orders from his son, they would not follow him. They would lose all respect.

Lars took a closer look at the man facing him. God, he was big, with muscles that bulged his obviously expensive shirt. Lars noticed the man's boots. Again he got the impression they were very expensive. Who the hell was this Val Mack?

But Lars was no coward. He'd had his share of rough and tumble fistfights, and he was not a little man. He'd worked hard all his life and his shoulders and arms were packed with muscle. He slowly took off his fancy gunbelt and laid the rig on the bar. He was very conscious that the eyes of all his men were on him. He watched as Falcon pulled on a pair of thin black riding gloves he'd taken from a hip pocket of his jeans. Lars wondered about that. He was not yet experienced enough as a fighter to know that a thin leather covering on the fists both protects the hands and enables a person to hit harder.

Lars suddenly lunged at Falcon. Falcon sidestepped and gave the younger man a hard shot to the belly. The air whooshed out of Lars and he grabbed at the bar for support. Falcon stepped back and let him catch his breath.

Lars cussed Falcon after he'd sucked in some air and again lunged at him. Falcon lashed out with a right and left that both connected on Lars's face. The blows stopped the blowhard cold. Lars shook his head to clear the cobwebs and stood for a moment, glaring at Falcon.

"You know where you can find a cute little puppy for Jimmy?" Falcon asked.

Lars spewed out a few cusswords about Falcon's question, Jimmy Bailey, and dogs in particular, and stepped in. Falcon let the younger man's blows fall on his shoulders, doing no real damage, although Lars thought he was inflicting a great deal of abuse.

Falcon abruptly shoved the man away and popped him on the nose, bringing a thin flow of blood.

Lars backed away and wiped his nose with the back of his hand. He stared down at the blood for a second, then began yelling. He seemed outraged at the sight of his own blood. He wiped his nose again and lifted his fists, finally getting some smarts about fighting this man who stood in front of him, smiling.

Lars stepped up to the invisible mark and flicked out a probing left. Falcon slapped it away. Lars tried a right and Falcon slipped a straight left through the gap and again connected with Lars's nose, snapping his head back and bringing a grunt of pain. Before Lars could recover, Falcon was all over him with lefts and rights, the blows smashing into the man's face and mouth and nose. This time, one of the blows flattened Lars's nose.

Falcon stepped back, allowing the younger man to catch his breath. He had to breathe through his mouth because of his damaged beak.

Lars was game, Falcon had to concede that. He plowed in, his eyes wild with fury and his fists pumping and windmilling. He connected with a fist to Falcon's head that stung and another hard fist to Falcon's jaw that drove the bigger man back. Falcon quickly recovered and stepped right back into the fray.

Falcon busted Lars solidly on one ear, which brought a yelp of pain, and followed that with a shot to the gut. Lars doubled over and Falcon hit him with a uppercut that straightened the man up, his eyes glazed over.

Falcon bored in with hard lefts and rights, pinning Lars against the bar. Falcon sensed the fight was nearly over. He hit Lars twice more, a very solid left and right, and Lars slumped down to the saloon floor. Falcon backed up and waited.

But Lars wasn't going to get up for a couple of minutes; he was hovering between consciousness and unconsciousness.

Falcon lowered his fists and pulled off his gloves, tucking them in a back pocket. He stepped to the bar and finished his beer, then signaled the post owner for a refill. None of the Snake riders made a move except to lift their shot glasses.

Falcon was halfway through his beer before Lars groaned and tried to stand up on very wobbly legs and rubber knees. He didn't make it, slumping back down until he could will his head to cease its spinning.

"I expect you to personally bring Jimmy a puppy," Falcon said. "All bathed and prettied up. A nice friendly little dog. You hear me, Lars?"

Lars groaned a reply.

"I'll take that as a yes." He turned and looked at the Snake riders. "You boys be sure to remind Lars and his father about the puppy. I wouldn't want a disappointed little boy. Understood?"

Several of the Snake hands nodded their heads.

"That's fine," Falcon said. "I'm glad we got all that straightened out." He looked down at Lars. "Right, Lars?"

Lars groaned.

"I'm glad to hear it."

Falcon rubbed his jaw and smiled ruefully. Lars could hit, and hit hard, no doubt about that. He just didn't know how to fight. And Falcon doubted the young man would live long enough to learn, unless he had a drastic change in attitude.

Falcon finished his beer and turned to his men. "Let's ride, boys. We've got a ways to go." He looked down at Lars, sitting amid the cigar butts, squashed hand-rolled cigarette butts, and tobacco juice. "I'll see you in a few days, Lars. When you personally bring the puppy dog to Jimmy."

Falcon, Stumpy, and Wildcat walked out of the saloon, all of them wearing smiles.

A few of the Snake riders were also smiling.

* * *

"You really think Lars will bring Jimmy a puppy?" John Bailey asked his foreman that evening after supper.

Kip nodded his head in the fast-fading light of day. "Yes I do, John. The son got his butt kicked over this puppy. It's a matter of honor to the Gilman name now. Miles just might even come along with the son."

"Be a sight to see," John said softly. He grunted. "Been many a year since Miles has been over here."

"I said he *might* come along."

"I think he will, Kip, now that you mention it."

"Well, if he does, it'll be for more than one reason. And you know it."

"To check out the place. Yeah, I know it."

"Maybe he'll bring the kid with him."

"The kid?"

"The Silver Dollar Kid."

John spat on the ground. "It'd be like him to do that. He always did like to show off his pretties."

Kip chuckled as the shadows deepened around the ranch. "Maybe Miles thinks just the sight of the Kid will scare us all off."

John carefully rolled him a smoke then handed the sack and papers to his longtime friend. "That just might have done it 'fore Val Mack showed up. Or whatever his name is."

The foreman nodded his head in agreement. He rolled his cigarette and said, "Cookie thinks he knows who Val Mack really is. He just can't pull the name up. He swears he's seen him before." Kip thumb-popped a match into flames and lit up.

"And you know too, don't you, Kip?"

"I got me an idea, John. But it's so far-fetched it's unreasonable."

"Who do you think he is?"

"I think Val Mack is really Falcon MacCallister."

That shook the rancher right down to his boots. He cut his eyes and stared at his foreman for a long moment. "Jamie MacCallister's boy?"

"Yep. I seen the boy 'bout fifteen years ago down in Colorado. Just the one time it was. He's older now, heavier by a few pounds. But he's still the spittin' image of his pa.''

Cookie had limped up to lean against the corral rail. The older man nodded his head. "It's him all right. Now that you've dug up the name, it fits. I seen him years back when I was heppin' push them beeves up from the south. The boy was dressed all in buckskins and looked 'bout as wild and untamed as them Cheyenne he was travelin' with.''

"Well, I'll just be damned!" John Bailey breathed. "Falcon MacCallister workin' for me. Lord, the MacCallisters is the richest family in the state. Maybe in the whole west. They're worth millions of dollars, way I hear it.''

"For a fact, John," Kip said. "The grandpa found all sorts of gold and silver and marked the locations. He personally never had much use for wealth. He give it all to Falcon's pa. Jamie used some of the money to buy land—thousands of acres of land. He bought MacCallister's valley. That piece of land stretches for fifty, sixty miles, runs north and south, I believe, and it's about twenty or thirty miles wide. The MacCallisters own it all, 'ceptin' what they sold to friends. Then he bought the land east and west of the valley and bought mines all over the west. He done it all on the sly, without nobody 'ceptin' his wife knowin' anything 'bout it. He hired lawyers and bankers in big cities to invest his money wisely, and they done it, too. He bought stock in railroads and factories and inventions that nobody thought would prove out. But they did. When Jamie was killed a few years back, he was the richest man west of the Mississippi. He left it all to his kids. But most of them was already wealthy in their own right.''

"And Falcon, so the stories go, was always the wild one, sort of like his pa," Cookie said. "Always wantin' to see new country, and always takin' off to travel the high country alone. He finally settled down and married him some sort of Injun princess, a half-breed French-Cheyenne woman and they had several kids. She was kilt a couple of years back and Falcon hit the high lonesome, all full of grief, trackin' down the men who kilt his wife.''

"That's the story, all right," Kip said.

"But I heard somebody sayin' Falcon was wanted for killin' two lawmen over in Utah . . ." John paused and sighed. "All right, now the pieces of the puzzle is comin' together. Those lawmen was Noonan's. Brothers of Nance Noonan, wasn't they? A federal marshal and a local sheriff, way I heard it."

"That's the way I heard it," Kip said, pinching out the butt of his smoke.

"And Falcon MacCallister is workin' right here on the Rockingchair range," Cookie breathed. "Hard to believe."

"You know all these old mountain men know who he is," Kip said. "They was all friends of Falcon's pa. That's why they all come arunnin' when Falcon sent out the word for help."

"Do we let on that we know?" Cookie asked.

John Bailey was silent for a moment, then he sighed and said, "We might as well. One of us is sure to let it slip accidental." He smiled. "I sure would like to be there when Miles hears the news."

Laughing, the three men walked toward the bunkhouse, to confront Falcon.

Sixteen

Within forty-eight hours the news had spread all over that part of Wyoming: Falcon MacCallister was working for the Rockingchair spread, and it was he who'd bought all those sections of land, and had all that money deposited in the local bank.

Miles Gilman sat in his darkened study and watched the evening shadows creep slowly around the room. He'd already sent a wire about Falcon to the local deputy federal marshal's office down at the territorial capital and received the bad news: The warrant had been lifted on Falcon. Falcon MacCallister was as free as an eagle.

"Falcon MacCallister," Miles whispered. "Of all the people in the west to show up and take sides with John Bailey, it would have to be him. Damn!"

Miles sighed heavily and lifted the glass of whiskey. He started to take a sip, then grimaced and placed the glass back on the side table. Outside, several of the hands were playing with the little puppy he'd gotten for his son to take over to the Rockingchair . . . whenever Lars was able to get out of bed, that is. Falcon had really given him a beating. Maybe tomorrow they could both ride over. Seventy-two hours was long enough for Lars to lollygag about in bed, getting waited on hand and foot by his sister. Disgusting!

Miles stood up and walked over to the window, watching for a moment as the hands played with the dog. It was a cute puppy. Miles had always like dogs.

He shook his head and turned away from the window.

Matters were going sour—he could feel it in his guts. But turning back was impossible . . . Miles knew that much for a certainty. Everything was in motion and rolling. It couldn't be stopped. This was one train that was going to go straight to the end of the track, and anyone who tried to stop it was going to get run over, and that was that.

And if that person's name happened to be Falcon MacCallister . . . too bad.

Nance was bringing a number of men up with him. My God, the man had seven brothers and about fifteen cousins alone. Probably forty hands, most of them drawing fighting wages. Add that number to Miles's crew and Rod Stegman's hands . . . God, it was an army.

An unstoppable army.

Miles sat down and picked up his glass of whiskey. Took a sip. He felt better after thinking it through. Yes, he did. He felt a few hunger pangs touch his stomach and wondered if the cook had any supper left.

Miles finished his drink and walked to the kitchen. Lars was sitting up in the den, Terri sitting beside him. Boy looked like a tree full of owls: both eyes discolored, lips still swollen some, one ear all puffed up. Miles wondered if his son had landed even one blow on Falcon. Probably not.

"We're going to take that puppy over to the Rockingchair in the morning," Miles told his son. "Be ready to go at dawn."

"I'm going too," Terri announced.

Miles nodded his head, knowing it would be pointless to argue with the girl. "Fine. We'll make it a family affair. Where are your brothers?"

Terri shrugged her shoulders and looked at Lars. He mumbled, "Out with the herds."

Miles's other sons didn't stay at the ranch much, preferring the line shacks to the big house. Miles didn't understand that, but didn't dwell much on it. They were all growed-up men and could do as they damn well pleased . . . and usually did.

Miles fixed him a plate of food and sat at the table in the kitchen and ate. Listening to Terri comfort Lars was enough to make a buzzard puke. He finished and walked back into the den.

Lars's sister had certainly done her part to spoil the boy rotten. She needled and poked fun at him, but loved him one hundred percent nonetheless.

"Daddy," Terri said.

"Yes, darlin' girl?"

"How come we don't just ride up into ol' man Bailey's yard tomorrow and just shoot all them people right down dead when they aren't expectin' it? That way, don't you see, we could just have done it."

Miles cleared his throat. Sighed. There was no doubt that Terri was as pretty as any sunset that God had ever graced the earth with. Unfortunately, while He blessed Terri with uncommon good looks, He shorted her on smarts. Terri could sometimes be as dumb as a post without even trying.

"Well, darlin', you see, there's gonna be six or eight rifles on us the whole time we're at John's spread. We try anything funny, and we're dead, baby."

"Oh," Terri said. "Well . . . I guess John doesn't trust any of us very much, does he?"

"Uh . . . no, darlin', he don't."

"Well, that explains that, I guess."

Miles suddenly decided he needed another drink, and headed for the study. He really loved his only daughter, but he also wished some nice young man would come along and marry her and take her away. Sometimes Terri near'bouts drove him slap nuts!

"Brought a pup for you, boy," Miles told Jimmy.

"He says it," Falcon said, looking at Lars. "Let him say it."

"Here's your dog, boy," Lars mumbled. The young man's lips were still swollen from the beating Falcon had given him. He spoke in low tones.

"Thanks, mister," Jimmy said, taking the squirming puppy and running off to play.

"Miles," John greeted the man.

"John. It's been a while."

And that was the extent of their conversation.

Lars wasn't looking at anyone. He sat his saddle and kept his eyes downcast. But Terri was staring at Falcon, as was the lone hand with them. A young man with silver dollars on his hat, vest, and gunbelt.

"I've heard of you, Falcon MacCallister," the kid said. "I reckon you've heard of me."

"Can't say as I have, boy."

The kid flushed at the slight. "I been around quite a bit, you know."

"I didn't know it, but I'm sure glad to hear it. A young man ought to get around and see the country. It helps to broaden his horizons."

Big Bob Marsh and the other mountain men were out of sight, in the barn, bunkhouse, and house, all armed with rifles and ready to bang in case of trouble.

And their absence did not escape the eyes of Miles Gilman.

Miles made another stab at conversation. "John, sell out to me and move away. You know I'll give you a fair price."

John Bailey shook his head. "Miles, do you know how many years we've been out here?"

"A long time, John, that's for sure."

"Twenty-six years, Miles. At least, that's my count. This is home. I've buried both kin and hands over yonder on the hill, and that's where I plan to be buried when it comes my time. I'm not sellin' out, to you or anybody else."

Miles shook his head slowly. "Then I guess we got nothin' else to talk about, John."

"I reckon not, Miles."

Gilman cut his eyes to Falcon. "The name MacCallister don't mean a whole lot up here, mister."

"Then I'll have to see to it that I leave some sort of lasting impression on the good people of this part of the country," Falcon replied evenly. Then he smiled. "Won't I?"

Terri was still staring at Falcon, thinking: Lordy, what a handsome man. 'Bout the handsomest man I ever did see. And worth millions of dollars, too. My, my. She batted her eyes at him. Falcon ignored her.

"What's the puppy's name?" John asked. "The dog's got to have a name."

"We didn't name it, John," Miles told him. "Thought we'd leave that up to the boy."

John nodded his head in agreement.

The Silver Dollar Kid continued to stare at Falcon, as did Terri.

"Well, uh, how's Martha, John?" Miles asked.

"She's well, Miles. We were speaking of you just the other day. The times we had, uh, before the troubles."

Miles nodded his head. Then he frowned and said, "Before the troubles, John? Well, we been fightin' Injuns, outlaws, bad weather, low prices, squatters . . . seems like trouble's all we've known. But . . . I reckon I know what you mean."

"I figured you would, Miles," John said softly.

"Them days is gone, John. They ain't never gonna come again. It don't do no good to think about them."

John shrugged his shoulders. "If that's the way you feel about it, I reckon not."

Lars raised his battered face to Falcon. In a low, calm, and very deadly voice, he said, "I'm gonna kill you, MacCallister. I'm tellin' you that right now."

Falcon smiled at him. "You going to do it facing me, boy, or back-shoot me?"

"There ain't no Gilman ever back-shot no man!" the father hotly protested.

"Just asking," Falcon replied evenly.

"I'll call you out, MacCallister," the son said, in that same low, deadly voice. "Count on it."

"If you feel it has to be that way," Falcon told him.

Jimmy ran past the men standing by the corral, talking with

the visitors on horseback. The little puppy was barking happily and the boy was laughing. Neither of them realized they were running past life and death being discussed so lightly on this sunny summer morning.

"No man does to me what you done and gets away with it," Lars said, his voice never changing from that low, deadly tone.

"You could have walked away from it," Falcon reminded him.

"You know better," Miles stepped in. "That ain't the way it's done out here. But I ain't my son, MacCallister. If me and you ever tie up, the outcome will be different."

"I doubt it," Falcon told the rancher. "But no one needs to tie up with anybody. There's land aplenty here for all. You and John Bailey came in here with a few head each of cattle and built a home, helped settle this land—probably did settle this part of the territory all by yourselves. You were friends for years while all that was going on. Then one of you got greedy and wanted what the other had, and good close friends became enemies. It can stop right here and now and . . ."

"No, by God, it can't!" Miles almost shouted the words. "It's gone too far for that. And John knows it. I've got to have grass and water for my cattle, and for my partner's cattle, and by God I'm going to get it."

"No matter who gets hurt in the process?" Falcon asked.

Miles Gilman refused to reply to that. He sat his saddle and glared at Falcon.

Martha and Angie stepped out of the house and began walking toward the gathering by the corral. Both of them carried rifles.

"Oh, Martha!" Miles blurted, embarrassment coloring his face. Faced with the situation, the rancher could not help himself. "Since when do you need a rifle to face me?"

"Since your riders began paying us visits at night, Miles," the woman said, walking up to stand by her husband. "And your son there leading them."

Miles's mouth clamped shut. He could not deny the charge with any conviction. But he had not authorized the raid, and had almost hit Lars when he'd heard of it. But now, sitting his saddle, he recalled his words of only a few days back, to start the killing of Rockingchair hands and either drive the rancher and his wife and family off their ranch or bury them. He shook his head and sighed in remembrance and experienced a few seconds of regret . . . but the contrition quickly passed.

"Did your daddy really fight at the Alamo?" Terri asked Falcon, lightening the moment without realizing she had done so.

Falcon could not help but smile at the young woman's words. He understood right then that he was not dealing with the brightest female in the territory. "Yes, he did."

"My, my," Terri said. She shifted her gaze to Angie. "I haven't seen you in a long time, Angie. I believe you were wearing that same dress last time I saw you."

Falcon immediately backed up, putting some distance between himself and the two young women. Both John and Martha had told him there had never been any love lost between Terri and Angie, beginning when they were little girls.

"Oh, I probably was," Angie replied very sweetly. But her eyes were flashing warning signs. "This is a ranch where everybody works, Terri. I don't sit around on my butt and stuff my face with imported chocolates the way some do."

Terri had to think about that for a few seconds. Then it finally dawned on her that she'd been insulted. There really wasn't anything wrong with Terri's mind: She just hadn't used it very much. It was soft from lack of exercise, like much of the rest of Terri.

But not Angie. Angie had been milking cows and chopping wood and working the fields since she was knee-high to her mother. Angie was tanned of face and strong of arm.

"Are you talkin' about me, Angie?" Terri demanded.

"I'm sure standing right here talking to you, aren't I?"

"You still got a smart mouth, don't you?"

Terri was off her horse in a flash and marching up to Angie.

"Now, girls!" Miles said.

"Now, girls!" John said.

The Silver Dollar Kid was sitting his saddle, his mouth hanging open.

Falcon backed still further away, sensing there was going to be one hell of a fight here any second.

Martha shook her head and backed up.

"You take back what you just said about me!" Terri demanded.

"Go jump in the creek!" Angie told her.

Terri rared back and took a wild punch at Angie and the fight was on.

Seventeen

Terri missed her wildly thrown punch and fell off balance. Angie seized that opportunity to slap her across the face. Terri screamed and the horses went into a panic. The Silver Dollar Kid's horse reared up and the Kid hit the ground, dumping him right in the middle of a huge pile of fresh horse crap . . . and that horse must have been suffering from a slight bowel problem: The pile was very large and wet.

"Oh, God!" the Kid hollered, as his hands went wrist-deep into the pile and his butt splattered into the mess. "Oh, phew!"

Terri grabbed Angie and tried to throw her to the ground but Angie was too strong. She broke free and popped Terri on the side of the face with a small hard right fist.

Terri screamed and Miles's horse began bucking and pitching and snorting. "Whoa, damnit!" the rancher hollered.

Miles grabbed for the saddlehorn, missed, and went sailing off the hurricane deck, landing on his butt on the ground.

Terri managed to land one punch on Angie's cheek, but it was a glancing blow and did little except further enrage the woman. Angie hollered and swung a fist, connecting solidly with Terri's jaw and knocking her to the ground. Angie straddled Terri and began pounding her face.

"By God!" Miles yelled. "I'll not tolerate that." He jumped to his boots and ran to his daughter's assistance.

Lars had sat his saddle for a moment, just looking at the melee. Then he slowly turned his horse and rode off without a change of expression. He had one thought on his mind, and this was not the time to act on it.

Miles grabbed Angie's shoulders and tried to pull her away from his daughter. Martha yelled out her concern and John put a hard hand on Miles's shoulder and spun him around, giving him a solid shot to the jaw with a work-hardened fist that knocked Miles to the ground.

"All right, by God!" Miles hollered, crawling to his hands and knees. "I should have done this a long time ago."

"Get up and do it, you son of a bitch!" John yelled.

John was about ten years older than Miles, but unlike Miles, John had never stopped doing hard brutal work every day of his life. He was in excellent physical shape, while Miles had grown soft.

Falcon had stepped away from the fighting, keeping an eye on the Kid. But the Kid was busy at a watering trough, concerned only with getting the horseshit off of him. Right now, he was doing a dandy job of spreading it all over himself.

"Yuck!" the Kid hollered, as the crap seemed to grow on his hands and forearms.

Angie and Terri were both cussing and duking it out, as were their fathers.

The mountain men left their hiding places to stand and stare in disbelief at the goings-on.

"Oh, for Heaven's sake!" Martha yelled at her husband and daughter.

Miles was huffing and puffing while John appeared to be enjoying himself. He was certainly getting the better of the younger man, landing lefts and rights on Miles's face.

Lars had completely disappeared from sight, riding slowly back to the road that would either take him to town or to the Snake ranch. He had not looked around once during his slow departure.

"By God, I'll teach you a lesson with my bare hands," Miles puffed, swinging at John and missing.

"Well, you're doin' a piss-poor job of it," John told him, just a split second before smacking his once best friend and longtime neighbor in the mouth and busting his lip.

Miles yelled and bored in, swinging both fists and hitting nothing but air.

John sidestepped Miles's charge and stuck out a boot, tripping the man and sending him sprawling to the ground. Miles ate a little dirt and came up roaring like an angry grizzly. He charged at John and grabbed the man in a bear hug, each of them going hard to the ground, kicking and cussing and yelling and spitting and trying to hit the other, neither of them succeeding in doing any damage.

Angie and Terri were standing toe-to-toe and slugging it out, cussing each other.

Martha had walked over to stand beside Falcon, a very disgusted look on her face.

Jimmy and his little puppy were down by the creek, playing, unaware that anything except conversation was going on by the corral.

"This is positively disgraceful!" Martha said.

"That's certainly one word for it," Falcon agreed.

Angie and Terri both stepped in a puddle of water and lost their balance, both of them hitting the ground. Falcon seized that moment to grab Angie by the neck of her dress and haul her away, physically slinging her in the direction of her mother. Terri crawled to her feet and Falcon pointed a finger at her.

"It's over," he warned her. "Settle down."

Terri's nose was bleeding, one lip was puffy, and her hair was all a mess. But she was game. She very bluntly told Falcon what he could do—which was impossible—and charged him. She slammed into the man, knocking him to one side. Falcon tripped and went sprawling to the ground. Terri stepped all over him in her wild charge to get to Angie and the two women went at it again.

"Whore!" yelled Terri.

"Slut!" yelled Angie.

"Well, the hell with it!" Falcon said, crawling to his feet.

John and Miles had lost their six-shooters, Angie had propped her rifle up against the corral, and Terri's pistol was lying in a big pile of horse crap. There was no danger of anyone starting any gunplay.

Dan Carson had followed Lars when he rode off. He returned and told Big Bob Marsh, "Lars is gone. Headin' into town. We'll not see him again this day. What's happenin' here?"

"Craziness," Big Bob replied. "I reckon the best thing we can do is just let them fight until they're plumb wore out."

Falcon had crawled into the corral, putting the corral bars between him and the combatants.

Martha had walked back to the house and slammed the front door in disgust.

The four participants in the free-for-all were still at it, but rapidly running out of steam.

The Kid had removed his gunbelt, hanging it on a peg and doing his best to clean all the crap off his hands, arms, and jeans. He had taken off his shirt, which he had managed to smear quite liberally with horseshit.

He wadded up his shirt and turned to stuff it into his saddlebags when he noticed the six mountain men, all armed with rifles, all looking at him. The Kid smiled rather weakly and held out his hands wide, signaling that he wanted no trouble at this time.

Mustang walked over and gathered up the Kid's guns, stuffing them into his saddlebags and buckling the flap securely.

John took that time to give Miles a solid shot to the jaw and Miles went down in a heap, not quite out, but very close.

Terri and Angie were also running out of steam, but of the two, Terri had fared the worst: One eye was closing, her nose was bleeding, and her mouth was all puffy. Angie gave her one more good pop to the jaw and the woman went down on her butt. This time she stayed there.

"That's it," Falcon said, stepping out of the corral and motioning for the others to join in. Together, Falcon and Big Bob and the others managed to get Terri and Miles on their boots and get between the Baileys and the Gilmans and keep them separated.

"Get them on their horses and get them out of here," Falcon told the others.

"I'll kill you, you bitch!" Terri squalled.

"You've not heard the last from me, John," Miles warned.

"Anytime you want to really settle this, Miles," John told him, "just let me know and we'll stand up and face each other with guns."

"I just might do that, by God."

"Anytime," John told him. "Now get off my property and don't ever come back. I might just decide to shoot you on sight."

Miles cursed the man under his breath and managed to get into the saddle. Puma had shucked all the cartridges out of his pistol and stuck it back into Miles's holster. Stumpy had done the same with Terri's pistol.

The Kid had gotten his crap-smeared behind into the saddle and was waiting patiently.

Angie came to her father's side and put an arm around his waist. She was a mess, but not near the mess she'd left Terri. Father and daughter stood and watched Miles, Terri, and the Silver Dollar Kid ride off. John had a lump on one side of his jaw and a busted lip, but other than that, he was unhurt.

"The fat's in the fire now, folks," Kip said. "From now on, it'll be shootin', not fists."

"You're probably right about that, Kip," John said, then grinned. "But damn, that sure was fun!"

"John, Angie!" Martha called from the front door. "You get yourselves in here and let me clean you up. And I mean, right now! Kip, you get down to the creek and see about Jimmy."

"Yes, ma'am," Kip said, and vacated the scene promptly.

Laughing, arm in arm, father and daughter walked toward the house.

"It's gonna get dirty from now on, Falcon," Wildcat said. "Real low-down dirty."

"It had to come, boys," Falcon said. "We all knew that. From now on it's going to be pistol play instead of cattle work."

Puma grunted. "That suits me. Sooner we get done here the sooner I can get back home and see my Jenny."

"You think that beast misses you, huh?" Big Bob asked.

"Shore she does," Puma replied indignantly. "Jenny's my baby."

Big Bob walked off, muttering to himself about grown men that keep cougars for pets.

During the next week, Falcon visited each of the farmers and small ranchers north and south and east of the Rockingchair, warning them that everything was about to pop. He brought them spare weapons and ammunition and made certain each person who was of age knew how to use the weapons. After talking with each family member, Falcon felt sure that every family would stand and fight, and fight to the last person.

He reported as much to John and the rancher agreed.

"They'll fight, and they'll put up one hell of a fight," John said. "The ranchers have been here, some as long as me. They've fought Injuns and outlaws. The farmers are all combat veterans from the War Between the States. A couple of them officers. They're all good people. Not a quitter among them. Martha's met all the ladies and speaks highly of them."

"John, I have to ask this: Do you want to take the fight to Miles and the others?"

The rancher was reflective for a moment, then sighed and shook his head. "I should, I know I should, but I just can't do it, Falcon. It just isn't in me."

"I know, John," Falcon replied easily. "It's got to be all them. I understand."

"You think I'm wrong, don't you, son?"

"Speaking frankly, yes I do, John. But it's your decision to make."

"They've got to start it, Falcon," the rancher said stubbornly.

"And you don't think they have already?"

"That's my decision. Can you and the other men live with it?"

"Oh, we can live with it, John. Problem is, can you and your family live with it, and do you have the right to speak for all the others?"

"I've spoken with my family. We all agree that Miles has got to make the first move. After that . . ." He shrugged his shoulders. ". . . I guess anything goes."

"All right. We'll wait for them to open the dance. But I warn you of this: When they strike up the band, rules go right out the window. I don't fight by rules, and neither do any of the boys. It's going to get down and dirty real quick."

"When the other side starts it, Falcon, deal the cards and let the chips fall."

Falcon smiled his reply. He was a gambler, and now the game was getting to his liking.

The first bunch of Stegman and Noonan's hands rode in. Stumpy was posted up on a ridge and was watching them through field glasses as they rode across the grasslands. He reported back to Falcon.

"They're hired guns, all right," the older man said, after pouring himself a cup of coffee and taking a seat at the table in the bunkhouse. "I recognized a couple of them. They're experienced shooters."

"Where are they out of, you reckon?" Wildcat asked.

"Some was sittin' Texas rigs," Stumpy said. "I seen one that I know is out of New Mexico and another that's made quite a name for hisself out of Utah. The rest . . . ?" He shrugged. "From all over where scum gathers."

"How many in this first bunch?" Dan Carson asked.

"I counted ten."

"Probably more than that unless he took off his boots and used his toes to count with," Big Bob said.

The insults started flying then, and Falcon laughed and walked out of the bunkhouse. Kip was leaning against the corral, smoking a cigarette. He looked up.

"Trouble, Falcon?"

"It's gathering, for a fact." He explained what Stumpy had seen that morning.

"They can gather until Hell freezes over," Kip said. "But until they actually do something, John isn't goin' to strike."

"I know. I just thought he'd want to know."

Kip nodded his head. "The herds won't be far behind, will they?"

"Oh, probably no more than two or three weeks would be my guess."

"I'll tell John."

Kip walked to the main house, leaving Falcon alone by the corral with his thoughts. Falcon knew there were others he could call in to assist in this fight, but he also knew that numbers alone would not win it for John and the others. All more men would accomplish would be more deaths.

Dan Carson walked out to join him. The older man shaped himself a cigarette and handed Falcon the makings. The two of them smoked in silence for a moment.

"You know the easy way to do it, don't you?" Dan broke the silence.

"Oh, sure. But do you think John would go along with that?"

"He might not have a choice in the matter."

Kill Noonan, Stegman, and Gilman. Take out the leaders and the rest would break up.

"He'll never go along with it, Dan. Put it out of your mind."

"It was just a thought."

"I had the same thoughts, believe me."

"It's what Jamie would have done."

"Oh, I know that. Pa wouldn't hesitate for a minute. Neither would I, for that matter. But this isn't our show. We're just the soldiers in this little war."

Dan chuckled and Falcon cut his eyes. "Something funny about that?"

"The soldiers always have the solution, boy. The men who do the actual fightin' always know the simple way. It's the generals and the politicians who drag it out."

Falcon had to smile, knowing the mountain man was right in what he said.

One by one, the others joined them at the corral, standing and smoking in silence. Finally Cookie made up the last of the nonfamily group. Kip was considered part of the Bailey family.

"John is one of the most decent men any of you will ever run up on," Cookie said. "He's honorable clear through. He still thinks there's hope for Miles."

"He's wrong," Big Bob replied. "Miles Gilman's power-hungry. I can't speak for his other kids, but Terri and Lars is just like him. Terri's lazy and worthless and Lars is just plumb crazy in the head. That whuppin' you gave him, Falcon, shoved him over the edge."

"I know that now," Falcon admitted. "I wish I hadn't done it."

The others looked at him, Mustang saying, "It wouldn't have taken no big push, boy. He was set to step over the line. Borned that way."

"And the daughter ain't no different," Puma allowed. "That girl's not right in the head."

"You mighty right about that," Cookie said. "She's just mean, that's all. She's always been that way. She's just plain low-down dirty mean."

"She really is?" Dan questioned.

"She really is. She's just no good," Cookie allowed. "She's done some dastardly things."

"Well, I'll be damned. Pretty thang, though."

Cookie grimaced. Obviously, he did not share Puma's sentiments.

"Miss Angie damn shore wound her clock for her though, didn't she?" Wildcat asked with a grin.

All the men, including Falcon, got a chuckle out of that. After the quiet laughter died away, Falcon said, "We'd better start posting guards now. I hate to do it, but I think it's the smart thing to do."

"I was gonna suggest that," Mustang said. "Miles ain't never gonna forget that whuppin' John Bailey hung on him. He was some hot about that."

"He sure was," Stumpy said. "And him and that boy of hisn both meant what they said about killing you and John, Falcon."

"I know," Falcon's words were soft in the fading afternoon light. "There are threats, and then there are threats. Both father and son meant theirs." Falcon began assigning men to guard times. When that was done, he added, "And trouble could come any night. Including tonight."

Eighteen

Falcon had just gone on his watch, midnight till two, when his eyes detected the slightest movement from the direction of the creek. There were no cattle grazing in that area. He waited, watching. There was another movement, off some twenty or thirty feet from the first one. Falcon knelt down, picked up a pebble from the ground, and tossed it against the side of the bunkhouse. That would be all the signal the mountain men would need. They had spent their entire lives living on the edge of danger, and the slightest sound would bring them awake.

Within seconds, the front door to the bunkhouse was cracked open a few inches. Falcon hooted as an owl, then followed that with a nightbird's call. The door closed quickly, the mountain men picking up on one of the Cheyenne signals for danger.

But there was no way Falcon could signal those in the main house. They would have to come up alert and ready at the sound of the first shot. Falcon had told John about his plans to mount a guard and the rancher agreed it was the prudent thing to do, especially after hearing Stumpy tell of the bunch of hired guns he'd seen riding in.

Out of the corner of his eye, Falcon saw the front door to the bunkhouse open, and three men dart out, a few seconds apart, rifles in their hands. One headed for the barn, another took up position behind the woodpile, and the third bellied down behind the rocks of an old well off on the far side of the bunkhouse.

Falcon heard another nightbird call, coming from the main house, and he smiled. John was up and had seen what was going on. The old Indian fighter had been sleeping very lightly. He would have his family up and the adults ready at rifle slits, Jimmy safe behind cover. His puppy, whom he had named Freckles, cuddled safe with him.

Falcon smiled, thinking, *Come on, boys. Hit us with your midnight raid. We're ready.*

Falcon looked very carefully all around him, moving his head slowly, ears straining to pick up the smallest of sounds. There! And there! And over there! The hired guns had managed to surround the spread before one moved at the wrong time and Falcon detected the movement.

Falcon heard Hell snicker softly in his stall. He wouldn't make a sound if it was someone familiar, so that meant that a mercenary had made his way into the barn. The mountain man waiting in the barn would not give away his position until the first shot was fired outside, or unless the gunhand spotted him, but if the hired gun somehow got into Hell's stall, he would never leave it alive, or at best would leave crippled, for the big mean-tempered horse would kill him or stomp him.

Falcon waited for the hired guns to make the first move. He didn't think it would be long in coming, for if one was already in the barn, the rest were almost in position. And that surely meant that several were closing in on the main house, set some hundred or so yards up a slight incline from the bunkhouse. Falcon hoped John and his family were ready.

That was answered a heartbeat later when a rifle cracked from the house and a lifeless form came rolling down the incline a few yards.

"Go!" someone shouted. "They've spotted us. Burn the place down."

When the torches the gunhands carried were ignited into flame, Falcon and his men opened up, laying down a hail of gunfire. The men carrying the torches went down almost immediately, mortally wounded. The torches began burning themselves out harmlessly on the ground.

"It's an ambush!" one of the gunslicks screamed.

That's all he got to say before Falcon drilled him in the belly with a rifle shot.

Then the night exploded in gunfire as the night raiders were caught out in the open: dark shapes that clearly stood out as they tried to run for cover.

Many of them didn't make it, for the raking gunfire of the ranch defenders was merciless.

The firefight was over in a few minutes, the survivors making it back to their horses and heading hard for home range, leaving their dead and their badly wounded behind.

The defenders left their positions warily, but all the fight was gone from those wounded left behind. Several of them were calling for doctors. Most would not live long enough to see a doctor.

Martha and Angie stayed in the main house with Jimmy. John and Kip walked among the dead, dying, and wounded.

"You know any of them, Kip?" John asked.

"No. I never seen any of them before."

Kip held the lantern while John knelt down beside one hard-hit gunhand. The young man had taken two .44 slugs in the belly. He couldn't have been more than twenty years old.

"Boy," John said, "you got parents somewhere?"

The young man nodded his head.

"You want me to notify them?"

"No," the young man gasped. "I ain't got nothin' to say to them two."

"That's mighty hard of you, son."

"They threw me out. Hell with them."

John left him and walked to an older man who had taken a slug through his chest. There were pink bubbles forming on his lips. He was lung-shot. John squatted down beside him.

"Forget it," the hired gun said. "I ain't got nothin' to say to you. Leave me die in peace."

John walked over to another gunslick and knelt down. "I

got money in my pocket,'' the man whispered, ''and my Ma's name and town writ down on a piece of paper. You see she gets the money?''

''I'll see to it,'' the rancher said. ''You have my word.''

''Kind of you.'' Then the man closed his eyes and died.

John patted the man's pockets until he found his wallet. There were fifty dollars in the worn leather purse and a piece of paper. He stood up and shook his head. ''Fifty dollars,'' he said softly. ''The man died for fifty dollars.''

''Nobody forced him to sign on with Gilman,'' Kip reminded his friend. ''Or whoever he was workin' for.''

John Bailey sighed. ''You're right about that, Kip.'' He looked around him. ''Falcon?''

''Right here, John.''

''Are there any wounded who can drive a wagon?''

''Oh, yes. One here with just a crease on his head. He's fine otherwise.''

''Have the boys hitch up a team, please. We'll put the dead and the wounded in the wagon and take them to town.''

''All right, John.''

''You think they'll be back this night, Falcon?'' Kip asked.

''No. I think they're through for this night. Has anybody counted the dead?''

''Hell, we ain't found 'em all yet,'' Dan Carson called. ''Here's another one that's hard hit and ain't gonna make it.''

''I don't wanna die!'' the hired gun gasped, his words drifting all around the minibattlefield.

''You should have thought about that 'fore you decided to fight for pay, boy,'' Dan told him, a hard edge to his words. The older man had seen death come riding up on all kinds of horses during his hard life in the wilderness.

''Them ain't very kind words, mister,'' the belly-shot gunhand moaned.

''Wasn't very kind of you and your friends to come in here shootin' up the place and disturbin' our rest neither,'' Dan told him. ''Hasn't anybody ever told you that older folks need their rest?''

''You're makin' light of my dyin'!'' the man gasped.

"Well, I damn shore wish you'd hurry up and ex-pire, boy," Puma told him. "I was havin' me a dandy dream 'fore all this crap started."

"Oh Lord!" the man cried.

"He's tryin' to sleep, too," Big Bob Marsh said. "Now make up your mind whether you're gonna live or die and get on with it."

"Y'all ain't decent," another wounded man said. His wounds were painful, but not life-threatening. "I ain't never heard such hard talk in all my borned days."

"Stick around, sonny," Mustang told him. "It's liable to get a lot worser"

"Mama!" yet another dying man hollered.

"It's gonna be a long night," Wildcat bitched.

Noonan and Stegman arrived the next day, riding far in advance of the herd being pushed up into north Wyoming. They sat in Gilman's study, drinking whiskey and listening to yet another one of the survivors of the abortive raid on the Rockingchair tell what happened.

Finally, Stegman waved him silent. "Get out," the .44 owner told him. "I'm sick of hearin' all these damn excuses."

Alone in the study, the door closed even to Gilman's family, Noonan said, "Miles, you was supposed to have all this area clean for us when we arrived. What the hell happened?"

"Falcon MacCallister," Gilman said bluntly. "That's what happened."

"One man is responsible for this holdup?" Stegman asked. "I don't believe it."

"I do," Nance said, before Gilman could reply. "I'll believe anything about those damn MacCallisters. The old man, Jamie MacCallister, ended up ownin' an entire county down in Colorado, plus bits and pieces of practically half the damn state. Made friends with all the damn Injuns. None of 'em would ever bother no one who lived in that damn valley of his. I don't know how he done it. Plus, I hate that damn Falcon MacCallister. I hate all MacCallisters. Ever' one of them."

Neither Stegman nor Gilman had a reply to Noonan's hate-filled comments. Both men knew that just the mention of Falcon's name could send Nance off into a towering rage. They waited until Nance had calmed down a bit.

"He's organized and armed all the small ranchers and farmers in this part of the state," Miles said. "He's armed them with weapons taken from the men I hired to run them out!"

"Where is he getting supplied?"

"From the old trading post."

"Well, hell, man!" Nance yelled. "Put the damn trading post out of business! Burn it down. Blow it up. Kill the bastard who runs it."

"Can't do that, Nance," Miles spoke calmly, hoping that if he stayed calm, some of it would rub off on Noonan. "The place is a stage stop and is also a remount station for the cavalry. We don't want private detectives and the cavalry taking sides with the small ranchers and farmers."

Nance thought about that for a moment, then slowly nodded his head. "Yeah, you're right about that. Damn! The federal marshal for this area?"

"He won't bother us."

"You're sure about that?"

"Positive."

"And the county sheriff is out of it?"

"All the way."

Nance stared at Miles for a moment. "Six old men join up with Falcon MacCallister and bring everything to a halt. Incredible."

"You know who these old men are, Nance?"

"No, I don't. What the hell difference does that make?"

Miles named them all and Nance's mouth dropped open. Miles had just named some of the most famous mountain men of the west: army scouts, Indian fighters, explorers, trailblazers, and so much more.

Nance got up to pace the room for a moment. He stopped, poured another drink, then sat down. "Books and stories have been written about those men. We can't afford to have the eastern press get wind of this. They'd come swarmin' in here.

But neither can I afford to have this drag on for months. I've got cattle comin' in and they're gonna need graze and water. Money is not the answer—MacCallister could buy and sell all three of us. And I'm not kiddin' about that. What's a fortune to us is nothin' but pocket change to Falcon. And if all the MacCallisters was to get involved in this fight . . ." He shrugged muscular shoulders and let that trail off. ". . . They'd just hire a damn army to come in and wipe us out, right down to the last man. There's as many of them as there is my kin, practically, and they've got the money to do whatever they damn well please. If I had any sense I'd back off and out of here and just look somewheres else. But this is personal, 'tween me and Falcon, and by God I intend to see it through to the finish."

"I've got to stay," Stegman said. "I got no choice in the matter. And you know that, Nance."

Again, Noonan nodded his head. "I know, Rod, I know. Don't worry: I'm not goin' to quit on you."

"We've got to give this situation some hard head ruminatin'," Rod said. "Miles's way ain't workin', that's plain to see. So we got to come up with another plan."

"Good thinkin', Rod," Nance said, very sarcastically. "Excellent." But the sarcastic words were lost on his brother-in-law. He cut his eyes to Miles. Went right by him, too. Nance knew that when it came to thinkin', Miles and Rod weren't among the best. They were men of action, first, last, and always. If there was to be any planning, it would be up to him to come up with it and spell it all out, carefully.

"We can outlast them," Miles said. "If you had to, Nance, you could graze your cattle south and west of here until all this was settled."

Nance changed his opinion of Miles . . . a little bit. That wasn't a bad plan. "If it comes to that, yeah. But we've got a few weeks before the herds arrive. We might get lucky 'tween now and then."

"Let's just ambush MacCallister and have done with it," Rod growled.

As if that hadn't been tried about two dozen times over the years, Nance thought. *The man's as savvy as his father.* Nance stood up. "Let's have some breakfast," he suggested. "Think on this some. Maybe get some rest. More men will be comin' in today and tomorrow. I want the next move we make to end it. I want to see Falcon MacCallister *dead!*"

Nineteen

The Noonan clan began arriving and settling in. The families took up residence in the ranch houses that had been vacated when the former owners were either run out of the country or killed by the hired guns of the cattlemen's association. There were eight Noonan brothers, counting Nance, six cousins, and a small army of kids, ranging in age from toddlers to grown men in their early twenties. The Noonan clan swelled the population of the county by about a hundred and they claimed thousands of acres of land. Each family had six to ten hands, most of them hired guns. Stegman claimed as his own what had been the third largest ranch in the area and moved in his family and a few of his hands. The rest of he and Noonan's cowboys were pushing the herd up and were still several weeks away.

The businesspeople in the town of Gilman were overjoyed at the prospect of new customers. A new café had been added, as well as a new saloon and several other businesses. The new saloon was called the Purple Palace, but was soon shortened to just the Palace. It was anything but a palace, but no one seemed to object to its rather raw and austere interior. The dozen girls that worked at the Palace livened up the joint considerably as soon as the sun went down: They had to wait until it got dark before making an appearance, for most of the soiled doves were so ugly they could have made a living haunting graveyards.

"Good God!" Wildcat blurted, at his first glimpse of the ladies employed by the Palace. "I'm glad I waited 'fore eatin' lunch."

Falcon chuckled at the words of the older man and cut his eyes to Stumpy, who had just walked up to stand with the men on the boardwalk after seeing to their horses. Stumpy grimaced at the sight of the soiled doves, lounging under the awning of the Palace.

Stumpy said, "I'll bet when them gals was borned their mamas didn't know if they was gonna walk or fly!"

"Be kind, boys," Falcon said. "You know what they say about whores having a heart of gold."

"I ain't found one yet that did," Wildcat said. "And I have had a bit of experience with whores."

"No!" Stumpy gasped. "I never would have guessed that of you, Wildcat. I'm plumb shocked to hear it. I don't know whether I want to associate with you no more, seeing as how you cavort about with loose women and all."

Then there was no more time for banter as a dozen horses came galloping into town, the riders reining up in front of the Palace, to go stomping and cussing and laughing inside the saloon, the soiled doves latching onto them immediately.

"Double N hands," Wildcat observed. "Seem like a real nice bunch of boys, don't they?"

"Certainly some I'd take home to meet my sister," Stumpy said. "Providin' I had a sister, that is."

"I didn't even know you had a mama," Wildcat told him.

The two mountain man would spend the next ten minutes insulting each other, while Falcon went into the bank to see about some land that the bank had foreclosed on.

The president of the bank, Willard, almost had a heart attack when Falcon strolled in. But he knew perfectly well that if the MacCallisters took a notion to do so, they could buy the bank and put him out slopping hogs somewhere. He forced a smile and greeted Falcon.

Falcon came right to the point. "The small ranch just west of the Rockingchair . . . you just foreclosed on it and I want to buy it. How much?"

Willard breathed a sign of relief. "That was the Rone place, Mr. MacCallister. It's already been picked up. Honestly, it has."

"I doubt if it was done honestly," Falcon replied. "But probably legally."

Willard stood passively and said nothing. Falcon was one of the bank's biggest depositors—he couldn't afford to anger him.

"All right, Willard," Falcon said. "Thanks." He turned and walked out of the bank, stepping back out onto the boardwalk just in time to see Jim Wilson and his family rattle into town in a wagon.

The Wilsons had moved into the area just before Falcon had arrived, having inherited a farm from Wilson's older brother, who had been killed by night riders. The farm was a large one, for the elder Wilson had bought a number of sections over the hard months before his death from people who had given up under threat from Gilman. Jim wasn't about to give up his land, determined to make a go of it. Jim's wife, Peggy, was a tiny thing, but with steel in her backbone and a set to her jaw that told anyone with half a brain this was one woman who wouldn't easily give up. The Wilsons had four kids, two boys and two girls. The boys were fourteen and twelve, the girls were ten and eight. Jim was a former captain in some unit of the Tennessee Cavalry: a highly decorated Confederate officer. He was quiet and soft-spoken, but a man with no back-up in him.

Since Falcon had suddenly become one of the county's money-men, his money had become good all over town, and that was something that not even Gilman could prevent. Falcon had also passed the word that the farmers and small ranchers, who had heretofore been prevented from shopping in town, had better be welcomed with open arms in every store. Miles Gilman had not even tried to stop the store owners from doing business with the farmers and small ranchers, knowing when it was wise to hold his cards and when it was smart to fold and let someone else have the hand. There was always another shuffle and deal.

Falcon watched a couple of Double N hands as they stood under the awning in front of the Palace and scowled at the Wilsons as they rattled and bounced into town. Then the hired guns stepped back into the saloon.

Be trouble in a few minutes, Falcon thought. He lifted his eyes, looking for Wildcat and Stumpy. They had spread out, across the street and left and right of the front of the Palace. The two experienced frontiersmen were ready for whatever trouble came their way . . . probably looking forward to it.

The boardwalk in front of the Palace was soon crowded with Double N hands, all of them with bottles of whiskey in their hands, drinking and getting themselves primed and cocked for trouble.

The Wilsons stopped in front of Dean's General Store and got out of the wagon.

Falcon moved half a block closer to the store, staying in the shadows. So far, he was sure he had not been spotted by any of the Double N hands.

The Double N hands were making some pretty vulgar comments about the Wilsons, and getting louder with them. There was no way Jim and his family could keep from hearing the filthy talk.

Falcon moved closer to the general store and watched the Wilsons climb down from the wagon and enter the store. Several Double N hands began walking toward the store, swigging whiskey as they walked. Falcon moved to the end of the street and crossed over. The Double N hands paid no attention to him; just another cowboy crossing the street.

The cussing had gotten louder and more vulgar. Falcon decided it was time to step in before Jim took some sort of action and got himself hurt or killed.

There were four Double N hands entering the general store when Falcon stepped up on the boardwalk from the street. Falcon heard one make a very filthy comment to Peggy.

"Now that's enough of that kind of talk!" Jim shouted.

Dirty laughter followed that, then: "Pig farmer is gettin' mad, Jess."

Falcon had reached the front doors when Jess said, "Man's got a big mouth for someone who ain't wearin' a gun."

Falcon stepped through the open doors and stopped just inside the store. He stood for a moment, allowing his eyes to adjust to the gloom.

"What the hell do you want, mister?" a Double N hand demanded of Falcon.

"Oh, maybe some peppermint candy. Yes, that would be a very nice treat today."

"Oh, my!" another of the Double N men mimicked nastily. "The big man wants some peppermint candy. Quick, get him some candy."

"Ooohh!" the fourth Double N hand said. "I bet he's a real tough feller, all right. What's your limit, cowboy? Two pieces of peppermint candy?"

The four Double N guns burst into hard and mean-sounding laughter.

Falcon smiled and stepped toward the counter. Peggy had the two girls close to her. The youngest was pale and frightened.

"Let him through, boys," Pete hollered. "Mr. Two-Guns has to have some candy."

"What do you reckon he's got them guns loaded with?" another Double N rider yelled. "Sugar cookies?"

That got the hired guns started again. They howled and slapped each other on the back and cussed, the filth rolling from their mouths.

"I really wish you boys wouldn't cuss in front of the lady and her children," Falcon said softly, moving closer to a barrel that was filled with ax handles.

"Oohhh, my!" a gunny hollered. "We shouldn't cuss in front of the pig farmer's woman and kids, boys. Mr. Peppermint Candy is takin' off-fence at our language. What do you think about that, Pete?"

Pete mouthed some very filthy words concerning Falcon and what he could do with several sticks of peppermint candy.

Falcon jerked an ax handle out of the barrel and popped Pete right between the eyes. Pete's hat flew off and his eyes rolled back in his head as he hit the floor, out cold.

Falcon spun around and jammed one end of the ax handle into the stomach of a Double N rider just as Jim jerked an ax handle out of the barrel and slammed the business end of it against the back of a third Double N gunhand's head. He yelled and went to the floor.

The fourth Double N rider grabbed for his pistol just as Falcon swung the ax handle, connecting with the side of the man's head. The Double N rowdy went down to the floor, blood suddenly leaking from a long cut on his jaw.

Falcon smiled at Jim. "You ready for a fight, my friend?"

"I'm ready, Mr. MacCallister," the farmer said. "But I'm not armed."

Falcon began jerking the Double N riders' pistols from leather and tossing them to a very startled storekeeper and his wife, both of whom were standing openmouthed behind the counter. They caught the six-guns, handling them as if they were live giant bees.

"Now neither are they," Falcon said, hauling Pete up to his boots and busting him right in the mouth with a hard fist. Pete went staggering and stumbling out the front door and fell off the boardwalk into the street.

Jim had jerked up another Double N rider and smacked him on the jaw with a work-hardened fist. The man followed his buddy out the front door and into the street.

Falcon put the toe of one boot hard into the stomach of a third hired gun just as the man was getting to his hands and knees. The air whooshed out of him and he stretched out on the floor, gagging and puking.

Jim was pounding a fist into the face of the fourth gunslick, smiling as he was doing so. After a few seconds, Jim jerked the man up bodily and sent him stumbling through the open front doors, off the boardwalk, and into the street. The hired gun landed face-first into a fresh pile of horse crap.

Falcon reached down and pulled up the last of the Double N men and sent him out the front door. He went off the boardwalk and impacted against Pete, who was just getting to his boots. Both of them went sprawling into the dirt of the street.

"Put those guns into a sack, Mr. Dean," Falcon told the store owner. "And put them with the other supplies Mr. and Mrs. Wilson decide to purchase."

"Ye . . . ye . . . yes sir, Mr. MacCallister," Dean stammered. "I'll do that."

"And anything the Wilsons want, let them have. Put it on my account, understood?"

"Yes sir! I certainly do. Anything at all. You betcha, Mr. MacCallister. Consider it done."

The remaining Double N hands were gathering outside the general store, standing over their fallen friends and muttering and cussing.

"What about them?" Jim asked, jerking his head toward the street.

"I'll worry about them," Falcon told him. "You folks just do your shopping."

"It's my fight, too," Jim reminded him.

"You're not carrying a gun, Jim. This is going to be a shooting fight."

"One man against six or eight?"

Falcon smiled. "I have a couple of boys outside. You helped out in here, now let me handle the outside. You and your wife go on shopping . . . and stay away from the front door and windows."

"All right, Mr. MacCallister. We'll do as you ask."

"Falcon. I told you, it's Falcon."

Jim smiled and nodded his head. Falcon turned and walked outside to stand on the boardwalk, over the moaning Double N hands, who were just now getting to their hands and knees. Double N riders were beginning to gather around, trying to help their buddies.

One of them nudged another and jerked his head. His friend cut his eyes. Stumpy and Wildcat were standing on the street behind them, ready to hook and draw.

Falcon detected movement behind him but did not dare take

his eyes off the Double N riders. Jim stepped up beside him, to his left, a rifle in his hands.

"I'll take that stocky one with the beard," the farmer said softly, but with steel behind the words.

"All right, Jim," Falcon said.

"And I'll make sure that tall skinny one never bothers another woman or child," Peggy spoke, walking up to stand on Falcon's right. The farmer's wife carried a double-barreled shotgun she'd taken from the gunrack. "And I loaded this up with buckshot."

"Ma'am," the skinny Double N rider said, his face suddenly paling at the thought of what that shotgun could do at this range. "I didn't say nothin' to you atall."

"Your friends did," Peggy reminded him. "Filthy things, and they thought it was funny to say them in front of children."

The tall skinny rider sighed. He didn't know how to reply to that, so he said nothing, just waited.

The Wilsons' oldest boy, James, walked out onto the board-walk, carrying a rifle. He stepped up to stand by his father. "I'm tired of people looking down at me and making fun of me because I'm a farmer. I'm not going to take it no more. I'm proud to be a farmer."

"Good for you, son," Jim said, his chest swelling with pride.

The Double N riders suddenly found themselves in a very bad situation. Two men behind them, men who, by the look of them, had been born with the bark on and ready to kill. Four people in front of them.

"That's Falcon MacCallister," one of the Double N men blurted. "I seen him down in Colorado one time."

That did it. All the fight went out of the hired guns, at least for the moment. None of them wanted to tangle face-to-face with Falcon MacCallister.

"We'll be headin' back to the saloon now," an older rider said.

"Fine," Falcon told him. "Me and my men will just stick around while the Wilsons do their shopping. I think it's a real shame when a decent family can't come into town and shop without being accosted by foulmouthed hoodlums." Falcon smiled. "Don't you, buddy?"

The Double N man muttered something under his breath.

"What was that, buddy?" Falcon questioned. "I couldn't catch what you said."

The man sighed and shook his head in disgust. He was in a hard bind and knew it. "I said you're right, Mr. MacCallister. That's what I said."

"Well, I'm mighty glad to hear that," Falcon told him. "That really makes me feel better knowing that someone is going to see to it that these punchers don't cause any more trouble. You are going to see to that, aren't you, buddy?"

This time the man's sigh was audible. "Yeah," he said, resignation in his voice. "I'm goin' to see to that."

"I have your word on that, buddy?" Falcon pressed.

"Yes, Mr. MacCallister," the Double N rider said. "You have my word."

"By golly, that shines," Falcon replied, a smile on his lips. "Yes, sir, it really does. And I know you're a man of your word, aren't you, buddy?"

The Double N rider had to smile despite, or because of, the situation. MacCallister had boxed him in verbally and there was no way out without appearing to be a man of no character; a man whose word meant nothing. The Double N spokesman had to hand it to MacCallister: He had cooled the situation without gunplay and done it smooth as glass. "I keep my word, MacCallister. You can count on that."

"That shines, buddy. That really shines."

"And you can count on this, too," the Double N rider added. "You can write in your tally book or tattoo on your arm or have it with your coffee: You and me will meet up another time when there ain't no women nor kids around."

"I'm sure we will, buddy."

"And my name ain't *buddy*. It's Les."

"All right, Les. I'll make it a point to look you up sometime."

"You be sure and do that, MacCallister. I don't take water for no man."

"I didn't ask you to take water, Les. If you think I did, I apologize for it. I just asked you to control your friends and not talk dirty around women and kids. That's all. What's wrong with that?''

Les looked at him for a moment. "Puttin' it that way, nothin', I suppose."

"Then we're all jam up and jelly, aren't we?"

"For the time bein', I reckon."

"See you around, Les."

Falcon stood on the boardwalk and watched the Double N riders walk back to the Purple Palace.

"Do I keep those pistols you took from those men, Falcon?" Jim asked.

"Yes. And you carry one with you at all times. Plowing, going to the well, slopping the hogs, *everywhere!* Understood?"

"I understand."

Falcon turned and started back into the store.

"Where are you going?" Jim asked.

Falcon smiled. "To get me some peppermint candy."

Twenty

Falcon had him a hunch that once Les knocked back a couple of shots of hooch, he just might come looking for him. If so, it couldn't be helped. Falcon hoped that would not be the case, but if it was, so be it. Falcon had other errands to attend to in town, and he wasn't going to leave because of Les's hurt feelings, or whatever might be eating at the Double N rider.

Falcon bought the Wilson kids each a peppermint stick, then stood in front of the general store, chomping on his own stick of peppermint candy. He finished the candy, then stepped back inside and ordered a few supplies that were needed back at the ranch.

When he again stepped outside, he glanced down the street toward the Purple Palace. Les was standing outside, drinking from a bottle of whiskey and glaring down Falcon's way.

"Damn!" Falcon muttered.

He looked across the street from the store. Stumpy and Wildcat were still there, waiting for the trouble they both sensed was coming. And they both knew that Falcon would not leave town simply to ride away from that trouble. That wasn't the way of a western man.

Les knelt down and placed his bottle on the edge of the

boardwalk, then stepped out into the street. He motioned to Falcon.

Falcon sighed. There it was.

The Double N crew exited the saloon, crowding the boardwalk in front of the Palace, watching and waiting. They stood in silence, waiting for the hook and draw from the two men who would face each other in the dusty street of the little town.

Reverend Watkins appeared at the far end of the street, holding a Bible.

"Don't do this!" the minister shouted. "A minor disagreement is not worth the life of a man."

Les paid the preacher no attention as he walked to the center of the street and stopped, slowly turning to face Falcon's direction.

Falcon stepped off the boardwalk and walked slowly toward the center of the street.

"Somebody stop them!" Reverend Watkins shouted. "This is madness, I say, madness."

"You think a few words are worth dying over, Les?" Falcon called.

"No man talks to me the way you done," Les called.

"I avoided trouble, Les. That's all."

"Well, you got a whole bunch of it now, MacCallister."

"This is stupid, Les. No point to it."

"I say different, MacCallister."

"Stop this!" Reverend Watkins yelled. "Somebody stop these men."

Les took a step and Falcon did the same. They were half a long block apart.

The shopkeepers and businesspeople of the town had, to a person, stepped outside to stand in silence on the boardwalk, watching the two men walk slowly toward the violent death of at least one of them.

Stumpy and Wildcat had moved up the block, to stand across from the Purple Palace, facing the Double N crew. But all doubted there would be any interference. This was between Les and Falcon; to interfere would not be the western way. It would be in violation of an unwritten code of conduct. In the west, if a man strapped on a gun, he was expected to use it if he was called out. If he refused, he was branded a coward, and nobody, even those who might be opposed to six-gun justice, would have much to do with that man from then on. In the days of the wild west, there was no place for a coward.

"Oh, Lord!" Reverend Watkins lifted his face toward the heavens and began his prayer. "I beg You to . . ."

"Shut up, Preacher!" Les called. "This ain't none of your concern."

Watkins stepped out into the street.

"Get him out of here," Falcon called. "Somebody get the preacher off the street."

The bank president stepped off the boardwalk and hustled toward the minister. He took him by the arm and forcibly pulled him off the street and over to the edge of the boardwalk.

"This is wrong!" Watkins said.

"It's the way it is," Willard said. "And you can't change it, so don't even try."

Falcon and Les each took a few more steps.

Jim Wilson and his oldest son stepped out of the general store, each with a rifle in his hands.

"We're out of it!" one of the Double N hands called. "Just take it easy. No matter which way it goes, we're out of it. You can put up them rifles."

"Stand clear, Jim," Falcon said, his voice carrying back to Jim. "The hands won't interfere."

"How do you know?" Wilson called.

"That's just the way it is out here. Stand clear and stay out of it."

The two men in the street took another step toward each other. A man stepped out of the hotel to stand on the boardwalk. A stranger. Falcon cut his eyes. He had never seen the man before. He wondered if it might be the deputy federal marshal. The man was neatly dressed and clean shaven, his hair trimmed. He wore one pistol, tied down. Might be him. Then Falcon quickly returned his eyes to the man called Les.

The two men were walking steady now, rapidly closing the distance between them. The townspeople were quiet, no one saying a word, no one moving, no one taking their eyes off the life-and-death scene being played out in the street in front of them.

A dog suddenly darted out into the street, between the two men. The men stopped their walking for a moment, until the little dog had cleared the street.

The sun had climbed high into the blue of the sky, and it was hot. Falcon could see the sweat staining the front of Les's shirt. Falcon stopped about forty feet from Les. He would walk no farther; he would make his stand here and wait for Les to make his play.

Reverend Watkins was praying.

Les was no braggart. He offered no boasts about what he was going to do. He just grabbed for his gun.

Falcon shot him, clearing leather and firing before Les could even get the muzzle of his .45 clear of his holster. Falcon shot the Double N rider in the right shoulder, his six-gun dropping into the dust of the street from suddenly numbed fingers.

"Son of a bitch!" Falcon heard one of the Double N riders exclaim in awe at his speed and skill.

Falcon had placed his shot carefully, to wound and not to kill. But he was well aware that those days were rapidly drawing to a close. With the number of hired guns growing, the days of anyone being selective about killing were almost over. And Falcon was somewhat saddened by that thought. It meant that very soon the blood would start to flow indiscriminately . . . unless a miracle occurred, and Falcon doubted that would happen.

He walked up to Les, who was on his knees in the street, his good hand pressing against the wound in his shoulder. "You satisfied now, Les?" Falcon asked.

The man looked up at him, the shock wearing off and his eyes reflecting the pain that was beginning to tear through his body. "I reckon, MacCallister. You're the best I ever seen, for a fact you are."

Falcon pointed up and across the street. "Some of you boys take him over to the doc's. He's hurt, but he'll live."

"Wait a minute," Les said, struggling to get to his boots.

"Who are them old men with you, MacCallister? Them ol' boys over yonder." He cut his eyes.

"Wildcat Wheeless and Jack Stump."

"Jesus Christ," another of the Double N hands muttered. "Them men are legends. They workin' for you, MacCallister?"

"Working for John Bailey. Along with Big Bob Marsh, Puma Parley, Mustang, and Dan Carson."

"Shhh-it!" another hand said, his voice filled with awe.

Out of the corner of his eyes, Falcon watched a couple of the Double N hands exchange knowing glances. The expression on their faces stated very plainly that they wanted no part of those legendary old mountain men: men who had fought everything from Indians to grizzly bears . . . sometimes with nothing but a knife.

Falcon figured that come the evening, several of Noonan's men would be riding out, heading for safer locales.

But that still left the farmers and small ranchers (those that were left, that is) badly outnumbered.

"I got me some money stuck back in my poke," Les said, still hesitant to move from the dusty, bloody street. "I think I'll mend my shoulder here in town, away from the em-ploy of Nance Noonan."

"And just see what happens?" Falcon asked.

"Something like that."

"Better go see the doc now."

Les nodded and allowed himself to be led off, walking slowly toward the doctor's office.

Falcon turned his head. The neatly dressed stranger who had watched the hook and draw from the boardwalk was gone.

Falcon walked back to the general store and stepped up onto the boardwalk. "Jim, you folks get your shopping done and get clear of the town. We'll hang around until you're finished. A few of those Double N boys will be sure to get liquored up and come trouble-hunting after a time. Get enough staples to last you for a time."

"That's probably an excellent idea, Falcon. We'll take your advice and do that."

"And stay out of town for a time. If you have to come to

town, several families come together and come armed and ready to use those guns.''

The farmer nodded his head in agreement and walked back into the general store.

Falcon picked out the empty brass from the cylinder of his .44 and reloaded. Stumpy and Wildcat were still across the street, sitting in the shade of the awning, waiting.

One of the Double N men had ridden out, probably heading back to Noonan's headquarters to report on what had happened in town.

Two more Double N hands had just plain ridden out, heading in the opposite direction. They were the men Falcon had seen exchange glances. They were pulling out for good. It was one thing to make war against men who were not experienced gunhands, and women and kids. It was quite another matter to be facing some of the meanest men west of the Mississippi; men who played deadly games with no rules except those they made up at the moment.

Falcon felt there would be a few more hired guns who'd pull out, but by and large, the exodus was over. The men who were staying would fight until the finish, earning their forty or sixty dollars a month.

Standing on the boardwalk in front of the general store, Falcon rolled him a smoke and stepped back into the shadows. He still had some errands to attend to, but he would wait until the Wilsons were through with their shopping before seeing to them.

The town had settled down, the residents vanishing back into their stores and homes. The long street was quiet. Reverend Watkins had ceased his praying and gone back to his church.

The town of Gilman had the appearance of being just another sleepy western town stuck in the middle of nowhere.

But Falcon knew there were tensions and hatreds bubbling just under the surface, ready to erupt with volcanic fury at a single word or gesture.

And when the rage finally reached the boiling point, the range would run red with blood.

Twenty-One

Night riders struck that same night, burning out and killing a farmer who worked the land on several sections south of the Rockingchair. Falcon rode down to see the family the next day, Big Bob and Puma with him.

They found a very tired-looking woman loading up a wagon with a few meager possessions she had managed to drag from the flames before the fire consumed everything else they owned. Several children helped their mother load the wagon. About a hundred feet from the still-smoking ashes was a fresh-dug grave.

Falcon stepped out of the saddle and walked over to the woman, who was looking at him warily, through very weary eyes.

"I work for the Rockingchair, ma'am," Falcon said. "Is there anything I can do to help you?"

She shook her head. "No. We could have used your help last night, though."

"I wish I could have been here. Do you need any money?"

Again, she shook her head. "We had a few dollars tucked away. That will be enough to get us back to civilization. Damn this country! Damn it to hell!"

There was nothing Falcon could say that would ease the woman's pain. He stood silently with hat in hand and let her vent her rage.

Big Bob and Puma stood off to one side, both of them helpless to act in the face of this tragedy. But they would act, soon. There would be a payback, in blood and pain and fire. This senseless killing and burning could not go unavenged.

"Then let me buy your land, ma'am," Falcon said. "I'll pay top dollar. How many sections did you folks own?"

"Four. You just make me an offer, any offer, and I'll sure take it."

"Any offer I make will be fair, ma'am. You can count on that."

"You're Falcon MacCallister, aren't you?"

"Yes, ma'am."

"Heard of you. Heard good things about you."

"I was going to come see you folks. I've been visiting families north and east of your location."

"How do we handle this sale? I want to get gone from this evil place."

"I'll get a piece of paper and pencil and you write out a bill of sale and I'll give you a check or cash money. But a better way would be to follow us into town. Let me check you all into the hotel. You can clean up and I'll treat you to a new set of clothes at the store. We'll see the banker and have the transfer of title done legal and I'll have funds transferred to any bank of your choice in the nation. How about that?"

"You'll do that for us?"

"I certainly will."

"Let me say good-bye to my husband. Give me a few minutes alone with him, won't you?"

"You take as much time as you like, ma'am. We'll finish loading up the wagon. That oldest boy of yours needs to have a doctor look at those burns."

"Doctors cost money," she said simply.

"Don't worry about that. Go say good-bye to your husband. Take as much time as you like. We'll get busy here."

Big Bob and Puma were angry to the core. Falcon could tell

that by their silence as they worked. It was one thing to fight a grown-up man, but to burn out a family, destroy everything they had worked for, torment women and children, kill the father right in front of his family's eyes . . . that was the work of craven cowards, men too low-down to live.

"Settle down, boys," Falcon spoke the words in a low tone. "Just settle down."

"You settle down," Puma told him. "We get this poor woman and what's left of her family on the road, the war's on."

"And we better not meet up with no .44 or Snake or Double N riders neither," Big Bob added. " 'Cause if we do, I'm gonna read to them from the Scriptures. Count on it."

A quaint western expression meaning there would be blood on the land.

"In spades," Puma added.

"All right," Falcon said simply.

"Damn right it is," Big Bob said.

"There ain't even no goddamn lard left to smear on those children's burns," Puma said, his voice shaking with rage. "Goddamn men who would do this. Goddamn 'em right straight to the pits of Hell."

Falcon kept his silence. There was no point in talking . . . not at the moment. Falcon understood that the mountain men were about to declare war, and it was not going to be pleasant. Falcon knew he had to handle this in a very delicate way, for if he attempted to get bossy with these old boys, they would just tell him to go to hell.

It was the condition of the kids and their pain-filled eyes that did it. Falcon knew that, for he felt the same way. Making war on adults was one thing, making war on kids raised the hackles on any decent man.

The wagon was loaded and the team hitched up. The woman wiped her eyes and turned away from the fresh mound of earth.

"I'll come back and fix up a marker for your man, ma'am," Big Bob gently told the woman.

"That's kind of you, but there's no need," she told him.

"My man loved the land. Let him become a part of it. It's the way he'd want it."

"Yes, ma'am," the big man replied softly, but with unmistakable rage just behind the words.

Be blood on the moon very soon, Falcon thought. *The fuse is lit and there is nothing anyone can do to stop it.*

Falcon and his friends trailed the wagon and the family over the long dusty miles into town. They made it just in time, for the bank was only a few minutes away from closing time. Willard almost went into apoplexy when the woman walked in with Falcon, for he knew with some degree of certainty what was about to take place, and was powerless to do anything except go along with it.

Puma took the kids over to the general store to have them outfitted with new clothes while Big Bob took the boy over to the doc's to have his burns attended to. By the time all that was done, Falcon had bought the sections of land and the woman was picking out a couple of new dresses at the store.

Falcon arranged for rooms at the hotel and got the family settled in. Then the three men went over to the café for an early supper.

While waiting for their food, Big Bob asked the waitress, "You see any Snake, .44, or Double N riders?"

"Not a one today," she told him. "I 'spect some of them will be coming in later on this afternoon."

Big Bob smiled ever so slightly and thanked her. Falcon watched as the big man cut his eyes to Puma and received a small smile in return. Falcon knew then the two men had already agreed on some sort of plan and the best thing he could do, hell, the only thing he could do, was stay out of their way.

Before leaving the ranch, Falcon and Big Bob and Puma had packed a bit of grub and secured bedrolls behind their saddles. They had planned to spend a couple of nights out. They would not be expected back at the ranch.

Working on his second huge slab of apple pie, Big Bob looked at Falcon, who had finished his meal and was drinking a cup of coffee. "You can go visitin', if you like. Count your money, or somethin'. Don't interfere with me and Puma."

"I wouldn't dream of it, Bob," Falcon replied.

"Good," the big man said.

"But do you mind if I sort of tag along with you?"

"Long as you don't make no speeches to none of them hired guns," Puma said. "Me and Bob is fixin' to settle accounts for that good lady over yonder, and her kids."

"I promise, no speeches."

"Then you're welcome to come along with us."

"Thank you."

"We might need an extra gun," Big Bob said. "But bear in mind I said gun, not no long-winded talks."

"Anything you say, Bob. This is your show."

"Good."

"But the other boys will be upset they weren't invited," Falcon added blandly.

"That's their problem," Puma said, after taking a slurp of coffee. "And don't be tryin' no slick snake-oil words to talk us out of doin' this deed, Falcon. It won't work."

"I had to try."

"Well, stop tryin'."

The man who owned the leather and gun shop walked into the café and sat down at the table next to the three Rockingchair men. "I just heard what happened to that farm family, Mr. MacCallister. I want you to know I don't hold with night riding, and I 'specially don't hold with the harming of women and kids. And I'll tell Gilman the same thing."

Falcon nodded his head. "How many others in town feel the way you do?"

"More than you might think. It's just that Gilman and his toughs have a lot of the townspeople buffaloed, that's all. Hell, man, we *want* other folks to come into the area. That's business for us. It wouldn't make any sense for us to want to keep people out."

"I did wonder about that," Falcon replied, motioning for the waitress to come refill his coffee cup. Big Bob and Puma rose from the table and walked outside, to stand on the boardwalk.

"Those ol' boys of yours is on the prod, aren't they?" the shop owner asked.

"All the way on the prod."

"It's a good way to get themselves killed."

Falcon smiled. "Those men don't have any plans to get planted anytime soon, mister. I can assure you of that. My advice to you is when you see .44 or Snake or Double N boys come in, you gather up your family, go home and close the door, and stay there, because it's going to get wild in this town shortly after any of those night-riding bastards hit the street."

"Not every rider from those ranches took part in that raid," the citizen pointed out.

"But they know those who did," Falcon came right back. "And that makes them just as guilty."

The citizen looked at Falcon for a long moment, then took his coffee cup and moved to another table. Falcon smiled and lingered for a time, smoking and drinking his coffee. He paid for the meals and walked outside. Big Bob and Puma were across the street, sitting on a bench about a hundred feet from the entrance to the Purple Palace.

Falcon looked out toward the edge of town. In the distance he could see a moving dust cloud. Riders coming in. He didn't have to point it out to Big Bob or Puma; they'd probably seen it before he had.

Falcon glanced up at the sky. There were clouds rolling in. It had been several weeks since a good rain, and they were due for one. From the looks of the sky, they were going to get a good soaking.

The dust cloud grew closer. Falcon could count six, no, eight men riding into town. He stepped back into the shadows created by the boardwalk's awning and waited. He wasn't sure what Big Bob and Puma had in the way of plans, but knowing them as he did, Falcon had a hunch it would be very direct. He had noticed that before coming to town with the woman and her kids, the mountain men had each dug out a spare pistol from their saddlebags, loaded it up full, and shoved it down behind their belts. Whatever the two men had in mind, Falcon would be comfortable betting a bundle that when it started it was going to be very quick and very nasty. And very bloody.

The riders had reached the edge of the town and stopped. Falcon couldn't figure what they were up to. Then they all lined up abreast and Falcon got it then: They were going to race up the main street, probably to the Palace saloon. They would create enough dust to cover everything in town, plus endangering anyone who might be caught in the street.

And that's not all they were going to do: They were also going to irritate the hell out of Big Bob and Puma, for the men had washed very carefully and spent several minutes getting the trail dust out of their clothes before going to the café.

Falcon rolled him a smoke and looked carefully up and down the street. It was deserted. Somehow the residents of the western town had smelled the invisible odor of trouble on the hot summer wind and everyone had headed for the inside.

The riders came in a rush, whooping and hollering and galloping their horses as fast as they could run up the main street of town. The dust the pounding hooves kicked up was terrible, a thick choking cloud that hung over that section of town for a moment, and then settled to cover everything.

"Stupid," Falcon muttered. "And arrogant." He brushed the dust from his shirt, then took his hat and slapped the dirt from his trousers. "That makes me mad!" he said.

"The men were only being exuberant." The familiar voice came from Falcon's left.

Falcon cut his eyes. Reverend Watkins. He sighed. Falcon really did not feel like putting up with the preacher this day.

"A little dust is no reason to start trouble," the preacher said.

"I don't intend to start any trouble, Preacher. But look around you: There's no one on the street. Doesn't that tell you anything?"

"Not really," the minister replied. "Is it supposed to tell me something?"

"How long have you been out west, Preacher?"

"A few months. Why?"

"And you came from where?"

"Boston. Why?"

"Just curious, Preacher. That's all. Just curious."

The riders who had galloped into town were a mixed crew of Double N, Snake, and .44 hands. Most of them wore two guns, tied down. They were a loud and profane bunch as they swung down from the saddles and swaggered about, making sure that anyone out and about both saw and heard them.

Big Bob and Puma rose slowly from the benches and began slapping the dust from their clothing. Falcon watched as the two mountain men also furtively slipped the hammer thongs from their six-guns.

"Boston is a lovely city," Reverend Watkins said.

"I know," Falcon replied, not taking his eyes off the milling gunhands. "I've been there."

"*You* have visited Boston?"

"Yes. Also New York City, Baltimore, St. Louis, and a few other large cities. You'd better get off the street, Preacher. All hell's about to pop here in a minute. A stray bullet doesn't care who it hits."

Watkins ignored the advice. "How did you like our lovely city?"

"Too damn big," Falcon told the preacher. "Too crowded for my tastes."

"Yes. Well. I suppose to a western man it would seen so."

"Get off the street, Preacher! Damnit, do what I tell you to do."

The gunhands had noticed Puma and Big Bob. The hired guns were snickering and poking one another, whispering among themselves, making, Falcon was sure, any number of crappy comments about the two older men, and making them loud enough for the older men to hear.

The gunslicks were not aware of it, but they were talking their way into an early grave. Once, when Falcon visited New Orleans, he heard a Cajun make a comment about a man with an alligator mouth and a hummingbird ass. That pretty well summed up the hired guns.

Far in the distance, thunder rumbled. That storm was still many miles away. But the storm that was building on the main street of town was growing in quiet intensity, without the added attraction of lightning and thunder as a prelude.

The lightning and thunder would come along soon enough, in the form of gunsmoke and lead, to be followed by blood and pain.

Falcon unconsciously touched the butt of his second six-gun, stuck down behind his gunbelt. Watkins's eyes followed the movement.

"You are going to start trouble!" the preacher exclaimed. "But those cowboys haven't done anything."

"Shut up, Preacher," Falcon told him. "You don't know what you're talking about. Get off the street."

"You men over there!" Watkins suddenly shouted at the gunslicks. "It's a trap. You'll all be killed! Run for your lives!"

"Son of a bitch!" Falcon cursed, as the hired gunnies grabbed for pistols.

One of them pointed a gun at Big Bob and Bob jerked iron and drilled him in the belly.

The summer breeze that had been whispering on the main street of Gilman suddenly erupted into a full-blown storm.

Twenty-Two

The gunhand screamed and dropped his pistol, both hands holding onto his perforated belly. He sank to the dirt and horse crap of the street and stayed there, on his knees.

Another of the land-grabbing crew spotted Falcon as he stepped forward on the boardwalk and figured he was part of the setup. He snapped off a shot that missed Falcon and blew the preacher's hat off his head. Reverend Watkins let out a startled whoop and jumped for the protection of the nearest doorway.

Falcon triggered off a round that caught the night rider in the shoulder and spun him around. He dropped his pistol and fell back against the boardwalk, out of this fight.

Big Bob and Puma had their fists full of guns and were letting the hammers fall and the lead fly. The battle on the dusty street was over and done with in fifteen seconds. The Snake, Double N, and .44 riders were down, several of them dead or dying, the rest wounded.

Big Bob and Puma were unscathed, as was Falcon. Horses were settling down after some wild seconds of bucking and rearing, with some of them breaking loose from the hitchrails and galloping away up the street.

As the gunfire faded into no more than a hard memory, and the gunsmoke blew away in the quickening breeze that was preceding the summer storm, the doctor stepped out of his office, black bag in hand, and stood for a moment, looking at the carnage in the street. Then he stepped off the boardwalk and walked over to the nearest wounded man and knelt down.

The man that Big Bob had drilled in the belly was still. Falcon walked across the street and looked down at him. He was dead, on his knees in the dirt of the street. Falcon noticed that his boots were run-down at the heel and both soles had holes in them. The dead man was no more than twenty-five years old, at the most.

"That one shot my husband!" the woman's voice came from the balcony of the hotel.

Falcon turned to look at the settler's wife. She was pointing at a man who had been wounded in the leg and was stretched out in the street, his leg broken by the .45 caliber bullet.

"I'll never forget his face," the woman added, then turned and walked back into the hotel.

The night rider with the busted leg cussed the woman, loud and long.

"Here now!" the doctor admonished him. "There'll be no more of that."

The night rider cut his eyes and cussed the doctor.

"What a nice bunch of boys," Puma said, stepping off the boardwalk and walking over to stand beside Falcon. "You can tell right off they had proper raisin'."

The night rider with the busted leg cussed Puma.

The doctor looked up at Falcon. "This the bunch who burned out the farmer last night?"

"Yes."

Another night rider told Falcon what part of his anatomy he could kiss.

"That's disgustin'!" Big Bob said to the wounded man. "You ought to be ashamed of yourself, boy."

The gunhand directed his obscenities toward Bob.

"You started it now," one of the slightly wounded paid guns

said to Falcon. "There'll be no stoppin' our boys once they hear about this."

"Where's the damn law in this town?" Puma asked one of the citizens who were gathering around to gawk at the dead and the wounded.

"There ain't none," the citizen said. "The last marshal we had quit."

"This one just died," another citizen said, standing over a man sprawled facedown in the dirt.

"Good," Big Bob said.

On the boardwalk, Reverend Watkins had found his bullet-perforated hat and was now raising his voice in prayer.

Several rather ample ladies from his church had gathered beside the minister and were singing "Rock of Ages."

"I always did favor that song," Puma said. "Almost brings a tear to my eye."

"That's good," Big Bob told him. "Your face could stand a little water on it."

Several more ladies had joined their church sisters on the boardwalk and a choir was now in full tune.

"If he passes the collection plate, I'm gone," Puma said.

"You men are disgraceful!" a citizen told Puma.

"I know it," the mountain man said sorrowfully. "But mama done her best to raise me right."

"Oh, Lord!" a wounded night rider suddenly hollered. "I need something for the pain! My belly's on fire!"

"You want me to kick him in the head?" Big Bob asked the doctor. "That would shore shut him up for a time."

"I think you men have done enough for one day," the doctor replied, not looking up from his emergency ministering to the wounded.

"Hell, I was just tryin' to hep," Bob said.

"Let's go get us a drink," Puma suggested. "I don't think we're wanted here."

"Yeah," Bob said, doing his best to keep a hurt expression on his face. "I feel plumb left out and rejected."

"Good," the doctor said. "Please do leave."

"Grouchy thing, ain't he?" Puma said. "Come on, Bob. My feelin's is hurt."

The two mountain men walked off toward the Stampede Saloon.

The two night riders who were only slightly hurt had already limped off to their horses, ignoring any medical help, and ridden out of town. The doctor looked up at Falcon. "That puncher who told you there'd be no stopping them now wasn't joking, Mr. MacCallister. This shoot-out just started the war."

Falcon shrugged his heavy shoulders. "Then you'd better tell your carpenter to start knocking together a lot of caskets. You're going to need them."

Falcon walked off toward the Stampede, to have a drink with his friends.

Gilman, Stegman, and Noonan didn't wait long to strike again . . . they sent night riders out that same night. But this time the night riders ran into a hail of gunfire and were beaten back by a settler and his family. The farmer lost his barn to fire, but his house and possessions were saved. The next day, Falcon and his men and the farmers who lived within half a day's ride of the settler's place were there, raising a new barn. By that evening, the farmer was back in business and Stegman, Noonan, and Gilman were furious.

"You let them get organized!" Noonan fumed at Gilman.

"I didn't *let* them get crap!" Miles raged right back.

"The hell you didn't!" Noonan shouted.

"All right!" Stegman said. "Settle down, the both of you. My God, men, listen to yourselves. You're both losing it. You're going into a panic. Settle down and let's make some plans on how best to deal with this situation."

Stegman uncorked a bottle and poured them all stiff drinks. "That's better, boys. Much better," he said, after a moment of silence. "Now then, let's go over what we're up against. First of all, we have MacCallister. One man. About six old farts, all of them with one foot already in the grave. A few ranchers, and a handful of farmers. That's it. That's what we're facing. And that's all we're facing. Without MacCallister, the opposition would fall apart. He's the brains behind it all. So we take him out.''

"I've tried to do just that a couple of times," Gilman said, disgust in his voice. "It isn't that easy, believe me."

"Then we keep trying until we do take him out," Stegman replied. "We've got the men, and our payroll is costing us a bundle. I don't know about you boys, but I can't keep paying for much longer. The payroll will break me."

"It'll damn sure do that," Gilman muttered. "I'm going to have a cash flow problem before much longer."

Even Noonan agreed with that, nodding his head solemnly. "Yeah, me too. Hard money is gettin' tight. We gotta do something and do it damn quick."

"The problem is, one of them, anyways, is that MacCallister could buy us all if he took a notion," Stegman continued. "It's common knowledge that he's a millionaire. The whole damn family together is worth millions and millions of dollars. They're the richest family in Colorado." He waved a hand. "But that's ain't neither here nor there. Our problem is right here, with just one MacCallister . . . Falcon."

"Let's each pick five of our best men and send them after Falcon," Noonan suggested.

"That's a good start," Stegman agreed. "Let's keep it rollin'."

"We've damn sure tried everything else," Gilman said. "And nothin's worked so far. What the hell do we have to lose?"

"Nothin'," Stegman said. "Personally, I'd like to get this war over with and get rid of about ninety percent of these lazy gunslingers we got on the payroll. Some of these men don't know the ass end of a cow from the front end. All they do is eat and sleep and gripe."

"Kill the kids," Noonan said quietly. "That will take the guts right out of Bailey and we'll be shut of the main player in this little war. He'll fold up like a house of cards."

"I don't know about that," Stegman said. "We start killin'

ranchers' kids and the whole county will turn against us. You'd better give that some thought.''

"So we make it look like an accident," Noonan pressed on, leaning forward in his chair. "We kill some nester kids first. Nobody gives a damn about nesters' kids. I think Bailey will get the message pretty quick.''

Gilman laughed. "For a fact, some of them damn nesters probably wouldn't even miss a kid or so for a week. They breed like rabbits.''

The three powerful ranchers all enjoyed a good laugh at that. They each had another drink and were silent for a time. If their plans worked out, the three men would soon control the largest county in Wyoming. They would be running more cattle than anyone else. They would have an empire.

"What about this Silver Dollar Kid?" Noonan asked. "You're payin' him top dollar, Miles. And so far he ain't done nothin'. Turn him loose against MacCallister. Hell, if he's as good as his reputation, he just might get lucky.''

"I been savin' him," Miles said. "But now might be the time. I'll cut him loose in the mornin'. He's lightnin' fast, for a pure-dee fact.''

"Just to be on the safe side," Stegman said, "let's go ahead and each of us pick five men to go against MacCallister if this fails. We've got to start thinkin' ahead.''

"All right," Noonan said. "I can name five of the slickest gunhands anywhere around in one minute.''

"Me too," Gilman said. "God knows they're costin' me enough money.''

"That's the truth if it was ever spoke," Stegman agreed. "But first, let's figure how to get MacCallister into town to face the Kid.''

"I want to be there to see it," both of the others said as one. "I don't want to miss this.''

"Oh, we'll be there," Stegman said. "I wouldn't miss seein' MacCallister take lead. That'll be a tale we can tell our grandchildren.''

"And that will also whip the townspeople back into shape," Gilman mused softly. "They been gettin' a little uppity since it appears MacCallister is gainin' the upper hand. I got to slap them back down a notch or two.''

"I noticed right off they was sorta snooty," Noonan said.

"Look," Stegman said, "we can't be too obvious about this. As much as we might like to make it plain that we're behind it, it'd be better if the showdown between the Kid and MacCallister, when it comes, looks as though it just happened. We'll just send the Kid into town and he can get him a hotel room and he can wait it out. Lord knows, from what I've seen of him, he don't know nothin' about ranchin'.''

"For a fact," Gilman said. "He's sorta goofy in the head.''

"That ain't all he is," Stegman said drily, with a look of disgust on his face. "He makes my skin crawl just bein' around him.''

"Whatever else he might be," Gilman said, "he's the fastest gun I've ever seen. If anyone can take MacCallister, it's the Kid.''

"All right, Miles," Noonan said. "Cut him loose and let's see what happens.''

Miles Gilman stood up and poured them all drinks. He held his glass out. "To the death of Falcon MacCallister!''

The three of them solemnly clinked glasses.

Twenty-Three

The sky opened up shortly after the shoot-out on the main street of town and the rain didn't stop for two days. During that time, everybody stayed close to their respective ranches. When the storm clouds finally blew away and the sky cleared, The Silver Dollar Kid got his go-to-work orders and rode into town and got him a room at the hotel. That was noticed by all the residents of course, but no one really paid much attention to it. The Kid was a quiet type who didn't drink very much and took his meals alone and at odd times of the day when the dining room at the hotel was least likely to have many customers.

The Kid lounged around town for the better part of a week waiting for Falcon to make an appearance. Not only didn't Falcon come into town, no one from the Rockingchair came into town. Then on a Saturday morning, the Kid looked out his second-floor window and smiled. Falcon MacCallister was just stepping down from the saddle in front of the general store. John Bailey and his family were just reining up in the buckboard in front of the dress shop. The Kid stared at the lettering on the shop window. He never could figure that out. *Shop* was spelled with two p's and two e's. Stupid.

The Kid buckled on his gunbelt and slipped into his fancy

vest. He went downstairs to meet Falcon, certain that after today, his name would be right up there with Hardin and Hickok and Earp and Masterson and all the rest. He would be the man who outdrew Falcon MacCallister. He would be a legend. Tough men would step aside for him and singers would write and sing songs about him. There would be newspaper articles written about him, some penny dreadful books published, and maybe even some plays done about his life. The Silver Dollar Kid was sure all those things would happen . . . just as soon as word got out that he had killed Falcon MacCallister.

The Kid walked through the lobby of the hotel and stepped out onto the boardwalk, looking first left and then right. The shops and businesses were busy with customers. That was good. The Kid wanted lots of people to see him gun down Falcon MacCallister. He touched the butts of both guns. He was ready.

The Kid walked slowly up the boardwalk, toward the general store. He met a dozen people but spoke to none of them. He had just one thought on his mind: killing Falcon MacCallister.

Falcon was standing on the boardwalk in front of the general store, chatting with a local. He saw the Kid walking up the boardwalk and immediately sensed the Kid was going to brace him. It was in the way he was walking, the stiff back and the way the Kid held his hands.

"You'd better back away," Falcon told the citizen. "I've got trouble coming straight at me."

The local stepped to one side, then backed up until he was standing in the doorway of the general store, out of the direct line of fire.

"Falcon MacCallister!" the Kid called, stopping about a hundred feet from Falcon.

Falcon turned to face the Kid.

"I'm callin' you out, Falcon MacCallister."

"Why?" Falcon asked.

That confused the Kid for a moment. There was a look of puzzlement on his narrow face. " 'Cause you're you and I'm me, that's why," he finally said.

"It was that way yesterday, last week, and last month," Falcon said calmly. "Why brace me now?"

The conversation was getting just a bit philosophical for the Kid. He narrowed his eyes and stared hard at Falcon. "Don't try to weasel out of this, MacCallister. You knew it was comin'."

"I did?"

That brought the kid up short again. This just wasn't going exactly the way he'd had it all worked out in his mind. He'd envisioned crowds of people lining both sides of the street, standing silently and watching while he gunned down Falcon. He hadn't expected a damn conversation with MacCallister.

"Yeah, you did!" the Kid yelled in frustration.

"Oh," Falcon said. "Well. If you say so, Kid. Tell me, what are we fighting about?"

Again, the Kid was brought up short for a moment. He stared at Falcon, anger clouding his features, darkening his face. Finally, he said, "To see who's the better man with a gun, damn you, that's why."

"Oh. Is that all? OK. You're a better man with a gun. Does that make you happy?"

Several men along the boardwalk laughed at that. The Kid looked as though he was about to cry. This just wasn't working out the way he'd planned.

"No, you bastard!" the Kid shouted. "You got to face me and hook and draw."

"Aww . . . do I have to?"

For a moment, the Kid looked as though he was going to jump up and down on the boardwalk and have a temper tantrum. "Yes, damn you, MacCallister. You have to face me. I'm callin' you out, right now, right here. I'm sayin' you're a yellow dog and you don't have the courage to face me. I'm sayin' you got no guts and you're a damn coward."

The men along the boardwalk knew then that Falcon could not get out of this fight. No western man would stand and take those insults without reacting.

And Falcon was no different. He sighed and shook his head. "I wish you hadn't said those things, Kid," Falcon told the younger man.

"Well, I said 'em, and I meant 'em, you yellow bastard! Now step out into the street."

Falcon stepped off the boardwalk and into the street. There was nothing else he could do. The unwritten code had just been violated.

The Silver Dollar Kid stepped off the boardwalk and walked slowly to the center of the street, turning to face Falcon. The silver dollars on his vest, hat, and gunbelt twinkled in the sunlight.

John Bailey and his family stood inside the general store, looking out one of the large front show windows at the life-and-death drama that was taking place on the main street of town. They did not speak.

"Your play, Kid," Falcon spoke softly. "You wanted this, now you have it. But I wish it didn't have to be."

The Kid was all raging torrents inside. Outwardly, he was calm, but inside he was a spewing volcano. This was the moment he had lived for since he was just a pimply-faced boy. He was finally facing a top gun.

The entire town had turned out, lining both sides of the street. The townspeople and those who had come into town to shop stood silently on the boardwalk, not moving, not speaking. Watching and waiting.

"You got anything you want to say before you die, Mac-Callister?" the Kid called.

"I have no intention of dying this day, Kid. You've got it all wrong."

"What do you mean? I'm the Silver Dollar Kid. No man has ever beat me to the draw."

"You never faced anyone worth a damn, Kid," Falcon's voice carried up and down the street. "All you've ever faced was two-bit wanna-bes and kids. I'm telling you right now to back away and get out. Or die where you stand."

"You're ... tellin' *me?*" the Kid was amazed. Nobody talked to him like that. Nobody. It just wasn't done. And he had faced men who were good with a gun. There was that marshal down south, and that gambler who cold-decked him that time. And that cowboy who was supposed to be good with a gun. The Kid laughed at Falcon. "I know what you're tryin' to do, MacCallister. It won't work. You're just tryin' to save your own skin.''

"You're a damn fool, boy," Falcon told him, his words hard and cold. "What's Gilman paying you, seventy-five dollars a month? You ready to die for a few dollars? Is that all the value you place on your life?''

"You got it all wrong, MacCallister. I'm not the one goin' to die this day. You are!''

Falcon slowly shook his head. "No, I'm not, Kid. Be smart. Turn around and walk away. You've got a long life ahead of you. Don't end it in this street.''

The Kid laughed at Falcon's words. "Time for talkin' is all over, MacCallister. You can't talk your way out of this.''

"I tried," Falcon said. "Nobody can say I didn't try.''

"Now!'' the Kid shouted, and drew.

The Silver Dollar Kid was fast. If anything was ever written around him, that would surely be mentioned. He was only a hair slower than Falcon, and he got off the first shot. But he missed, the bullet digging up the dirt in front of Falcon. Falcon didn't miss. His bullet hit the Kid just under the V of the rib cage and turned him around. The Kid lifted his .45 and thumbed the hammer back. Falcon shot him again, the slug striking the Kid in the chest and dropping him to the dirt. The Kid's .45 slipped from his fingers just as he slumped over on one side, blood leaking out of a corner of his mouth.

Falcon walked slowly up to the young man and stood looking down at him. The Kid seemed to be having a difficult time focusing his eyes. He opened his mouth to speak, but nothing came out except a mumble that Falcon could not understand.

The Kid tried to pull his second Colt from leather but he could not make his finger close around the butt. He finally gave it up and lay still in the dirt.

"My aim was off," the Kid managed to say.

Falcon said nothing in reply.

The town doctor walked over and knelt down, examining the Kid. He stood up, looked at Falcon, and shook his head.

"He just wouldn't listen. I tried to talk him out of it, Doc.''

"I know you did. I heard you. No one can fault you for this shooting."

Reverend Watkins and some ladies from his church had gathered on the boardwalk and were singing.

"I'm too young to die. I don't want to die," the Kid muttered, his face pressing into the dirt.

None of the men gathered around said anything.

"It wasn't supposed to be this way," the Kid whispered. "I was gonna be famous."

Falcon picked out the empty brasses and dropped them into the street, filling up the cylinder with fresh rounds.

Two little boys darted out and grabbed up the empty brasses and dashed back behind the crowd on the boardwalk. None of those gathered around the dying young man noticed them. Somewhere in the town, several dogs started barking.

Reverend Watkins started praying for the Kid's soul and for the Lord to forgive Falcon for what he'd just done. The ladies broke out in fresh song.

The Silver Dollar Kid closed his eyes and died.

Falcon turned and walked away.

When the news of the Silver Dollar Kid getting gunned down by Falcon reached the hired guns in the county, some twenty of them packed their war bags and quietly rode out. They wanted no part of Falcon MacCallister. While the Kid may have been goofy in the head, he was still fast as a lightning bolt with a six-gun. Falcon outdrew him. That was it for those hired guns. This war was over for them.

Stegman, Gilman, and Noonan at first did not believe it when they heard the news about the shoot-out, for all three of them had seen the Kid practice and knew how fast he was. This meant that finding anyone now to go up against Falcon Mac-Callister face-to-face was going to be very difficult, if not impossible.

"Turn the boys loose and ambush the bastard," Noonan ordered. "It's the only way."

The fifteen gunslicks picked by the cattlemen's alliance met and discussed plans on how best to kill Falcon MacCallister. A gunslick named Wilbur felt sure he could take Falcon face-to-face. So did a hired gun who went by the name of Dooley, as did another mercenary who was called Ed.

"The Kid was all mouth," Wilbur said. "He wasn't as good as people thought he was."

"Yeah," Dooley agreed. "And neither is MacCallister. I can take him."

"So can I," Ed announced.

The twelve others in the group said nothing. To a man, they all secretly believed they were faster than Falcon, but would keep their mouths shut about it for the time being. They all knew that the Kid may have had an off day. He might have had the sun in his eyes. His hand may have been sweaty when he drew. There were a dozen reasons why Falcon dropped the Kid, but none of the fifteen believed any of those reasons would ever happen to them . . . when the time came for them to face Falcon MacCallister. And that day would come.

When the Silver Dollar Kid was buried, there were no mourners at the church or at the graveside service: just Reverend Watkins and the two grave diggers. Not even the ladies from the church choir showed up. The Kid didn't even have enough money in his pocket to buy a decent headstone. The undertaker had to rip the silver dollars off the Kid's hat band, vest, and gunbelt to pay for the services. Neither Stegman, Noonan, nor Gilman attended the funeral services for the Kid.

And no one knew what name to put on the simple marker. No one knew the Kid's Christian name.

THE SILVER DOLLAR KID was carved into the wooden marker, and the date of his demise. In a couple of years, the wooden cross would rot and fall apart and be no more, and no one would remember where the Kid was buried.

There were countless graves such as the Kid's scattered all over the west; too many for anyone to guess as to their number.

"The Kid was nearabouts as fast as Falcon," John Bailey told the mountain men and his foremen about the fight. "Maybe a shade slower—it was hard to tell. But he missed his first shot, and more important, he wasn't as calm as Falcon. The

Kid was sweatin' like a pig. Falcon never even broke a sweat whilst they was standin' in the street under the sun. I never seen a man that calm and steady.''

"Of all them boys, Falcon is the most like his daddy," Wildcat Wheeless said. "Damn near the spittin' image of him in looks, and his temper'ment is just the same. In the weeks that Falcon's been here at the Rockingchair, I bet ain't none of you seen that man get really mad, have you?''

John and Kip had to admit that was the truth.

"You don't want to, neither," Wildcat continued. "He's just like his daddy when he gets riled: pure hell to behold."

"That there is a fact," Stumpy said. "When he gets tired of foolin' with this cattlemen's group, he'll end this fight, John, and it won't make no difference if he has to kill five more or a hundred more. He'll do it."

"That's what I'm afraid of," John admitted. "And it won't make no difference what I tell him, will it?''

"Not a bit," Big Bob Marsh said. "Not one little bit."

Twenty-Four

Falcon and Big Bob and Dan Carson stood over the blanket-covered body of the boy and exchanged glances. The mother and father were in the next room of the three-room house, both of them crying. The boy had been walking to the barn just after dawn when the rifle shot came out of the early-morning mist and cut him down. At approximately the same time, a teenage girl had been gunned down about ten miles to the north. John Bailey and Kip had gone to that farm to pay their condolences to the family when they heard the news.

"It just don't make no sense to me," the father said, wiping his eyes and blowing his nose. "He's just a boy. He wasn't armed. It's just murder. That's all it is."

Falcon and Big Bob and Dan Carson quietly left the farmhouse and the grieving family and the neighbors who had come to pay their respects.

"We've got to end this thing," Big Bob said, standing by his horse. "We've got to end it now!"

Dan nodded his head in agreement. "Killin' growed-up men is one thing. Killin' kids is something I can't abide. Let's take the fight to them for a change."

Falcon was strangely silent as he stood by his horse, looking

over the saddle at the death house and at the small group of
farm men who were standing outside, smoking and chewing
and talking in low tones. The grave had been dug, but the
mother of the boy just could not yet stand the thought of seeing
her son put into the ground.

"Falcon?" Big Bob said.

"I heard you," Falcon replied softly.

"Well?" Dan asked.

"It's got to stop," Falcon said, his voice no more than a
whisper. "I don't know how we're going to do it, but we've
got to stop it."

"I know how," Big Bob said. Falcon and Dan looked at
him. "We kill Gilman, Stegman, and Noonan. That'll stop it.
Real quick like."

"After the killing of these kids, those three men are going
to be surrounded by hired guns. Getting close to them is going
to be next to impossible."

"I once slipped into an Injun camp to rescue a pal of mine,"
Dan said. "Are you tellin' me I can't get close to them men
if I take a notion to?"

Falcon smiled. "You were thirty years younger back then,
Dan. Give that some thought."

Dan started to protest, but Big Bob waved him silent. "He's
right 'bout that, Dan. Can't argue 'gainst the truth, so don't
even try."

"We either avenge the killin' of these kids," Dan said, "and
do it right quick, or every farmer and small rancher in this part
of the country will start packin' it in. You both know that.
Folks ain't gonna stand for their kids gettin' murdered by them
night-ridin' back-shootin' bastards."

"That's a fact," Big Bob said. "I done spent near'bouts
most of the summer here. I'd sure hate for all that time to have
gone wasted. I think we got to do something, even if it's wrong.
And I'm purty sure the rest of the boys will feel the same way
'bout it."

The wailing of the grief-stricken mother increased as the
sound of hammering came from the house. The quickly knocked
together casket was being closed for the final time.

"No!" the mother sobbed, the one-word protest easily reaching the ears of the three men standing by their horses near the corral. "No! Wait just a few more minutes."

"Damn!" Big Bob said. "I can't hardly take this. This really cuts agin the grain."

Dan gathered up the reins. "Let's ride, boys." He swung easily into the saddle, doing it with the agility of a man thirty years younger.

Falcon and Big Bob stepped into their saddles and turned their horses' heads.

"Oh, God, no!" the woman screamed. "He's just a boy. Just a boy. He never hurt anybody."

"I'm fixin' to shoot me some night riders and baby killers," Big Bob said.

"I'm with you," Dan said. "I'm real weary of this dilly-dallyin' around with scum."

Falcon said nothing. The three men rode away, leaving the sounds of the nearly hysterical mother behind them. Halfway back to the Rockingchair, they ran into a mixed group of Double N, Snake, and .44 riders. The riders immediately spread out, covering the road. If Falcon and Big Bob and Dan were going to get by, they would have to leave the road.

"I don't think so," Big Bob said, and hauled iron and started shooting, Dan a half second behind him. The action was so unexpected it caught Falcon completely off guard. By the time his mind had registered what was happening, there were four empty saddles in front of him and three riders sitting their saddles with their hands in the air, stunned and disbelieving expressions on their faces. Four riders lay on the road, dead or dying.

"This is the way it's gonna be, boys," Big Bob said. "From now on. Ever' time I see you bastards, I'm gonna start shootin'. I ain't gonna say a word. I'm just gonna plug you."

"That goes double for me," Dan Carson said. "I just seen a little boy get put in the ground, a little boy that was gunned down by one of you or some of your friends, and it pissed me off somethin' fierce. I ain't gonna put up with child killers."

"So you that's left, pass the word," Big Bob said. "If you

work for the .44, the Snake, or the Double N, you're dead. From now on, that's the way it's gonna be. The only way you're gonna stay alive is if you're not wearin' a gun. We won't shoot no unarmed man. Now gather up your dead and wounded and get gone."

The cattlemen's alliance riders, badly shaken by what had just taken place, got the dead across saddles and the wounded in saddles, and rode out, back to home range.

"Well," Falcon said, "it's open warfare now, boys."

"That's the way I like it," Big Bob said. "This way it don't leave no room for doubt."

"None atall," Dan said.

"They've gone slap crazy," Stegman said, stunned by the news. "The whole bunch of them. Nobody goes around just blowin' people out of the saddle on sight!"

" 'Bout a dozen more boys just packed up and rode out," Noonan announced, turning away from the window in the study of Gilman's house. "There'll probably be more that follow them."

"Them boys that brought the dead and wounded back said it wasn't Falcon who opened the dance," Gilman said. "It was them crazy ol' mountain men."

"What the hell difference does it make who started it?" Stegman asked. "It's started and the boys is spooked, and I mean spooked something awful."

It was the day after the shooting in the road, and the three main players in the cattlemen's alliance were meeting, trying to decide what course of action to take. None of them had ever had to face something like this. A range war was one thing; they'd all been through that before. But this? . . . Hell, this was unheard-of.

"We could back off and wait them out," Gilman said. "Those mountain men are wanderers. They won't stay for no long length of time."

"Can't none of us afford to do that," Stegman said, nixing

that suggestion. "Not and keep all these hired guns on the payroll. We'd go broke 'fore they left."

" 'Sides," Noonan added, "I got seven brothers and their families on my back. Plus thousands of head of cattle only a few days away. I got to have range and water and then ship out to the army and back east 'fore winter. I ain't got no choice in the matter. None of us do."

"Them ranchers over west of us say we bit off more than we can chew," Stegman said. "I got that word a few hours ago. They're not gonna support us. No way, no how. They said killin' them kids done it for them."

"They can afford to get all righteous about it," Gilman said. "They've shipped their cattle and don't have a damn army on the payroll."

Gilman walked to the window and looked out at the low hills that surrounded his ranch complex. It was about an hour before dark. He turned just as one bullet smashed through the window and hit a water pitcher on the table and another bullet tore through another window and knocked a chunk of plaster off the wall. The three most powerful ranchers in the area hit the floor. Outside, hidden riflemen in the hills close in opened up and started spraying the lead around.

The riflemen were the mountain men, Falcon, and the Rockingchair foreman, Kip. While John Bailey had not given his blessing to this type of action, neither had he forbidden it. He had just nodded his head when Kip told him what his men were going to do and walked back into his house without saying a word. The body of the dead girl he'd seen buried just hours before, a girl just barely in her teens, had affected him deeply. The rancher had no more patience with men who would condone such a thing.

The long bunkhouse of the Snake ranch was fully exposed. One rifleman in the hills could keep those inside pinned down. Two slugs had gone through the bedroom window of Terri, sending the young woman scrambling and cussing to the floor. She was still on the floor, hollering and cussing.

Lars had been caught outside, between the corral and the main house. He was now pinned down behind a woodpile with absolutely no place else to go. He could not move. He could do nothing except cuss and cringe each time a bullet came close.

The men in the hills had moved in quietly, each of them armed with several rifles and bandoliers of ammunition. In addition to the rifles, Falcon and the mountain men each also had a bow and a quiver of arrows . . . the arrows each had a stick of dynamite secured behind the arrowhead, and the fuses were cut short. Falcon and his friends were going to have some fun—fun for them, that is, not for the men trapped below the hills.

Falcon laid his rifle aside and picked up his bow. Using a cigar, he lit the fuse and quickly let the arrow fly. It landed in the front yard of the house and blew. The explosion knocked out the front windows of the house and caused Terri to very nearly go into hysterics.

"Jesus Christ!" Gilman yelled. "What the hell is going on?"

"Some son of a bitch is usin' dynamite!" Stegman hollered.

"Get them men out of the bunkhouse and off their asses and fight!" Noonan yelled.

The second stick of dynamite blew a few yards in front of the woodpile where Lars was huddled. The blast collapsed the woodpile, covering Lars with firewood, ants, and dust. He started hollering and cussing.

Big Bob let an arrow fly. It arched its way downward, landed a few feet from the side wall of the bunkhouse, and blew. The impact knocked a huge chunk out of the wall and blew out both windows, sending those men trapped inside scrambling toward the other end of the bunkhouse, most of them now unable to hear anything due to the nearness of the tremendous explosion.

Wildcat Wheeless hummed a dynamite-tipped arrow toward the complex. It landed on top of the main house, directly above Terri's bedroom, and blew, knocking a huge hole in the roof and covering Terri with splinters, dust, bird shit, and chunks of roofing material. Terri really started cussing and hollering and raising a fuss.

"Lars!" Gilman shouted. "Come help your sister, damn you, boy!"

"How?" the young man returned the shout. "I got a pile of wood all over me and I can't move without gettin' shot."

"Where's all them damn hired guns of yours?" Stegman demanded from his position on the floor.

"Out looking for MacCallister," Gilman hollered, over the rattle of rifle fire and the yelling of trapped men.

Noonan put his head down on the floor and cussed just as another stick of dynamite came sailing through the air and the arrow point stuck into the side of the house. The dynamite blew and a huge hole was torn out of the kitchen wall. The Chinese cook was last seen hotfooting it toward the barn, screaming in some incomprehensible language. The cook grabbed the first horse he came to and was gone, galloping off into the hills, waving his arms and still screaming in that strange language.

Puma let fly an arrow that sailed right through a bunkhouse window and blew. Half the roof collapsed, part of one wall disintegrated, and a dozen hired guns were out of the fight with broken arms and legs from falling debris and the concussion of the explosion.

The few horses who had been in stalls in the barn panicked and kicked free and were gone, racing wildly off into the hills. One hired gun apparently forgot where he was and what was taking place and went running off after his horse. Mustang knocked a leg out from under him with a well-placed rifle shot. The man rolled on the ground, yelling from the pain in his broken leg.

"All of them at the house!" Falcon yelled to the man nearest him, and Stumpy passed the word around the low hills. Arrows were fitted and fuses were lit. The arrows were sent humming through the air, the fuses sputtering.

Eight dynamite-tipped arrows landed on, in, or very close to the big ranch house and blew. The front porch collapsed, one side wall was blown wide open, and another part of the roof was destroyed. This time the blown-open roof was over the study, and Stegman, Noonan, and Gilman were covered with debris. Noonan had part of a support timber land on his noggin and the impact knocked him goofy. Stegman was trapped under several hundred pounds of roofing material. Gilman got hammered and bruised and cut with flying stones from the fireplace, which blew apart from the explosion.

Over the hollering of trapped men in the bunkhouse, the vocal ragings of Lars, pinned under several cords of firewood in the side yard, and the yelling and cussing of the ranchers trapped under piles of crap in the study, Terri's voice was clear as a bell.

"Get this goddamn crap off me!" the young lady hollered. "Help, help!"

The men in the hills started shooting fire arrows into the jumble of confusion. Soon tentacles of smoke began arching upward from the wreckage of the house and the bunkhouse.

Lars managed to kick free of the firewood and jump up, looking for a bucket. Big Bob let fly another arrow and the stick of dynamite blew while still about fifteen feet in the air, just above and behind Lars. The concussion lifted the young man off his boots and turned him a slow flip in the air. He landed on his belly on the ground, the impact knocking the wind from him and the force of the explosion leaving him momentarily even nuttier and more addled than before. The young man managed to get to his hands and knees and began crawling around in circles, reciting a nursery rhyme remembered from his childhood.

"Somebody help me!" Terri screamed. "I'm trapped in here. Help, help!"

Several of the hired guns came staggering out of the ruined bunkhouse, their hands filled with pistols, firing wildly up into the hills. Rifles cracked from hidden positions and the hired guns went down in lifeless heaps.

More fire arrows were arched into the ranch house and the bunkhouse and soon both structures were blazing uncontrollably. Falcon and his men slipped away, back to their horses. They rode away from the scene of burning devastation, heading deeper into Snake range, all of them smiling. They were not yet through with Miles Gilman. The score in this deadly game was beginning to inch toward a tie.

Gilman was ruined: His home was destroyed and the large bunkhouse was rapidly turning into ashes. Only his barn remained intact. He'd lost more than twenty of his hired guns, most of them out of the fight with broken arms and legs and heads. Six of them were dead.

And Falcon and his mountain men still had half a night's work ahead of them.

"When we reach the main herd," Falcon called, "start them running toward the grasslands and keep after them; keep them moving. It'll take weeks for Gilman to round them all up."

"That's where Stegman's first herd is," Big Bob called, a slow grin working its way onto his face.

"You bet," Falcon called. "And when we push Gilman's beeves into that herd, we use dynamite to get them all in a stampede."

"Hell," Dan yelled over the pounding of hooves and the rush of the wind. "Some of these cattle will travel all the way to the mountains."

"That's my plan," Falcon said.

Laughing, the men rode on into the deepening dusk. They were going to have a good time this night.

Twenty-Five

When Gilman got word the morning after the attack on his ranch, he knew he was finished as a power in the county. Night riders had hit his herds after his ranch was destroyed and scattered them all to hell and gone. It would take weeks to round up the cattle, and even then many would never be found. Half a dozen of his regular hands had been wounded in the raids and another half dozen had quit. His two sons who had preferred the range to the ranch had been among the wounded. They were not seriously hurt, but they were out of it for a time. Lars had packed up a few things and moved into town with his sister, swearing he would shoot Falcon MacCallister the first chance he got. Miles Gilman had him a hunch that Lars would not live out the week, but made no attempt to dissuade his youngest son. All the steam had gone out of Miles for a time. He just sat among the ruins of his ranch and wondered why everything had gone to crap in such a hurry.

Nance Noonan and Rod Stegman had left Miles sitting amid the ruins of what had been his ranch. The only thing that remained was the barn. Miles appeared to be a broken man. And whether he would snap back or not was no concern of Noonan and Stegman's. Those two had suddenly been forced into a defensive posture, all because of Falcon MacCallister and six old mountain men.

The deputy federal marshal who had talked with Falcon in the darkness of the Rockingchair barn that night sat in his hotel room and chuckled at the developments. This was turning out to be the easiest assignment he'd ever had. All he was going to have to do was sit around and relax and drink coffee and let Falcon MacCallister and his friends handle the situation. He'd been warned by his superiors back in the Washington not to get directly involved; just hang around and keep tabs on the trouble in this part of Wyoming. Well, he was hanging around, for a fact, and he sure as hell wasn't getting involved.

The deputy U.S. marshal stretched out on his bed in his hotel room and decided to take him a little nap. Sure wasn't much else to do. The deputy federal marshal glanced out the window as three men came riding into town on Double N–branded horses. Three of the Noonan brothers. The Noonan brothers were easy to identify: They all bore a strong resemblance; they all looked like something that had just crawled out of a cave. It had been several days since the raid on the Snake ranch, and there had been no trouble.

The deputy U.S. marshal had had the thought just that morning that it was time for something to pop. And something sure was about to pop, for coming in from the other end of town was Falcon MacCallister, riding alone.

The deputy U.S. marshal slipped into his coat and left his room, walking down to the hotel lobby and taking a seat by a front window. He wasn't going to get involved in any fracas, but he did want a front row seat to this upcoming fight . . . and he was certain there was going to be a fight. The three Noonan brothers were riding stiff in the saddle and the smell of trouble was in the air. The deputy U.S. marshal had worn a badge for a long time; he knew trouble when he saw it.

Falcon stepped down from the saddle in front of the general store. He'd promised Jimmy some stick candy and decided he'd get that first and stow the peppermint candy in his saddle-bags, then he'd go see Willard at the bank. It was then Falcon noticed the three men reining up in front of the Purple Palace

Saloon and stepping down from their saddles. They slowly turned as one to face him. They were half a long block apart. Falcon silently cursed. He recognized the men as Noonans. Had to be. Hell, they all looked alike. They were all as big as bears and their facial features made them look like apes.

"You've done all you're gonna do, MacCallister," one called. "You've interfered in affairs that ain't none of your business for the last time. I'm tellin' you that now."

"You boys have to be related to Nance," Falcon returned the call. "You sure look alike."

Falcon had to get off the street. Had to pull these Noonan brothers with him. The street had a dozen or more people on both sides, on the boardwalks, including some kids. If lead started flying now, some innocent people would get hurt.

"Time for talkin' is over and done with," one of the three brothers said. "Your time is over."

"Who am I talking to?" Falcon said, stepping up onto the boardwalk and taking a couple of steps toward an alley. Just a few more steps and he'd be in the alley.

"Howard, Mark, and Nap Noonan," another of the brothers called. "The three brothers who is gonna kill you."

"Oh, I don't think so," Falcon said, then quickly stepped into the alley and ran down to the end, stepping out behind the general store.

"Get that son of a bitch!" one of the brothers hollered. "Take the alley, Nap."

Falcon took half a dozen steps and crouched down behind the privy that was shared by the general store and a farm supply business.

Nap came boiling out of the alley, six-gun in hand. He looked left and right as he muttered to himself about killing Falcon. He wanted to shoot Falcon in the belly and watch him die.

Nice fellow, Falcon thought.

"Where are you, you bastard!" Nap said.

"Right here," Falcon called, then quickly shifted to the other side of the rear of the privy.

Nap triggered off a shot that knocked a chunk of wood from the privy.

"No doubt about them wanting to kill me," Falcon said, as he leveled his .44 and put a round into Nap's belly.

Nap grunted and sat down on the ground, a strange expression on his apelike features. Then he hollered as intense pain struck him hard. "Howard, Mark!" Nap screamed. "I been hit. The bastard done shot me."

Keeping the two-hole privy between himself and the badly wounded Nap, Falcon quietly slipped back a few yards and slid down into a ditch behind the long block of stores. He crouched there, waiting for the other Noonan brothers.

He could hear a lot of excited voices from the street side of the buildings, and a number of running feet as the shoppers went scurrying for cover.

Falcon cut his eyes to his right just as another of the Noonan brothers came around the corner of a building.

"Nap!" the brother called. "Hang on, boy. I'm comin' to help you."

"Be careful, Howard," Nap called weakly. "The bastard is hidin' in the ditch. Kill him for me, brother. The son of a bitch has done me in. Kill him."

Falcon shot Howard in the chest and the man staggered backward, dropping his pistol, grunting and cussing. A six-gun barked and Falcon's hat flew off his head. Falcon threw himself to one side and bellied down in the ditch, leveling his .44 just as the third brother stepped out the back door of a store. Falcon drilled him in the belly and the brother fell back into the store.

"Mark!" Howard called. "Boy, come help your brother. I'm hard hit. I done lost my gun."

"Stay where you are, Mark," Nap called, his voice getting weaker. "That MacCallister is still alive and waitin'. Save yourself."

Mark stepped out of the rear door, one hand holding his bloody stomach, the other hand holding a pistol. Falcon shot him in the chest and Mark tumbled face first onto the ground and lay still amid the broken bottles and debris.

Three of the Noonan brothers were down and dying. Falcon wondered how many more brothers there were. He'd heard there were seven or eight of them all told.

But these three were finished. Nap had fallen over on his face, kicked a couple of times, and now was still. Mark was still on the ground behind the store. Howard was still alive and cussing Falcon. But his pistol was six feet away from where he sat on the ground, his back to a building. Falcon looked around for his hat. It was ruined, laying a few feet away from him, full of huge holes front and back.

He picked up his hat, stuck his fingers through the holes, and sighed. It was his good hat, too.

"You played hell, boy," Howard gasped. "You're as lucky a man as I've ever seen."

"I had a good teacher," Falcon told him, rising to his boots in the ditch. "My father."

"Nance will kill you for shore over this, MacCallister."

"I doubt it."

"If he don't, I got three strappin' sons who'll avenge their pa's dyin'."

"Not if they're smart, they won't." Falcon walked over to where the man sat on the ground, his back to a building. "You got any words you want me to repeat to anybody special?"

"I reckon not."

"Your wife?"

"She died years back. You go to hell, MacCallister."

Falcon stood silent, looking down at the man. The town's doctor appeared at the other end of the alley, his black bag in hand.

"You want me to call Reverend Watkins?" the doctor asked.

"If you want to," Falcon told him.

"I don't need no damn preacher," Howard said.

"Suit yourself," the doctor said, walking up and kneeling down. He pried Howard's hand away from his chest and opened the man's shirt.

"Don't bother," Howard said. "I know I'm dyin'." His voice was very weak and both Falcon and the doctor had to strain to hear his words. "I want . . ."

Whatever it was Howard Noonan wanted, he took the request to the grave with him. He died before he could finish the sentence.

"I only came into town to see the banker and to buy some peppermint candy," Falcon said.

"Nobody is blaming you, Mr. MacCallister. Most of the town is behind you and John Bailey now. Now that Miles Gilman's stranglehold is broken. But I have to warn you: Lars is in town. That young man is, well, seemingly not right in the head."

"He just needs a little straightening out." Falcon looked at his hat. It was ruined. Falcon left the doctor and entered the general store through the back door. The Deans were both standing behind a counter, looking at him as if he had suddenly grown horns and a tail. Falcon waited on himself, selecting a new hat, then picking out a dozen peppermint sticks. He laid the money on the counter, then stowed the candy in his saddle-bags. He was aware the entire time that Lars Gilman was standing in front of the hotel, watching his every move. He hoped the young man would not brace him, but he knew there was only a very slim chance he could mount up and ride out of town without Lars calling him out.

Falcon turned away from his horse. Lars was walking toward him, walking slowly up the boardwalk. The rancher's son was going to brace him. It was in his walk and his bearing. Falcon sighed.

Falcon waited for a moment. Lars pointed toward the street and stepped off the boardwalk.

"Kill him, Lars!" Terri shouted from the open hotel doors. "Kill him!"

The deputy U.S. marshal looked at the young woman. He wondered if the entire Gilman family was addled in the head? He had certainly never seen a stranger bunch.

Lars ignored his sister and stopped in the center of the street. The wind picked up and created a dust devil that danced wildly in the street for a moment, then vanished.

Falcon stepped away from his horse and walked to the center of the street. He called, "Don't do this, Lars. Go on back to the Snake and help your father. But don't do this. It's going to get you killed."

"The Snake is ruined. You and them old men did it," Lars shouted over the distance. "There ain't nothin' left."

"Kill him, Lars!" Terri screamed.

The deputy U.S. marshal shook his head at the venom in the young woman's voice. He'd never heard such hate-filled words.

"The land is left, Lars," Falcon called. "You and your father can rebuild and become a part of the community. You're a western man. You know how forgiving western people are. Everything that's happened will soon be forgotten."

"Too late, MacCallister," the young man called, then resumed walking toward Falcon.

"It's never too late, Lars. There's been enough killing. Too much. Let's stop this."

The townspeople had gathered on the boardwalk on both sides of the street. Many of them nodded their heads silently at Falcon's words. Falcon was trying to bring the bloodshed to a halt. Lars was pushing for more blood to be spilled. The sentiment among the townspeople had changed drastically and dramatically.

"Stop this!" Reverend Watkins shouted. "Stop this killing at once."

"Shut up, you crazy psalm-singing fart!" Terri screamed. "Shut your goddamn mouth."

"I'll pray for you," Reverend Watkins called from across the street.

"Stick it up your butt!" Terri responded.

The deputy U.S. marshal shook his head in wonderment. He'd never heard a lady use such language.

"Your soul is in terrible danger, Miss Gilman," Reverend Watkins called. "I'll pray that you never see the flaming pits of Hell."

Terri told the preacher where to stick his words. Sideways.

The deputy U.S. marshal's eyes widened at that. "My word!" he said.

Terri ran over to where he was sitting and got all up in his face. "You got a problem with something I said, you goofy-lookin' prairie dog?" she screamed at the man.

The marshal resisted a nearly overpowering urge to take the

young woman across his lap and spank her butt . . . something her father should have done years ago.

"Back off, Miss Gilman," the deputy U.S. marshal said softly. "Right now."

Something in his words caused Terri to momentarily shut her mouth and step back. She recovered enough to cuss him and return to the open hotel doors, giving him a few dark glances on the short walk.

In the street, Lars was working himself up into a frenzy of hate. He stood in the center of the main street and cussed Falcon. Falcon stood tall and did not respond to the profanity . . . not at first. But he soon grew weary of the cussing. He had taken just about all he was going to take from the Gilman family.

"Shut up, Lars!" he told the young man. "Shut up and go on home, back to your Pa. And take your sister with you."

Please do, the deputy U.S. marshal thought. What a great relief that would be.

"Don't just stand there, Lars!" Terri screamed. "Jerk iron and kill him!"

"Your time has come, MacCallister," Lars shouted. "Today's the day you die."

Falcon shook his head. "Wrong, Lars. I'm telling you for the last time: Turn around, get on your horse, and ride out of here. There's been enough killing for this day."

But Lars had worked himself up into a mindless frenzy of hate. There was nothing on his mind except killing Falcon MacCallister. Everything else was clouded over with shadows of loathing for everything connected with Falcon.

"You ready to die, MacCallister?" Lars screamed.

"No. Not this day, Lars."

"Draw, you bastard."

"After you, Lars."

"Now!" Lars screamed, and grabbed for his gun.

Twenty-Six

Lars dropped his six-shooter.

The pistol hit the dirt of the street and a small dust cloud rose from the impact. The blood drained from Lars's face as he found himself looking down the barrel of Falcon's .44.

"You dumb bastard!" Terri squalled from the hotel.

Falcon slowly let the hammer down on his pistol and holstered it. "It's your lucky day, Lars. God was looking after you."

"Goddamn you!" Terri screamed from the hotel door. She jerked out a pistol and leveled it at Falcon.

The deputy U.S. marshal lunged out of his chair and slammed into the young woman just as she pulled the trigger. The shot went wild and Terri hit the floor, losing her grip on the six-shooter. She banged her head against the floor. The marshal grabbed the gun and stood up, shoving the short-barreled pistol behind his belt.

"You son of a bitch!" Terri screamed at him.

"Oh, shut up," the marshal said. "You have the foulest mouth I have ever heard on a woman."

That set her off like a firecracker. She sat up on the floor and started cussing, the vulgarities directed at the deputy U.S. marshal.

"Can I pick up my pistol?" Lars asked.

"Not unless you have a death wish," Falcon told him. "Just let it lie, Lars. Go on back to your Pa. He needs you now more than ever."

"Pa don't need no one."

"Yes he does, Lars. He needs the support of his kids. You especially."

"You really think so?"

"Don't listen to that son of a bitch!" Terri screamed. She had overheard Falcon's words when she had paused for breath. "He's lyin'."

"Shut up, Terri," Falcon called. "You owe your pa, too. You should be ashamed of yourself being in town when he needs you back at his ranch."

"He doesn't have a ranch, you rattlesnake!" she squalled. "You burned it all down."

"It can be rebuilt," Falcon said. "But your pa needs the help and support of his kids to do it. He'll be doing it for you."

Lars turned slowly and began walking away from his pistol in the dirt of the street.

"Where are you goin'?" Terri shouted at him.

"Home to Pa," the young man replied.

"You yellow bastard!" his sister shrieked at him.

The townspeople were standing quietly on the boardwalks, listening to the heated words.

Lars paused and turned toward the hotel doors. "You're stupid, Terri. I just realized that. I been stupid, but I got over it, I hope. But you're really stupid." The young man walked on toward the livery.

Terri verbally unloaded on her brother, calling him every filthy word she could think of . . . and she knew plenty of them. Lars walked on without pausing or looking around.

Falcon turned and walked over to his horse. He was heading back to the Rockingchair.

* * *

John Bailey and Kip rode over to Snake headquarters—or rather, what was left of it—several days later. The first thing they noticed was that all the hired guns were gone. There were half a dozen cowboys helping haul lumber in, but no hired guns.

They also noticed that Lars was working right alongside his Pa, and no one was wearing a gun. John and Kip dismounted and walked over to Miles Gilman.

"You need some help, Miles?" John asked.

Miles paused in his sawing and looked at the man he used to call friend. "You volunteerin', John?"

"We're here, aren't we?"

"After all I've done, you . . ."

John waved him silent. "That's over and done with, Miles. In the past. We don't need to ever speak of it again. I thought me and Kip here might start movin' some of your cattle back onto your range. Some of my men spotted a bunch not too far away. That all right with you?"

Miles stared at John Bailey for a moment, then cleared his throat. "Sure suits me to a T, John. That would be right neighborly of you, sure would."

"We'll do that, then." He dug in his saddlebags and Kip did the same, both men coming out with packets of sandwiches all wrapped up in cloth. "Martha and Angie fixed these up for you men. Sandwiches and some cake. Cake is right tasty. I'll just set them over on that old table yonder. Me and Kip packed a bite for ourselves, so we'll be out for the night with your herd. We'll see you in the morning, probably."

"How about some coffee 'fore you head out, John? We found a pot and Lars just boiled up some. It's good and strong, just like me and you used to make, long years back," he added.

John smiled. "Coffee sounds good to me, Miles. We'll just help ourselves."

Miles smiled and then looked around as the sound of wagons

approaching reached the men. A dozen wagons were rumbling slowly up the road.

"What in the world . . . ?" Miles said.

"Folks from town and from some of the ranches and farms around the area," John told him. "They're bringin' in supplies and food and such. I 'spect they'll have some sort of shelter up for you and your hands before dark."

"My God!" Miles whispered.

John smiled. "Welcome back, Miles."

Miles turned to his old friend. "It's good to be back, John Bailey. I was lost there for some years, wasn't I?"

"Oh, you got sidetracked a bit, that's all."

"I feel like I've been livin' in a fog of hate, John."

"Well, you're out of it now, so welcome back." John took the tin cup of coffee his foreman handed him and took a sip. "Good coffee," he said with a smile. "Just like we used to make back in the old days."

"It is pretty good, ain't it?" Miles asked, returning the smile. "The womenfolk just don't have the knack of makin' good coffee."

"For a fact, Miles. For a fact. Theirs is just a tad on the weak side."

Both men stood for a moment, looking at one another. Miles slowly held out his right hand. John smiled and took the hand and gripped it tightly.

The war between the Snake and the Rockingchair was over.

Twenty-Seven

Nance Noonan buried his brothers in a lonely spot far from the town. The graves were not marked. Nance swore these would be the last brothers that would ever fall under the guns of Falcon MacCallister. He also swore that Falcon would die by the hand of a Noonan. The sons of Howard Noonan—Slayton, Bert, and Rawlings—had already taken an oath on the family Bible that they would be the ones to kill Falcon MacCallister. The Noonan brothers left alive, Penrod, Dale, Jack, and Hodge, had sworn among themselves that *they* would be the ones to kill Falcon. Of course, Nance had ideas of his own about that killing.

"He's mine," Nance swore. "I'm gonna kill that bastard personally. Bet on it."

"Not if I get to him first," his brothers and nephews all said.

Rod Stegman met with Nance Noonan several days after Howard, Nap, and Mark were planted. "What about Miles?"

"What about him?" Nance asked.

"What do we do about him?"

"Nothing. He's gone yellow on us and pulled away from our agreement. He's got half a dozen hands left and none of them much with a gun. Far as I'm concerned, he's out of it. Forget him. Hell, Rod, I think he's done throwed in with the small ranchers and them nesters. Him and John Bailey is back bein' big buddies and such.''

"I could have used his range."

"We'll take it when the time comes. Soon as I get finished with MacCallister, we'll take what range we need. Don't worry none about it."

"Nance, there ain't gonna be enough grazin' range for all our cattle. I got to worry about it."

"We'll do somethin' about it when the time comes, Rod. You got my word on that. Just relax. I'll take care of things, count on it.''

"How about them fifteen guns who was supposed to have taken care of MacCallister?"

"I called 'em off. I want MacCallister all for my own."

"Nance, you a good man with a gun, but MacCallister's fast as lightnin'. I got to say I don't believe you can take him in a face-on hook and draw."

"I do," the rancher replied.

Stegman knew that was the end of that discussion, for when Nance made up his mind about something, it was set in stone. Nance had always been that way, and it had gotten him in trouble many times. He would say no more about Falcon's abilities with a gun.

Nance rode back to his home range and Stegman paced the room he had turned into a study.

"What's the matter, Rod?" his wife asked from the doorway.

Stegman ceased his pacing and looked at his wife for a moment. "I got a bad feelin' about all this, Claire. A real bad feelin'."

"My brother knows what he's doing."

Stegman found his hat, plopped it on his head, and left the house. There was no point in discussing anything with Claire. If it involved Nance, Nance was always right and everybody else was always wrong.

But Stegman could not shake the feeling of impending doom. It clung to his mind like a leech. He saddled up and rode out to where part of his herd was grazing. He looked at the grass. This range wouldn't take much more. The herd would have to be moved and the move would have to take place soon.

Stegman cussed softly. He wished he'd never listened to Nance and made the move to this part of Wyoming. It wasn't going to work out. He could feel it in his belly. Stegman could read the attitude of the townspeople, and the people had turned against them.

It just wasn't going to work out.

"Never seen such a change in a man come so fast," John Bailey told Falcon. The men were standing by the corral. "It's like a dark cloak was suddenly lifted from around Miles's mind."

Miles had passed the word to the farmers that they could have some of his cattle to help them feed their families. The farmers were at first very suspicious, but soon realized the rancher meant what he said, no strings or tricks attached.

Miles had dismissed the few hired guns who had remained on the Snake, keeping only those men who could work cattle. He had gotten word to Nance and Stegman that he was through with the cattlemen's alliance. There was range enough for everybody. As far as he was concerned, the war was over. He wanted no part of any more trouble.

And Terri had come home.

Miles had told the hotel clerk he would no longer pay her bills and the desk clerk kicked her out of her room, much to the amusement of the deputy U.S. marshal, who had taken great delight in watching the entire proceedings. Terri had cussed the desk clerk, cussed the marshal, and cussed anyone else who came within hearing distance of her. But her cussing didn't help matters any: She was still without a place to stay. It didn't take her long to decide to go home.

What really irritated the young woman was finding out her father was seeing a farm woman who had lost her husband to an accident the year before. The woman was trying to farm six hundred and forty acres with only the help of her two young children . . . and not doing a very good job of it.

Miles had gently taken over providing for the family and was getting serious about the woman. That really irritated Terri.

"That damn nester woman had better not ever try to order me around," Terri said.

"You best shut your mouth," Lars told her. " 'Fore Pa gets a notion in his mind to take a belt to your butt."

"He wouldn't dare!"

Lars smiled. He knew his pa was not far from doing just that. He'd seen the look in his pa's eyes, and if Terri didn't button up her mouth and settle down and pitch in to help around the ranch, she was gonna have a sore butt.

Just as Miles had done, Lars had changed dramatically. That moment in the street when he had dropped his six-shooter and found himself looking down the barrel of Falcon's .44 had opened Lars's eyes and mind to just how precious living was. He still carried a pistol when he was away from the house— just as most cowboys did—but killing another human being was very low on his list of priorities now. He carried a pistol to shoot snakes and for self-protection . . . no other reason.

"Go make some biscuits, Terri," Lars told her. "And start dinner. We're gonna be hungry in an hour or so."

Terri cussed. "Where is that damn cook?"

"He took the stage to San Francisco," Lars informed her. "He won't be back."

"I ain't no goddamn servant!" Terri raged. She turned and looked into the eyes of her father, who had just walked up. Funny look in her pa's eyes. Terri decided she'd best go make some biscuits and start dinner.

"And shut your filthy mouth," her father told her, reading her mind, something that spooked the young woman. "I'll not put up with your swearin' any longer. And tomorrow is Sunday. We're all goin' to church. You'll wear a dress and Lars will drive you into town in the buckboard."

"*Church!*" Terri squalled.

"Church," her father calmly informed her. "Every Sunday

from now on. Get that through your head. That's the way it's goin' to be.''

"Wear a *dress?*" Terri hollered. "Them silly-lookin' dresses you bought me in town the other day?"

"Yes," the father replied.

Terri opened her mouth to cuss and Miles pointed a blunt finger at her, a clear warning in the gesture. Terri shut her mouth.

"And you'll ride with Mrs. Carter," Miles told the young woman. "And you'll be civil to her. Understood?"

Terri knew better than to argue. She had learned a long time back just how far she could push her father. "Yes, Pa. I understand."

"Good. Now go fix dinner."

When Terri had dutifully, if not happily, walked off toward the tent where the stove was located, Miles said, "She's comin' around, son. Slow but sure."

"If she'd just stop cussin'."

"That'll come in time. I'll see to it personal."

"Good luck," Lars said with a smile.

"It's Terri who's gonna need the luck," Miles replied. "Reverend Watkins has asked me if he could call on Terri, and I said yes."

Lars's smile broke into a wide grin. "This I gotta see!"

"Now be nice, son."

"Oh. I will, Pa. I will."

Father and son looked at each other for a few seconds, burst out laughing, and after a few minutes, went back to work, both of them still chuckling.

"It's gettin' plumb borin' around here," Puma Parley said over breakfast. "You don't reckon Stegman and Noonan have give up, do you?"

"Not those two," Falcon replied, buttering a biscuit. "The only way those two will give up this fight is if they're dead."

"That could be arranged," Stumpy said, a mean look in his eyes.

"Let them start it," Falcon echoed John Bailey's words. "When they start something, we can act."

"That man shore has funny notions about fightin' a war," Wildcat said.

"Shore do," Mustang agreed.

"I got me a hunch it won't be long 'fore Noonan or Stegman makes a play for us," Big Bob Marsh said. He looked at Falcon. "And you be careful, boy. Them brothers and sons and cousins of the three Noonans you killed is gunnin' for you. I got that word from one of the gals who works in the Purple Palace. And they mean ever' word, too."

"I know it," Falcon said, refilling his coffee cup from the huge pot. "That's why I've stayed out of town for the past week. I'm trying to avoid trouble."

Big Bob fixed him with a jaundiced look. "I reckon that's why you got all purtied up this mornin'. So's you can herd cattle in your good clothes, right?"

"I have to go to town to see the banker. It's something I can't get out of."

"Never saw a man with so much money," Dan Carson said with a grin. "The man don't even know how much he's worth."

Dan didn't know it, but he was telling the truth. Falcon really didn't know how much he was worth. He was worth several million dollars, he knew that much, but just how much he was worth he really had no idea, because his wealth kept increasing every month. He knew that sometimes the investments made for him lost money, but that was a rare event. Usually they just generated more money for him.

The gold and silver his grandfather and father had found had set up the entire MacCallister clan and made the kids rich.

Falcon drank his coffee and smoked a cigarette, listening to the mountain men talk about the day's work ahead of them. One by one they started drifting out, until Falcon was alone at the table in the bunkhouse.

Falcon was stalling, and he knew it. He really did have to go into town to see the banker, but he knew that when he rode into town, if there were any .44 or Double N hands in town, and especially if there were any Noonans present, there would be gunplay.

He pushed back his chair and stood up. There was no point in delaying any longer. He had to head into town. He checked his pistol, loading it up full, then shoved another .44 behind his gunbelt. He saddled up and swung into the saddle, pointing his horse's head toward town. If there was trouble waiting for him, so be it. He wasn't going to change his lifestyle because of the Noonan brothers or cousins or nephews or a bunch of .44 hands. He had never ducked trouble, and by God he wasn't going to start now.

The ride into town was uneventful. He met several farm families on the way in, stopping and chatting with them for a few minutes. They were heading into town to buy supplies. Falcon warned the families he met to be careful in town: There would likely be trouble.

"I have my rifle with me," one of the farmers said. "And my boy yonder is armed. We'll back you all the way, Mr. MacCallister. You just say the word."

"You stay out of it. But if I need help, I'll be sure to give out a holler."

Falcon rode on, a dark brooding feeling settling over him. He had always been able to sense impending trouble, and today the feeling was very nearly overpowering. There was danger waiting for him in town.

Falcon began to mentally prepare himself for the dilemma he would soon be facing. It was a trick he'd learned from his father and it had always stood him in good stead, never letting him down.

He reined up on the outskirts of town, giving the town a slow and careful once-over. Everything seemed normal and probably was, at least for the moment, for Falcon's decision to come into town had been made in the late afternoon the day before, and no one else could have known about it.

Falcon rode slowly into town. He was going to be in town for several hours—at least that was the plan right now—so he stabled his horse.

"Rub him down, Mr. MacCallister?" the stableman asked nervously.

Falcon picked up on the nervous tone and gave the man a curious look. "Yes. What's the problem?"

"Oh! . . . No problem, Mr. MacCallister. None at all."

Lying, Falcon thought. The man was lying. Falcon pointed a thick blunt finger at the stableman. "Don't lie to me, partner. You don't want me for an enemy. Now what's the problem?"

"They're all over town," the young man replied. "They come in every day and wait for you to show up. Now they're gonna be after me for tellin' you."

"No, they won't," Falcon assured him. "They'll never know. Just stay out of sight. Where are they and who are they?"

"They're all over town, Mr. MacCallister. In both saloons. In the hotel lobby. Everywhere."

"Rifles?"

"No, sir. Just pistols is all I've seen."

"All right, partner. You stay inside the barn and keep your head down. Understand?"

"You bet, Mr. MacCallister. I ain't leavin' the barn. Count on that."

Falcon took off his spurs and stowed them in his saddlebags, then went out the back way, slipping up behind the stores on that side of the street. No one was using any of the privies; no one saw him. He tried the back door of the hotel. Unlocked. He stepped into the darkness, his boots whispering against the floor. The door leading to the lobby was cracked open and Falcon walked to it and stood for a moment, listening. He could hear only a low murmur of voices, none of them sounding at all menacing, which meant nothing and he knew it.

Then one of the Noonan brothers (Falcon didn't know his name but they all bore a strong resemblance) walked up to the door. Falcon stepped back into the darkness. The man pushed open the door and looked inside.

"Settle down, Pen," another man's voice called. "Everythin's all right."

"I got me a bad feelin', Dale," the man called Pen replied. "I'm jumpy as a Mex jumpin' bean."

Falcon heard the sound of running boots striking against the boardwalk. "He's in town!" another voice called. "That goddamn stableman didn't warn us. I'll kill that bastard!"

"Forget the stableman for the time bein', Coe," Dale said. "He's nothin' and a nobody. He's just more scared of Mac-Callister than he is of us, that's all. He'll pay for thinkin' that. But we'll deal with him later. Now where the hell could MacCallister have gone?"

"I shore as hell didn't see him," Coe said. "He didn't come walkin' up the street, that's for shore."

"He's behind the stores," Dale said. "Got to be. The bastard done slipped in behind us."

"Alert the others to cover both ends of town. And put somebody in the livery. We got him now. He can't get away."

Trapped, yes, Falcon thought. *But you damn sure haven't got me.*

"I wanna shoot that scum in the belly just like he done our brother and watch him die," Pen said. "Maybe it'll take him a long time to croak."

I certainly have met some really nice people on this trip, Falcon thought.

"Let's get him, boys," Dale said. "Let's finish MacCallister once and for all."

Not likely, Falcon thought, pulling his second .44 from behind his belt. He cocked both pistols, stepped out into the lobby, and let them bang.

Twenty-Eight

Falcon put Dale and Coe on the floor in the first five seconds of the wild shoot-out, both of them hard hit in the belly and chest. The Noonan called Pen jumped out the front window to safety. He rolled off the boardwalk and disappeared from view.

Falcon kicked the guns of Dale and Coe out of their reach. They were down and badly wounded, but both were still able to pull a trigger . . . at least for a few more minutes. Ignoring their cussing, all directed at him, he quickly reloaded and returned to the back room, slipping out the back door. He cut to his left and ran a dozen or so yards before stepping into the rear of a dress shop. He stumbled through the darkness and made his way to the front of the shop. There were three ladies in the front, all pale and huddled together.

"Morning, ladies," Falcon said, smiling at them. "If I might make a suggestion, why don't the three of you get behind the counter and sort of hunker down? You'd be a lot safer, I assure you."

The women quickly took his advice and got down on the floor, behind the counter.

"Thank you," Falcon said, moving to the front window. "That makes me feel a lot better."

The main street was deserted. Falcon stood for a moment, behind a headless dress form that was draped with the latest creation of the shop owner. Falcon frowned at the model; it was cut sort of low in the front. He didn't figure any decent woman would ever wear something that revealing.

Falcon left the dress shop the same way he came in: through the back. He couldn't risk shooting from the store, even if he'd had a target. He didn't want a stray bullet to hit one of the ladies.

A man suddenly ran out from an alley, both hands filled with .45s. He saw Falcon and lifted his guns. Falcon shot him twice, the .44 slugs driving the man backward. He slumped against a building and slid down to the ground, both eyes wide in shock, staring at the blackness of death. Falcon stepped around the body and made his way cautiously up the alley.

A bullet cut a groove out of the building to his left, the slug just missing his arm. Falcon knew from the sound of the weapon that it was a rifle. He ducked down and rolled under the building to his right, wriggling and crawling to the other side, hoping he would not come nose-to-nose with a rattlesnake, who might be a little irritated at having his sleep disturbed.

"Did you get him, Jack?" someone called.

"I don't know. I think maybe I might have winged him."

Falcon peeked out from under the building and saw the rifleman, standing on the awning of a building across the street. Falcon leveled his .44 and shot the man. The man called Jack dropped his weapon and sat down hard on the awning. The sudden impact broke the awning and Jack tumbled to the boardwalk below. He hit the wood of the boardwalk and lay still.

"Where the hell did that shot come from?" another voice demanded.

"I couldn't tell for shore," someone answered. "Pen, you see where he is?"

"No. But the son of a bitch has kilt Coe, and Dale is hard hit. The doctor's with him now. I don't think he's gonna make it. He's shot in the belly."

"We'll get him, Pen," another voice called. "He's trapped here in town. He can't get out."

"You don't have me yet," Falcon muttered. Falcon looked down at his good clothes and saw that the front of his pants and shirt and jacket were covered with mud from his crawling under the building. That irritated him to no end. This was his best suit of clothes.

His shirt was ruined, with a long rip down the front and his suit jacket was stained, probably permanently.

Falcon cussed under his breath. He was so heavily muscled and his chest so broad and his shoulders so wide, it was almost impossible for him to buy a jacket off the rack. He'd have to have another jacket specially made.

"Damn!" he muttered.

"Somebody holler to me!" Pen shouted. "Somebody say somethin'. One of y'all's bound to spot him. He's gotta move sooner or later."

"He ain't movin' yet, Penrod," yet another new voice was added.

"Penrod?" Falcon questioned softly. "Penrod?"

A man suddenly darted out from a building, both hands filled with six-shooters. Falcon snapped a shot at him and knocked a leg out from under the gunhand. The man yelped in pain and rolled off the boardwalk, hitting the ground hard. He came up on his butt and started shooting wildly, hitting nothing but air and the wood of the storefronts opposite him. Falcon took aim and drilled the man in the chest. The man dropped both pistols and slumped over, his mouth hanging open and his head lolling to one side. Another one down and out of it.

"Jesus Christ!" Pen hollered. "Wiseman's down. Somebody spot that bastard and get lead in him."

Falcon ran back to the rear of the stores and this time he cut to his right, running back toward the livery.

A man stepped out from between buildings and Falcon collided with him, knocking the man spinning and cussing. The impact caused the man to drop his rifle and he clawed for his pistol. Falcon backhanded him with his .44 and the man dropped like a stone. Falcon noticed the man was carrying twin Remington .44s. He holstered his .44, grabbed the man's pistols, and checked them. Loaded up full. Falcon cocked both .44s and cut up between the buildings, walking slowly.

"Jeb?" a voice called from the street. "Are you all right, Jeb? Talk to me."

Jeb must be the name of the fellow I whacked upside the head, Falcon thought. Falcon stepped into a doorway and called, "No, Jeb isn't worth a damn, you silly bastard!"

"What!" the man shouted, then stepped out into the narrow space between the two buildings.

Falcon shot him twice. The man stumbled backward and tripped on the boardwalk. He rolled off into the street and lay still.

"Now we got him!" someone shouted. "He's in 'tween them buildings. He's done shot Luddy, too!"

"Where's Jeb?"

"I don't know . . ."

Falcon didn't hear the rest of it. He tried the side door knob, it turned under his hand, and he stepped into the darkness of one of the few empty buildings on the main street. Staying close to the wall, Falcon made his way to the front of the building and looked out through the dirty glass. The street, as much as he could tell through the filthy glass, was clear of people. He could see no one.

He took that time to punch out and reload the empty chambers of the .44s he'd taken from Jeb, and to catch his breath.

"Penrod!" a voice called, the words just audible to Falcon. "Can you see Jeb?"

"I ain't spied him since he went into the alley, Parnell. But there weren't no shots fired. Onliest one I seen was Luddy, and I think he's dead. He ain't movin'."

"Well, MacCallister's bound to be here on main street. Dave and Sonny is down at the livery a-waitin' on him. He'll not get out that way."

"And now he knows all about them two waitin' on him, you dummy!" Penrod hollered.

"Don't you be callin' my brother no dummy, you pissant!" another voice was added.

"Oh, shut up, Bud!" Penrod called. "And keep your eyes open for MacCallister."

Falcon smiled. It didn't appear that any of those after him this day were giants when it came to brains.

Falcon made his way across the large empty room and cracked open the back door. Jeb was still stretched out on the ground. He could see no one else.

Falcon stepped outside and looked quickly left and right. Nobody in sight. He began making his way slowly toward the livery. He saw no one on the short journey. At the rear of the livery, Falcon paused by the open doors and listened. He could hear nothing. Dave and Sonny were being very quiet.

Falcon picked up a stone and flipped it inside. The rock bounced off of something with a clatter amid the stillness.

"What the hell was that?" the voice reached him.

"I dunno," a second voice said. "Horse kickin' the stall, I reckon."

"Didn't sound like that to me."

"Well, hell, Sonny, check it out then."

"I'm a-goin' to."

The voices seemed to be coming from above him. Falcon guessed they both were in the loft. He heard what he believed was the creak of a wooden ladder. So at least one of them remained in the loft.

Sonny's boots hit the floor and his spurs dragged on something with a tinkle. *Real smart of you, Sonny,* Falcon thought. Another mental giant.

Falcon tossed another rock, throwing this one much harder. The stone slammed against the wood with a bang.

"All right now, by God!" Sonny said. "You gonna tell me that was a horse, Dave?"

"I don't know what the hell it was," Dave admitted.

"There ain't nobody down here!" Sonny said. "What's goin' on, Dave?"

"How the hell do I know? I'm up here, you're down yonder. You tell me!"

Sonny muttered under his breath. Falcon couldn't be sure of

the exact words, but they sounded suspiciously like *smartass* to him.

A glass bottle rattled behind him and Falcon whirled around. A man was standing only a few feet away, pointing a gun at him. His boot had accidently touched the empty whiskey bottle. Falcon jumped to one side just as the man pulled the trigger. Falcon hit the ground hard and squeezed off a shot, the bullet striking the gunman in the shoulder and turning him to one side. Falcon squeezed off another round just as the man recovered his balance and lifted his .45. The slug hit the man in the chest and knocked him down. He did not move. Falcon rolled into the ditch that ran behind the long row of buildings on that side of the business district.

"He's out back!" Sonny shouted. "Come on, Dave. Git down from that loft and come on."

Sonny appeared in the sunlight, pausing for just the briefest of seconds in the open barn doors. That was long enough for Falcon to snap off a round. Sonny's left leg buckled under him and he yelped in pain and fell backward into the semidarkness of the livery stable.

Falcon was up and running before the sound of the shot had echoed away. He could heard running boots slamming against the wood of the boardwalk that ended at the livery stable. Getting into the livery and to his horse was out of the question.

So much for trying to ride out of town.

"Where is he?" a voice demanded.

"How am I 'pposed to know?" Sonny shouted. "He's out back somewhere. Somebody yell for the doctor to come over here. I think my leg's busted."

"Hell with your leg," Falcon recognized the voice of Penrod. "Find that damn MacCallister and kill him!"

"Well, the hell with you too, you son of a bitch!" Sonny yelled. "I done been wounded, Pen! I need some medical attention for my leg."

Falcon could not contain his smile. This bunch certainly got shorted on good sense when the Lord passed out the brains. They must have stood up when the Good Lord said sit down.

"Oh, Lord!" Reverend Watkins's voice suddenly came ripping through the warm air of the small western town. "Deliver us from this pack of heathens."

"What the hell is that?" a voice called.

"That's the preacher," Dave called from the loft. "I can see him plain from up here. He's gatherin' a bunch of women around him on the other side of the street. I don't know what he's a-plannin' on doin'."

"I think he's a-gonna preach a sermon," another voice called from the front. "Or sing songs, maybe."

Falcon walked to the front of the narrow space between two buildings and peeked out onto the street. He had lost his new hat somewhere along the way and that annoyed him to no end. He sure was hell on hats this trip. He thought Dean at the general store had one more hat in stock that would fit his head. And Falcon didn't like that style. But he didn't appear to have much choice of selection.

"Jack's dead," a voice called. "MacCallister's done kilt another one."

"Somebody find that rotten bastard and plug him!" Penrod yelled. " 'Fore he kills all of us."

"I see him!" Parnell shouted, standing directly opposite Falcon on the other side of the street. "You mine, MacCallister," he said excitedly. "I gotcha!"

Falcon triggered off two fast rounds. Both bullets missed their target but came so close Parnell let out a whoop and hit the ground, crawling behind a water trough. Falcon whirled around just as a man appeared at the other end of the space between the buildings. Falcon plugged him and jumped out onto the boardwalk. He had no other place to go.

The gut-shot man dropped his six-shooter and sat down on the ground hard and started squalling in pain, both hands holding his bloody belly.

"The way of salvation is before you," came the harmonizing voices of the impromptu choir across the street.

"Who got shot?" Penrod called.

"Just follow the footsteps of the Savior," the choir sang.

"Will somebody please shut that damn singin' up!" Penrod hollered. "I can't hear myself think for all that squallin'."

"Matt, I think, Pen," someone shouted. "He's a-shore hollerin' to beat the band."

"Trust in the light of the Lord," the choir sang. "He will guide you through the storm."

Someone, Falcon guessed it was Penrod, put a round over the heads of the choir, the bullet smashing through glass. The choir scattered, running into a shop and getting all jammed up in the doorway.

Falcon had ducked into the Purple Palace Saloon, both hands filled with .44s. The soiled doves, all in various stages of undress, started screaming and running for cover. Falcon had never seen such ugly women in all his life. He was glad it had been several hours since breakfast. The sight of them was enough to cause a man to lose any recently ingested food.

"Excuse me, uh, ladies," Falcon said. He ran through the building and out the back door, jumping to the ground and cutting quickly to his left. He had no idea where he was going, but he damn sure wasn't going to stay in the Purple Palace.

"Cain't nobody spot him?" Penrod yelled. "Good God, he ain't but one man. Shoot the bastard!"

"Well, you ain't got no lead in him neither, big mouth," someone yelled. "So quit your bitchin' at us."

"Don't you git sassy with me!" Penrod hollered, the words reaching Falcon just as he paused for breath in a rear doorway.

I've got to get out of here, Falcon thought. *Somehow. It's a crazy house.*

Falcon slipped into the rear of the barbershop and walked into the main shop area. There were half a dozen men in the room. The locals turned and looked at him.

"Big doings in town today, huh, boys?" Falcon questioned.

"That is certainly one way of putting it," the new barber said. He hadn't been in town more than a couple of weeks and looked as though he would like to leave as soon as possible.

"This has got to stop, Mr. MacCallister," a local said. "There's going to be some women or kids killed."

"Well, I know how it can be done," Falcon told him. "Arm yourselves and put a stop to it."

Several of the locals smiled faintly. They had gotten to know Falcon over the summer months and all liked him.

"Trying to get the men in this town to pull together is damn near impossible," one of the locals said. "There are still some in this town who support Noonan and Stegman."

"I don't know why," Falcon replied. "But I suppose they have their reasons."

"I can sum it up with one word," another local said. *"Money."*

"Then they're fools," Falcon told him, walking to the front door. He could see no one moving on the streets or the boardwalks.

Then Falcon heard a shout that brought a smile to his face. "Yonder comes them old mountain men from the Rockingchair! All of them. They're ridin' hell for leather, too."

Falcon turned to the group of locals. "It'll be over in ten minutes," he told them.

Falcon MacCallister checked his guns and stepped out onto the boardwalk.

Twenty-Nine

Big Bob and his pals spread out just before they reached the town limits. They reined up and dismounted, quickly filling their callused hands with the butts of guns. They began advancing slowly into town, behind the buildings and straight up the boardwalks on both sides of the long street.

The Noonans and the .44 hands decided they wanted no part of the old mountain men coming at them with blood in their eyes. But for most of those who had lain in failed ambush for Falcon, it was too late. Dave cussed the advancing mountain men and leveled guns at them. Within a heartbeat he was filled with so many holes he died on his feet. Parnell ran out to help him and the mountain men drilled him, the impacting bullets turning the man around and around in the street, his body jerking from the hot slam of the .44 and .45 slugs.

"Hell's fire!" one of the others yelled, and hit the air, running all out to where their horses were hidden. Several others of the Noonan clan and of the .44 hands were right behind him. They leaped into their saddles and spurred their horses, quickly disappearing into the low hills.

There was a dead man sprawled on the boardwalk and Big Bob kicked him off into the street as he walked toward Falcon.

"You can't even go to town to count your money without gettin' into trouble, can you, boy?"

"Certainly doesn't appear that way, Bob," Falcon replied with a smile.

"Me and the boys kinda figured you'd get into a fight. We decided to follow you."

"Damn good thing you did, too."

"You shore left a passel of dead and wounded layin' about," Stumpy remarked, looking around him as he strolled up. "They must have irritated you somethin' fierce."

"They tried to ambush me."

"That would piss me off too."

"I count eight dead and two wounded," Mustang said, walking up. "One of 'em was draggin' a busted leg and crawlin' off. I let him go."

"I think that's the one called Sonny," Falcon said. "Dale's in the hotel lobby. He might live. There's another called Penrod."

"Penrod!" Puma blurted. "Penrod?"

"That's his name," Falcon said with a laugh. "I think he's related to the Noonans, but I'm not sure."

The doctor and the undertaker, newly arrived in town, were busy, moving from body to body.

"I feel in need of a drink," Wildcat announced. "But not in the Purple Palace," he quickly added.

"I was in there briefly," Falcon said. He shook his head. "Those, uh, ladies were, uh, not entirely pleasant to the eye."

"Only one of them is good-lookin'," Big Bob said. "Her name's Lilly and she runs the stable of gals. I been knowin' her for nigh onto fifteen years."

"You poke her ever' now and then, Bob?" Dan asked with a grin.

"My pokin' and who I poke it to ain't none of your damn business, Dan."

"I feel in need of a poke myself," Dan replied. "That's the reason I was askin'."

"Well, go ask her if you can poke her," Big Bob said. "But Lilly ain't cheap. And she's still right smart of a mover, too.

You better get cinched down tight when you climb on board and be shore to grab hold of somethin'. She can throw you.''

Laughing, Falcon walked on up the boardwalk toward the bank building. There would be no work done this day at the ranch. But he doubted there would be any further trouble in town . . . not once the survivors of the failed ambush got back to home range and spread the word.

But, Falcon thought, you never could tell. The shoot-out in town could bring the whole passer of them riding in. You just never knew.

Falcon spent an hour at the bank, dealing with Willard and one of his tellers. He made some arrangements for some of his money to be spent—mainly setting up through the bank lines of credit for half a dozen small farmers and several of the smaller ranchers. Then he walked over to the general store and found several nice shirts that would fit him and much to his surprise, a suit coat that would also fit him. He bought a pair of britches and changed clothes in the rear of the store. Then he bought the last hat in stock that was in his size . . . and in a style he did not like. He took his dirty clothes over to the laundry and cleaners to have them washed and pressed.

Big Bob Marsh approached him, a smile on his face. ''The mayor of the town done looked me up,'' Big Bob said. ''When the trouble's over, he wants me to be marshal of this town. I told him I would if I could have Stumpy as my deputy. He said that would be just fine with him.''

Falcon shook hands with the man and congratulated him. ''What does Stumpy think about all this?''

''Oh, I ain't told him yet. But he's been makin' noises 'bout it bein' time for us all to be thinkin' of settlin' down somewheres. He'll go along with it.''

''The work's just about done at the ranch, for sure,'' Falcon told him. ''Cattle are on good graze and by the time winter gets here, John will have several permanent hands hired. How about Puma?''

''Oh, he'll head back to the mountains and that damn cat of his. He ain't gonna farm and he ain't gonna settle near no town. He's done made that clear. He'll die up in the high country.

Hell, that's what he wants to do. I think he's got a right to do just that.''

"Man should be able to do what he chooses," Falcon agreed. "But it won't be lasting much longer. Not with so-called civilization fast coming this way."

"Well, it's gonna be a sorry damn day when that gets here," Big Bob said with a frown.

"I certainly agree with you, Bob. How about the rest of the boys? What are they going to do?"

"They're gonna stick around and farm them parcels of land you give out. I kinda figured they would. It's time for us to be thinkin' of warm fires and soft beds. Ain't none of us got that many more years ahead of us."

And their passing will be the end of another era, Falcon thought. An era of American history that will never come again. And how will it be marked?

"I got to find Stumpy and tell him the news," Big Bob said. "I can't wait to see his face."

"Those Double N and .44 boys might come back, Bob," Falcon cautioned. "I can't shake a bad feeling that fell on me a few minutes ago. You pass the word for the boys to be careful."

"Will do, Falcon."

As Big Bob walked away, Falcon consulted the clock in the bank window. It was just mid morning. Plenty of time for the Double N and .44 riders to reach home range, inform their friends what had taken place in town, and return en masse.

The feeling that the Noonans and the .44 bunch would do just that would not leave Falcon. And Falcon's men were going to do a bit of celebrating; they would stay in town all day, probably.

Falcon looked up the street: The farmers he had met along the way into town were just arriving in their wagons; wives, kids, and all.

Falcon spotted a young boy of about twelve sitting on the boardwalk and approached him, giving him a couple of dollars to situate himself on the edge of town, on one of the low hills, and keep watch. "You see riders coming, boy, you run find me and warn me, all right?"

"You betcha, Mr. MacCallister. I'll sure do it. You can count on me."

Falcon got himself a table at the rear of Rosie's Café and checked his guns . . . all four of them. He loaded them up full while he drank his coffee and ate his huge wedge of pie. He had seen Dan Carson go into the Purple Palace in search of Lilly to poke. Big Bob and Stumpy would be off together somewhere in town, making plans about when they became lawmen. Mustang was in the farm implement store, talking about plows and such, Wildcat with him. Puma Parley was wandering around town somewhere.

Falcon had not seen the man he suspected of being a deputy U.S. marshal. He had ridden out of town early that morning, the stableman had told him. He had him a bedroll and supplies for a couple of days with him.

The minutes ticked slowly by and became an hour, then two hours. Falcon sat in Rosie's and drank coffee and waited.

Shoppers had returned to the streets of the town, visiting and gossiping and shopping. The café began filling up and Falcon paid for his coffee and stepped out onto the boardwalk. The dark feeling of danger had intensified within him. He felt certain a showdown was imminent, and it would be a bloody one, he was sure of that.

More farmers and small ranchers had arrived in town with their families. Many of them would make a day of it in town, and were taking rooms at the hotel and the boarding house to spend the night.

Falcon walked down to the livery to check on his horse. Someone had tossed some loose dirt over the bloody spots on the livery floor. He left the livery to slowly walk the town. He spoke to the people he met and stopped a couple of times to chat with farmers and ranchers.

The crops looked good, cattle were fat, there was plenty of water this year, and everything looked good.

Except in town, Falcon thought. All hell was going to break

loose in town before this day was over. Now he was sure of it.

Falcon walked outside of town and climbed the low hill. The young boy smiled up at him. "I ain't seen a thing, Mr. MacCallister. But I'm keepin' my eyes open a-lookin'."

"Good boy. You keep sharp and there'll be a couple more dollars in it for you."

"Yes sir!"

Falcon walked slowly back to town, his thoughts dark. The feeling of impending danger had increased within him. More people had arrived in town and Falcon wondered why so many people were coming into town to shop on a weekday?

He watched with a feeling of dismay as John Bailey and his family came riding up the main street. Kip and the cook and the extra hand John had hired—a local young man still in his late teens—were not with them; they had stayed back at the ranch, taking care of odds and ends. Angie, Martha, and Jimmy were in the wagon, John on horseback.

"Damn!" Falcon swore just under his breath.

"Something the matter, Brother MacCallister?" The question came from Falcon's left.

He turned. Reverend Watkins was standing there, all spiffed up in his best suit.

"You're mighty dressed up this day, Preacher," Falcon said.

"I'm waiting for Miss Terri and her family," the minister said. "There is a box supper at the church this evening. Didn't you know?"

Falcon sighed. So that was it. Now Falcon remembered John and Martha talking about it. A box supper. That's why so many people were flocking into town.

"It slipped my mind, Preacher. Lots of people coming in, hey?"

"Nearly the entire population of this end of the county will be here," Watkins replied. "Every room at the hotel and at Mrs. Deekins's boarding house is taken."

"Interesting," Falcon muttered.

"People will be sleeping in tents and under their wagons,"

Watkins went on. "We're going to have a lovely service at the church. You will be there, Mr. MacCallister?"

"I'm sure," Falcon said, then excused himself. He walked off shaking his head. Reverend Watkins and Terri Gilman . . . Good Lord, what a pair. Falcon smiled at the thought as he walked away. Well, stranger things had happened, he supposed, but offhand he couldn't think of any.

At the general store he bought a bottle of sarsaparilla and some crackers for his lookout on the hill and carried them up to him.

"Ain't seen a thing, Mr. MacCallister," the boy said. "But I'm a-watchin'."

"Good boy."

Maybe I've just been imagining the danger, Falcon thought, as he walked back to town. *Letting my imagination run away in my head.*

But he didn't believe that for a minute.

Noonan and Stegman and their hired guns were coming to town, and they were coming to town on this day. And it wouldn't make any difference to them how many innocent people caught a bullet; men, women, or kids.

And it wouldn't make a whole lot of difference if Falcon and his boys rode out of town back to the ranch. Noonan and Stegman would just wait until the next time he came into town. Falcon was beginning to see Noonan's plan now . . . or he guessed it might be the rancher's plan: Noonan just might have in mind subduing the townspeople, kicking them back into submission by a huge show of force. Showing them he was boss and by God that's the way it was going to be from now on.

The more Falcon thought about it, the more convinced he became he was right. Today just happened by accident and it fit right into Noonan's plans.

Falcon stopped up short on the boardwalk. But someone had known about it: The new hand knew of Falcon's plans. Falcon had been currying his horse late yesterday afternoon and the young man had asked point-blank if he was going somewhere.

Falcon hadn't given it a second thought; he just told him about his planned trip into town today.

The hired hand had ridden out shortly after that and hadn't returned until long after dark. Had to be him. Falcon would have a little chat with Young Mr. Louis when he got back. That is, if Louis ever returned to the Rockingchair. If he had any sense, he wouldn't.

Falcon turned to look in the direction of the Double N and the .44 ranches. They were coming. He was sure of that. He just didn't know when.

He went in search of his crew and one by one told them of his suspicions.

"You think maybe we should all head back to the ranch?" Wildcat asked.

"Then they'd tear up the town just for spite and perhaps kill or injure some people just for the hell of it," Falcon said. "No. We'll stay. We're a thin line, but with any kind of luck we can make the difference."

"That church social couldn't have come at a worse time," Big Bob said. "You really think young Louis was spyin' on you?"

"Has to be him. Couldn't be anyone else."

"Is there anyone in town we can count on 'sides John Bailey?" asked Dan Carson.

"Damn few," Falcon replied, thinking fast. "Besides, most of the men I've seen aren't wearing a gun."

"I got me an idea," Mustang said softly, but with steel behind the words.

Falcon looked at him.

"When them hired gunhands come bustin' into town this time, let's us finish it once and for all."

"You got a plan?" Wildcat asked.

"Hot lead," Mustang replied. "That there's the best plan I can think of."

"Hell, Mustang," Falcon said. "There might be fifty or sixty riders come after us."

"The more the merrier," the aging mountain man said. "We'll make us a real party of it."

''Yeah, I like that idea,'' Big Bob said, a broad smile on his face. ''The more targets we have, the more likely we are to hit something.''

Falcon looked at each of his men. They were smiling at him. There was no fear in any of them. He slowly nodded his head in agreement. ''All right, boys. Did you all bring extra guns in with you?''

''Shore we did,'' Puma Parley answered for them all. ''We kinda figured there might be a real shootin' party here in town.

''How we gonna handle this?'' Stumpy asked. ''We got to have some sort of plan.''

''I got an idea,'' Dan said. ''It ain't real original, but it's somethin' them no-'counts shore won't be expectin', I betcha.''

''Well, boy, don't keep us in the dark about it, spill the beans,'' Big Bob urged.

Dan hunkered down by the side of the boardwalk and drew a line in the dirt with his finger. ''Here's what I got in mind. This here's the town limits, where them gunnies will be comin' in, hell-bent for leather. So, here's where we'll be . . .''

Thirty

"Get together as many men as you feel will stand firm and keep the people inside the church," Falcon told John Bailey.

The older man stared at him for a few heartbeats, then nodded his head. "The boil's comin' to a head today, isn't it, boy?"

"That's the way I've got it figured, John. They could come busting in here at any time, all of them."

John stood silent and rolled him a smoke. He lifted his eyes to Falcon. "Young Louis handed in his walkin' papers right after you left, Falcon. He was already packed up and ready to go. Is he tied up in all of this?"

"I think he was spying for Noonan or Stegman; reporting back to them."

John sighed heavily. "I never did totally trust that kid. Only hired him as a favor to his ma."

"Forget him, John. He's nothing and nobody. When word of his treachery gets around the county, he won't be able to get a job cleaning out privies."

"You can bet I'll personally see to that," the rancher said grimly. "You want me to pass the word to everybody about the raid?"

Falcon shook his head. "No. Because it might not happen.

I want you and some of those you can trust to get your rifles and throw up a line of defense around this church and grounds. If any of those bastards get close, put some lead in them. It's me they want anyway. They might just leave the townspeople alone.''

"I don't think so," John said. "I think Noonan and Stegman want to put the buffalo in on everybody." He smiled. "Look yonder, boy: There's Miles and his family comin' into town to socialize. We can count on him now. My, my, don't Miss Terri look mighty sweet all gussied up in a dress?"

"I never saw her in a dress before this."

"Tell the truth, I ain't seen her in one in years. Not since her ma pulled up stakes and went back east."

The men watched as Terri climbed down from the buckboard and walked over to Angie.

"Oh, Lord," Falcon said. "Here it comes."

"I don't think so," John replied. "I think we're about to see a makin'-up 'tween them two."

"I'm going to have to see it to believe it."

The two women chatted for a moment, then embraced. When they pulled back, both of them took out little bitsy handkerchiefs and dabbed at their eyes. Then they took hands and walked off together, chatting and smiling.

"Well, I'll be damned!" Falcon said.

"It's gonna be all right, boy," John said, unable to contain his wide smile. "Yes, sir. It's gonna be just fine."

Reverend Watkins joined the two young women and put his arm around Terri for just a moment. She smiled up at him.

"I don't believe it!" Falcon said.

"Oh, yeah. Martha heard that the preacher made a formal call on Miles to ask permission to come callin' on his daughter. He said yeah and they been an item ever since."

"Reverend Watkins and Terri Gilman!"

John chuckled at the expression on Falcon's face. Then he burst out in soft laughter. "Boy, if you could only see the look on your face. It's priceless."

Falcon took off his hat and scratched his head. "I've got to say that now I've seen it all."

John wiped laughter moisture from his eyes and said, "I'd better go see some of the men. You goin' to be around the church, Falcon?"

"No. Me and the boys will be in town, waiting for the action to start. Dan had him a pretty good plan, I think. We'll see how it works out."

Falcon smiled as John fixed him with a skeptical look. "It's a very simple plan. That's why I like it."

"I hope it works."

"Me too," Falcon said with a laugh. "See you around, John."

"Good luck, boy."

Falcon went back to the livery and got his rifle. He hid it under the dress shop. He took two of the pistols he'd taken from the dead and wounded in the earlier fight and hid them. Then he filled up a bandolier with .44 rounds and slung it over his shoulder and across his chest. His friends had stuffed their pockets full of spare cartridges. He was ready. Now came the hardest part: the waiting.

The noon hour passed and Falcon and his men ate a hearty meal at the café. The festivities at the church were supposed to get underway at mid afternoon. Already, people were finishing up their shopping and heading in that direction. John Bailey had quietly alerted about a dozen of the men and they had loaded up their rifles and tucked them out of sight but in very handy places. They all knew what to do when trouble started. If Noonan and Stegman tried to attack the church and the grounds around it, they would run into a hail of gunfire, from men who were very familiar with gunfire and knew their rifles as well as they knew the back of their hands.

Falcon put the church social out of his mind as he watched the shop owners shut down for the day, closing about three or four hours early so they could get ready for the social.

Big Bob walked up to stand under the awning where Falcon was just rolling a cigarette. Falcon handed him the makin's. Big Bob rolled and licked and lit. He inhaled, huffed out smoke, and then said, "I just heard that the Noonan that was hangin' on just died over to the doc's office."

"Dale?"

"I believe that's what the man called him. Yeah. That's right. Dale. Belly-shot, he was."

"That's him."

"I got me a notion that we ought to finish this little war today, Falcon."

"Sounds good to me, Bob. I'm for it."

"Me and the boys done talked it over. Them crazy damn hired guns is either gonna surrender or they's gonna die. One of the two. We all agree that there ain't gonna be no other option open to them."

"Suits me."

"I want this to be a nice peaceful little town when they pin them badges on me and Stumpy. Handle a drunk ever' now and then and maybe settle some family argument ever' so often. No shootin'. Me and Stumpy gonna get us a nice little house apiece and live quiet like."

"Tired of rambling, Bob?"

"I'm gettin' a mite weary of it, yeah. Stumpy, too."

"Then it's time to light for a spell."

"Yep. Shore is." Big Bob hauled out a watch about the size of your average clock and clicked open the lid. "They'll be comin' shortly now. I feel it in my bones. Your boy up yonder on the hill will be standin' up and wavin' and hollerin' in a few minutes."

"You're sure, huh?" Falcon asked with a smile.

"Yep. I'm shore."

Falcon hitched at his gunbelt and made no other comment about Big Bob's premonition. He had been raised around old mountain men and knew how finely honed their sixth sense was. They had lived their entire lives on the sharp edge of danger and their senses were twice that of any ordinary man.

Dan Carson walked up and paused for a moment. He wore two six-shooters in leather, had two more tucked behind his gunbelt, and another stuck down behind his belt at the small of his back. "Them ol' boys will be comin' in pretty damn soon, now, I reckon," he opined. "My blood is beginning to run hot. I 'spect we'd better get ready to greet them."

Falcon sighed and smiled. If another of his friends walked up and said something about the raiders coming in . . .

Puma walked up. Like Big Bob and Dan, he was fairly bristling with pistols. "Jenny's here," he announced.

Big Bob gave him a look. "That damn cat of yours is here, in town?"

"Yep. I can feel her near."

"But you ain't seen her?"

"I don't have to see her. I can sense when she's near to me. But I didn't come over here to jaw 'bout Jenny. Them raiders is on the way."

Falcon sighed.

"I figure they'll be here in 'bout twenty or thirty minutes."

Big Bob looked at Falcon and smiled. Then his smile faded and he said to Puma, "You keep that damn cat away from me, Puma, you hear me?"

"She ain't gonna bother you none. Relax. But I figure she's been real close by all the time. I been gettin' some messages from her."

"There ain't no goddamn way no goddamn puma can send no human bein' no goddamn message!" Big Bob snorted. "I swear, Parley, the older you get the crazier you get."

Puma Parley smiled and remained silent.

Falcon furtively looked all around him, thinking he might see Jenny skulking about the now nearly deserted town. Then he caught himself and felt rather foolish. He had to agree with Big Bob: Jenny was more than likely hundreds of miles away, and she certainly wasn't sending Puma any messages.

Puma walked away a few yards to stand smiling. "Yep," he finally said. "She's here, all right."

"Oh . . . to hell with you, Puma!" Big Bob said.

"I seen Miles Gilman," Wildcat said, in an effort to lighten the mood some. "He was squirin' around that farm woman, Mrs. Carter. They shore was lovey-dovey. I reckon that's gettin' some serious."

"Yeah," Mustang said. "And Terri and Reverend Watkins is seein' one another. I tell you what, they's some strange happenin's takin' place around this part of the country."

"For a fact," Stumpy agreed. "And they's gonna be some more things change in a few minutes."

"What are you talkie' about?" Puma asked, turning around to look at his old friend.

"Them raiders is almost here," Stumpy said.

Falcon looked up at his boy on the hill. The boy was sitting, staring out at the road that led to town, making no frantic signals to warn Falcon of any approaching riders.

"Yep," Big Bob agreed. "I do believe you're right, Stumpy. I can sense them gunhands gettin' closer, for a fact. I figure 'bout twenty minutes and we'll be shootin'."

Dan Carson nodded his head. "You're right, boys. They're almost here."

"Oh, now come on, guys!" Falcon said impatiently. "The boy up on the hill hasn't made a move to signal us. He can see for several miles."

"Oh, them raiders ain't come into his sight yet," Wildcat stated. "But they'll be plain to him in a few minutes. You just hold your water for minute or so. You'll see."

"Speakin' of holdin' your water," Big Bob said. "I reckon I'd better go shake the dew off my flower 'fore we has to go into action. It's uncomfortable havin' to pee and shoot at the same time."

"Yeah, I'm with you," Dan said. "Let's find us a privy right quick. We don't want to miss out on none of the fun."

The two men wandered down the alley. Falcon watched them go and shook his head in disbelief at their warning about the Double N and .44 riders approaching. Puma had already walked across the street, to take his position next to the far boardwalk.

Mustang hitched at his gunbelt and stepped off the boardwalk into the street. "I reckon we bes' get ready for some gunsmoke, fellers. For troubles a-comin', for shore."

Falcon looked up at the hill. The boy was sitting, staring out at the big empty, making no signals toward town.

Again, he sighed and shook his head.

"You told that boy that when trouble starts, to stay up yonder and keep down, didn't you, Falcon?" Stumpy asked.

"Yes. He knows to belly-down and stay clear."

"Good. I'd like this little fracas to end without havin' a single local gettin' hurt."

"They'll be comin' into sight now at any time," Puma said. "I can feel 'em gettin' closer."

"Oh, for heaven's sake!" Falcon said. "You guys are having fun with me, that's all."

"That there boy on the hill will be jumpin' up and down any minute," Puma said. "You'll see."

Big Bob and Dan returned from their visit to the privy. Big Bob said, "I reckon we all bes' be gettin' set for some action. You boys ready to let 'em bang?"

The mountain men nodded their heads. They were ready.

"Let's get set, then."

Falcon sighed. He lifted his eyes to the hill. The boy was standing up, waving his arms frantically.

"Well, I'll just be damned!" Falcon muttered.

"Told you," Wildcat said, stepping off the boardwalk into the street. "Let's get ready to smell some gunsmoke, boys."

Thirty-One

The seven men spread out across the wide main street of town. Puma, Mustang, Wildcat, Big Bob, Stumpy, Dan, and finally Falcon. Upon spotting the seven men, the huge gathering of hired guns reined up at the edge of town and let the dust settle and their horses blow.

"Must be fifty of 'em, at least," Stumpy said. "And another bunch comin' in behind that one."

"Yeah, but it's smaller," Big Bob called. "That'll be the bunch that Noonan and Stegman will be ridin' with."

"Get ready," Falcon called, just loud enough for his men to hear. "They're going to be coming up the street straight at us in a few seconds."

"Just like I figured they would," Dan said.

"Yep," Mustang said. "You called this 'un right, Dan."

"You boys all know what to do," Falcon said. "Soon as we empty the lead saddles, head for cover."

"You watch your butt, Falcon," Big Bob called.

"Good luck, boys," Falcon replied.

With a shout of defiance, the mounted mob put the spurs to their horses and lunged forward, galloping up the street toward the thin line of men. When they got within good pistol range, seven men each jerked two six-guns from leather and let them bang just as fast as they could cock and fire.

Twenty saddles were emptied in a matter of seconds. Horses were rearing up and bucking and screaming in fright. Wounded men were crawling around in the dirt of the street, most of them getting trampled on by the hooves of the horses that had been galloping directly behind them.

When the dust settled, Falcon and the mountain men were nowhere in sight and the horsemen were trapped in the center of the street.

Falcon and three of his men opened up from one side of the street, while the three other mountain men opened up from the other. More saddles were emptied and horses were going crazy from the smell of blood and the roar of gunfire and the screaming of the wounded gunhands.

Less than half of those who had arrogantly charged Falcon and his friends managed to get their horses turned around and gallop back out of town, and many of them were wounded. The street was filled with the dead, dying, and badly wounded.

Falcon and his men had not suffered even the tiniest of scratches.

Stegman was horrified at the carnage he was witnessing in the street, but Noonan was outraged. "Dismount!" he roared at his men. "Dismount and go after those bastards on foot and kill them. Do it! All of you."

A mob of hired guns spread out and began slowly working their way up both sides of the street, front and back of the businesses. There were Noonan and Stegman brothers and kids of the brothers and cousins and uncles and so forth. For many of them, this would be the last fight: Their blood would stain the streets and alleys and boardwalks and businesses of the small western town in Wyoming.

"Just stay inside the church," John Bailey told the people gathered for the church social. "Noonan and Stegman's men will not harm you. Preacher, get your choir together and give us some songs, will you?"

"My pleasure, sir," Reverend Watkins said. "Come, sisters,

let us raise our voices in song while the Philistines spill their blood in the streets.''

Falcon came up face-to-face with a bearded gunhand and shot him twice just as Big Bob lined up a paid gunny in his sights and blew him to hell. Dan Carson stood in the doorway of a back door and waited until a gunslick walked up . . . then he shot him in the head. Mustang stepped out of a building and blew one of the Noonan cousins out of one boot. The man was dead before he stretched out on the ground for the last time.

Puma called out to a gunslick, ''Hey, you ugly bastard! Behind you.''

The man whirled around and Puma gave him two .45 rounds in the chest.

Wildcat emptied one pistol into a knot of hired guns and sent two to the ground, mortally wounded. The other three jumped for cover and scrambled out of sight.

Stumpy leveled both pistols at several men who were trying to slip out the back of the building, and let his six-shooters bang. When the smoke cleared, two men were dead and the third was crawling away, out of the fight.

Suddenly there was a woman's scream: a terrible scream that cut the afternoon air. But after a few seconds, Falcon decided it wasn't a woman's scream; it was slightly off in timbre. A man staggered out from between two buildings, half his face gone and blood dripping from the terrible wound. The man tried to speak, but no words would come from his mouth.

''Jenny got him,'' Puma called. ''I told y'all she was close by.''

The man with half his face missing screamed in pain and then collapsed in the middle of the street and lay still.

''What the hell happened to Dick?'' someone called. ''I didn't hear no gunshot.''

''I don't know,'' a man called in reply. ''But half his face is missin'.''

A shot cut the afternoon and a gunslick grunted and took a header off the hotel roof. He smashed through the awning, bounced on the boardwalk, and lay still.

"Falcon MacCallister, you son of a bitch!" Nance Noonan shouted.

Falcon did not reply. He stayed between two buildings, pressed up into a doorway.

"You've played hell, for a fact," Nance shouted. "But this day ain't over."

For a fact, Falcon thought. *And if you had any sense, you'd pull up stakes and ride on out to another part of the country.*

Then Nance Noonan signed his death warrant when he shouted, "I know you got kids, Falcon. And I know where they are down in Colorado. I'll kill them, MacCallister. I'll make certain none of your stinkin' offspring lives. They're dead, MacCallister. You hear me? Your kids are *dead!*"

Falcon felt an icy sensation wash over him. It was as if someone had thrown a bucket of ice water on him. He did not know it, but he was smiling; but the smile was awful to behold. It was a curving of the lips that came straight from Hell.

"You're dead, Noonan," Falcon muttered softly, only the faint breeze hearing his words. "You're a walking-around dead man. No matter where you go, I'll find you and kill you."

A hired gun suddenly left cover and tried to make the side door to the general store. The guns of three mountain men barked and the man stumbled and went down to his knees. He stayed in that position for a few seconds, then toppled over and lay still in the mouth of the alley.

"I'm done, MacCallister!" a man called. "I'm out of here. I'm holsterin' my guns and gettin' my horse and ridin' out. Don't shoot. You hear me?"

Falcon maintained his silence.

"Me, too," another man shouted. "This is crazy. I ain't gonna die for no damn Noonan. I'm joinin' Pete and ridin' out. Don't shoot."

"You yellow-bellied bastards!" Nance shouted. "I've been payin' you top wages for months and now you turn yeller on me. You stand and fight, you scum."

"You go to hell, Noonan," another voice sprang out of an alleyway. "It's time, past time, you understood that you ain't gonna win this fight. It's over, man. And I ain't havin' no part of killin' nobody's kids."

"That goes double for me," yet another voice was added to the quitting voices. "I'm done here. MacCallister, my guns is in leather. I'm through. I'm headin' out the back alley and ridin' clear of this town. You understand?"

"Git gone then," Big Bob's voice shouted. "All of you who want to live, ride out and don't never come back to this part of the country. If I see any of you again, I'll kill you on the spot. Ride out and don't come back. Hold your fire, boys. Let them ride clear."

Nance cussed all those who gathered up their horses, swung into the saddles, and rode out. "You sorry bunch of yeller coyotes!" he shouted, his voice filled with rage. "You no-good scummy bastards. Take a man's money and then turn yeller on him. Goddamm you all to hell."

One of the men who had made up his mind to ride out told Nance how and where he could shove his words—sideways. Nance screamed his anger at the departing gunhands.

"How about it, Nance?" Falcon finally broke his silence. "You and me in the street. You have the nerve to face me man-to-man, you sorry piece of crap?"

There was no reply.

Falcon called again for Nance to meet him in the street. Nance made no reply to the deadly invitation.

"We're out of here, MacCallister," yet another voice filled the late-afternoon air. "We're done with this fight. They's five of us ridin' out. Hold your fire."

"Ten of us," another voice shouted. "That about does it, MacCallister. Tell your boys it's all over. We're through and done with it."

"Where's Nance?" Falcon shouted.

"He rode out a few minutes ago. He quit. Him and all his brothers and other kin with him. We ain't stayin' here and takin' no lead for him."

"Ride out then," Big Bob called. "But don't none of you never come back. You're dead if you do. You understand?"

"We understand. You've seen the last of us."

"Git gone, then!"

After a moment, Falcon yelled, "Where's Stegman?"

"Gone," Stumpy called. "I seen him ride out 'fore any of the others left."

"Anybody know where the doc is?"

"At the church, I think," Puma called. "I'm closest. I'll go get him."

"Take that damn cat of yours with you," Big Bob called.

"She's back in the hills," Puma shouted. "I seen her high-tailin' it after that no-'count scared her and she had to defend herself. Poor baby's scared to death, probably."

Big Bob had nothing to add to that, but Falcon could not help but smile as he imagined the big man muttering about Puma Parley's *poor baby*.

"I'll have to love on her and pet her for a couple of days to get her calmed down," Puma added.

"Oh, shut up about that damn beast of yours and go get the doc!" Big Bob yelled.

"You just don't appreciate God's creatures, Bob," Puma called. "They're wonderful critters."

"Go git the damn doc!"

"All right, all right. Keep your pants on, Bob. I'm a-goin'."

John Bailey and several other men came walking cautiously from the church to the main street, rifles at the ready. But they didn't need weapons. The fight was over. It had not lasted long, but it had been brutal and bloody. Twenty-eight hired guns were dead or close to death, another fifteen had suffered various wounds, most of the dead and wounded sprawled in the dirt of the town's main street.

"Good Lord!" the doctor blurted, upon sighting the carnage.

"Is it over here?" Puma asked.

"It's over," Miles Gilman said. "When the news of this spreads, Noonan and Stegman won't be able to hire any guns. Anyone with a gun for hire will stay far away from this part of the country. Count on that."

"I'm gone then," Puma said, walking up leading his horse. "I got to go find my Jenny. Poor thing's scared and alone up yonder in the hills."

"I owe you money, Puma," John said.

"Naw. Last week was payday and I ain't done nothin' the past week. We're even. See you, boys."

And with that, the mountain man was gone, swinging into the saddle and riding out without looking back.

"That's his way," Dan Carson said. "I been knowin' him for years and he always leaves out the same way. Just saddles up and goes, usually without so much as a fare-thee-well."

"I hope Jenny's all right," Wildcat said.

Big Bob rolled his eyes and shook his head.

"You folks go on and have your social," Falcon told the local men. "Me and the boys will help the doc and the undertaker get all this cleared up."

Miles Gilman and John Bailey started to protest and Falcon waved them silent. "Go on back to your womenfolk. Before some of them wander down here and see all this bloody mess."

"You got a point there, Falcon," Miles said. "All right. Come on, John. The biddin' on them box suppers is gonna be startin' 'fore long. And I don't want no one else to get what Mrs. Carter fixed."

Smiling, the two men walked away from the slaughter in the main street.

The bodies of the dead were carried off for a quick burial. The town's grave diggers would be working through the night. The wounded were taken to the doc's office, with most of those suffering from less serious wounds dumped on the boardwalk in front of the office. The doctor would get to them when he could.

Big Bob laid down the law to the less seriously wounded men. "Soon as you yahoos is able to ride, and that better be within a few hours, you plant your butt in the saddle and git gone from this town. I don't never want to see none of you again."

"You don't have to worry about that," a man with a bloody bandage around the upper part of his right arm said. "Once I git gone, I'll stay gone."

"I hope so," Big Bob told him.

Falcon walked up, leading his horse. "Where are you off to?" Mustang asked.

"I got things to settle with Nance Noonan," Falcon told him. He swung into the saddle. "He made his brags about what he was going to do. I aim to see that he doesn't do them."

"I'll get my hoss and go with you."

"No, boys. You stay here until John Bailey gets him a few permanent hands hired."

Wildcat noticed then that Falcon had tied him a bedroll behind the saddle and his saddlebags were bulging with supplies.

"Dean opened the general store for me," Falcon said. "And I stocked up with what I'll need on the trail. I met with Willard and he knows what to do with my money."

"No good-byes for John Bailey and his family?" Dan asked.

Falcon shook his head. "No. John will understand. I'll write him a letter once I get back to Colorado and make certain my kids are all right."

The men shook hands all around. "Good luck with your new lives, boys," Falcon told the mountain men. "I might drift back up this way one of these days."

That was probably a lie and the mountain men all knew it.

"See you, boy," Big Bob said, lifting a hand in hail and farewell.

Falcon sat his saddle for a moment, smiling at his friends. Then he turned Hell's head and rode out of town and out of the people's lives. He did not look back.

"I didn't like that man when he first arrived in town," the doctor said, walking up and wiping his hands on a bloody apron. "But I soon discovered that first impressions can be wrong."

"He's the spitting image of his pa, that's for shore," Stumpy said. "And behaves just like Jamie, too. Them Noonans is gonna be mighty sorry when Falcon MacCallister catches up with them."

"Takes a sorry son of a bitch to threaten to kill somebody's kids," Dan remarked. "I don't believe I ever heard anybody say they was deliberately settin' out to kill children."

"That's low, for a fact," Big Bob said. He smiled for a moment. "I got me an idea, boys." He motioned for his friends to follow him off a few yards. "I got me an idea on how to finish Nance Noonan's little empire. You boys interested?"

"Shore," Wildcat said quickly. "If it'll help Falcon, let's do it."

"It might involve some breakin' of the law, sorta," Big Bob cautioned.

"Oh, my!" Dan feigned great concern and alarm. "How awful. My goodness, Bob. How could you even think of doin' anything that might be agin the law?"

"I'm shocked right down to my socks," Stumpy said.

"You ain't wearin' no socks," Big Bob told him.

"Yes I is too!" Stumpy said. "I put me on a clean pair last week."

"Oh," Big Bob replied. "Well, 'scuse me. Gather round, boys. We gonna have some hard ridin' to do in a few minutes. This is what we're gonna do. . . ."

Thirty-Two

Somebody rustled the entire Double N herd that night and set Stegman's .44 herd into a wild stampede, running the cattle all over three counties. The men Noonan had left to guard the herd offered no resistance to the rustlers. A range detective later told a court of law that he'd heard that a group of men rode up to the herd early that night. They talked with the cowboys for a moment—it appeared that some money exchanged hands—then the Double N cowboys rode off and were never seen again. And neither was Noonan's herd.

The Nance Noonan empire was crushed, utterly destroyed in one night. Stegman's little domain was likewise trampled into the dust of northern Wyoming. The two men who were once cattle kingpins with dreams of starting a kingdom all their own were ruined financially.

And to make matters worse, they had Falcon MacCallister dogging their back trail with blood in his eyes.

Nance Noonan's wife had left him years back and Rod Stegman had sent his wife to visit friends in San Francisco the week before the slaughter in town. Rod had given her ample funds to see her through any hard times. Which was good thinking on Stegman's part, because she was never going to see her husband or brothers again.

Nance and his brothers and sons and Stegman and his brothers and sons were camped about twenty-five miles from town when a lone hand who'd decided to stay loyal to the brand rode in with the news of their herds.

"We still got some cattle bein' held in other places," Noonan said, after he'd finished stomping around and kicking this and that and cussing to beat the band. "There ain't neither one of us totally ruined."

Stegman looked at his brother-in-law without speaking. Nance just didn't get it: They were finished. They were dead men. Nobody makes threats like he was told Nance had made to a MacCallister and lives for very long. If it took ten years or a lifetime, Falcon would find them both and kill them. It wouldn't make any difference if Nance was to get down on his hands and knees and beg for mercy and forgiveness. . . . Falcon would just shoot him right between the eyes and walk off. And it didn't make one bit of difference that Rod hadn't been there when Nance made his threats or even if Rod would ride off now and turn his back on Nance Noonan. Not one bit of difference in the world.

Rod got up off his blankets and walked over to the coffeepot, pouring himself a cup. He looked around him. The kin of he and Nance were sprawled on the ground, and it was not a bunch to inspire a great deal of confidence.

"Should have stayed where we were," Rod muttered. "We had it made and didn't have sense enough to realize it."

Jack Noonan walked over to the coffeepot and poured himself a cup. He grinned at Rod, exposing rotting teeth. "Me and the boys been talkin', Rod. We figure we can take over that Colorado town where them MacCallisters is settled. What do you think about that?"

Rod Stegman just stared at the man. Take over a town where the MacCallisters lived? The man was a bigger fool than he looked.

"I been told them MacCallister women is fine-lookin'," Jack

continued. "Blond-headed and big-titted, all of 'em. Gits me excited just thinkin' about it."

The wives and kids of the Stegman and Noonan clan had been put on stagecoaches and sent off to safety before the raid on the town. Most would never see their husbands again.

"How's your wife, Jack?" Rod asked sarcastically.

"Ugly," the man replied.

A rifle shot split the night and Jack Noonan went down to the ground in a lifeless heap, the front of his shirt bloody.

Rod Stegman hit the ground and rolled behind a mound of earth. "Falcon MacCallister," he muttered. "Didn't take long for the bastard to find us."

"Douse them fires!" Nance hollered.

Another rifle shot blasted the night and one of the Stegman cousins grunted and sat down hard on the ground, both hands pressing against his bloody stomach. Then he started hollering as the pain hit him.

The fires were killed and the camp went dark. Max Stegman continued his screaming in pain.

"MacCallister!" Rod yelled. "Leave us be, man. You've done ruint us. We ain't got nothin' but the clothes on our backs. Go on and let us be."

The dark silence of the night was the only reply to the man's pleas.

"Shut up your damn beggin', Rod," Nance called. "Or I'll shoot you myself."

"You go to hell, Nance," Rod replied. "My life means more to me than a little bit of pride. I think you're crazy. You and that damn flappin' mouth of yours is what brought all this mess down on us."

Howard Noonan Jr. said, "Shut up your face, Rod. You yeller coyote."

Rod Stegman then offered Howard Jr. a few suggestions about where to put his words, his guns, and his horse. The saddle, too, if it would fit.

Some hundred yards from the camp, lying on a knoll, Falcon listened to the exchange and smiled.

He couldn't catch all the words, but enough of them to know those in the camp were falling apart.

Falcon backed off the knoll and walked to his horse. He mounted up and rode away. He had done all he could do for this night.

Tomorrow was another day.

Rod looked over at the dark shape of his cousin, still sitting on the ground, still screaming in pain. "Damn," Rod muttered.

"Jack's dead," one of Nance's boys called. "Gettin' cold already."

"Wrap him in his blankets, Wardell," Nance ordered. "We'll bury him in the mornin' and say some words."

Say some words? Rod thought. *To the Good Lord? You think He's gonna listen to anything we have to say? You're gettin' crazier with every passin' hour, Nance. The Lord quit us in disgust years ago.*

"He's gone," a lookout hollered. "I heard his horse a few seconds ago. He's headin' south from here."

"Then let's head north," Roan Noonan suggested. "And see if we can lose that crazy man."

We'll never lose him, Rod thought. *You people are walkin' around dead and don't even know it. Hell, so am I!*

"What do you think, Rod?" Nance called.

"I think we're dead men," Stegman said. "All of us. Falcon MacCallister ain't never gonna quit huntin' us until the last man is down."

"The last one of us ain't gonna be in the ground anytime soon," Nance came right back. "Tomorrow at first light, we're gonna start huntin' Falcon. The odds is on our side that we'll get him. Hell, we got him outnumbered by twenty-five or thirty men."

Wouldn't make any difference if we had him outnumbered a hundred to one, Rod thought. "All right, Nance," Rod called. "We'll try it your way come first light."

"I want four men on guard at all times," Nance called. "Work out the schedule and get in position. If we don't, Falcon will circle around and pick us off one at a time. The son of a bitch is worse than a damn stinkin' Injun."

"Hell, he married a squaw," Moe Noonan called. "That makes him just as bad."

"For a fact," Penrod said. "Anybody who would marry up with a red nigger is low as a snake's belly."

"We'd be doin' the world a favor by killin' all them half-breed kids of hisn," Hodge Noonan said. "That's the way I see it. An Injun is an Injun. I don't care what their last name is."

Max Stegman's cries were much quieter now: hideous moans in the night. He was almost unconscious. There was nothing anyone could do for him.

"You be right, brother," Penrod called. "You shore be right 'bout that."

Idiots, Rod Stegman thought. He wondered how he could slip away and get gone from this pack of fools.

But it was almost as if Nance was reading his mind. "Don't be thinkin' of takin' your kin and slippin' away, Rod. You're in this same as the rest of us: to the end."

Rod's temper flared white-hot. In the flames of the newly rekindled fire, he faced Nance. "To hell with you, Nance! I'm done takin' orders from you. Me and my kin is through with all this craziness. This thing 'tween you and Falcon is nothin' but revenge now. It's stupid. It ain't gonna solve nothin' one way or the other."

"You bracin' me now, Rod?" Nance asked, defiance in his voice.

"You bet I am, Nance. Yeah, I am. I'm done. At first light, me and mine are pullin' out and you and yours can go right straight to hell. 'Cause that's where you're headin' real quick if you keep on movin' toward Colorado with doin' harm to Falcon's kids on your mind. I ain't havin' no part of hurtin' no more kids. I'm through with it, and I'm through with you."

"You don't say?"

"I do say, Nance. It's over."

Both men were conscious of their kin moving around, lining up alongside one or the other of the two men who were facing each other in the flame-danced night.

"And I say you're with me to the end of this game."

"Go to hell, Nance."

"No man talks to me like that."

"I just did, Nance."

"You're a fool, Rod."

Stegman laughed. "That's sure the pot callin' the kettle black, Nance."

Nance's eyes narrowed in hate and anger. "You callin' me a nigger, you bastard?"

Rod sighed. He knew he was no mental giant, but compared to his brother-in-law, he was a genius. "No, Nance. That wasn't what I meant."

"You're a liar!"

"Forget it, Nance. Just forget it." He called over his shoulder. "That's it, boys. We're out of here tonight. Pack it up and let's get gone."

"You'll die here 'fore you walk out on me!" Nance yelled. "Drag iron, you coward!"

Nance went for his gun and Rod did the same. Both men were reasonably fast on the draw, but this time Nance was a hair faster. He shot his brother-in-law in the chest just as the camp exploded in sharp lances of gunfire.

Rod went down, falling backward and landing flat on his back on the ground. "Damn!" he whispered to the gunsmoke-filled night. His legs trembled once and then he was still. He closed his eyes and died.

The gunfight was over in only a few seconds. The Noonan crew had the Stegman crew outnumbered and outgunned, and it was carnage.

When the smoke had cleared and the men could once more hear, after their ears had cleared of the yammer of gunfire, Nance looked at the lifeless form of his brother-in-law and said, "We're better off without him anyhow. You .44 men that can still walk, drag your dead outta here and keep on goin'. I don't never want to see none of you again. If you're owed money, ask him for it!" He pointed at the body of Rod Stegman and laughed insanely.

Long after what was left of the .44 outfit had dragged their dead off and saddled up and got gone, Nance sat in the dark and sipped coffee. His thoughts were hate-filled. "Kill all them damn MacCallisters," he muttered. "Ever' one of them. God-damn Falcon MacCallister to hell. I'll burn that damn town to the ground. That's what I'll do."

Several miles away, Falcon rolled up in his blankets and dropped off to sleep. He didn't worry about anyone sneaking up on him, not with his big horse Hell picketed close by. His last thought before sleep took him was this: It would be good to see family again.

Thirty-Three

When Nance rolled out of his blankets the next morning, he found that half a dozen of his own kin had quietly packed up their few possessions and slipped away during the night, taking off for safer parts.

Nance cussed for a moment, but it was halfhearted. The move really didn't surprise him very much. He looked out past the camp: The bodies of Rod Stegman and his men had been dragged out a few dozen yards and covered with rocks and brush. He felt no emotion at the loss of his brother-in-law. The only emotion Nance was experiencing was the one involving his someday killing Falcon MacCallister. That emotion filled him with a great deal of satisfaction.

Nance didn't notice that he and his men were stinking and filthy, their clothing dirty and soiled. He didn't notice that they all looked like a bunch of bums. He didn't care about going back and trying to round up his cattle and starting over. He just wanted to kill Falcon MacCallister and the man's kids.

Nance Noonan had quietly slipped over the line into the darkness of insanity.

The only brothers he had left alive, Penrod and Hodge, were watching him closely. They knew something was very much wrong with their brother, but they didn't know what. Neither one of them was smart enough to understand it was insanity that had taken over their brother's mind. They would figure that out before too much longer.

Nance sat on the ground long after the sun had edged over the horizon and drank coffee and muttered to himself. He drew strange symbols in the dirt while his kin waited for him to tell them to mount up and ride.

But Nance was slipping deeper into the world of madness. He was no longer capable of telling anybody anything that would make any sense.

Most of Nance's cousins saddled up their horses and rode out without saying a word to Nance. Penrod and Hodge and the few kin who were left made no attempt to stop them.

Nance's brothers began talking, talking about Nance. Nance didn't hear them, or if he did hear the words, they didn't register in his sick mind. Words to Nance were now incomprehensible.

One of Nance's cousins walked over to him and slipped his guns out of leather. Nance didn't notice. He continued to hum and talk to himself and draw those strange symbols in the dirt. Occasionally, he would laugh out loud and look around him with eyes that were strangely vacant.

Nance soiled himself, peeing in his already dirty underwear. That was what finally got through to Penrod and Hodge.

"I think somethin' done snapped in his head," Penrod remarked in a low voice.

"He's gone crazy," Hodge said. "I seen an ol' boy lose his marbles one time. He acted just like Nance is actin'."

"What are we gonna do?"

"Hell, I don't know."

Only a few miles away, to the south, Falcon had fixed his breakfast, packed up his gear, and was riding back toward the camp of Nance and his Double N crew. He had made up his mind to finish this little war that day. Hell ate up the distance, moving Falcon closer to what he thought would be a showdown. It would be, but not the kind that he imagined.

Penrod walked over to his brother and shook him by the

shoulder. "Nance. We better get movin' now, boy. You hear me, Brother?"

Nance didn't look up. His brother's words were nothing but a roaring in his head.

"Nance, we got to do somethin', boy. We got to move out of here. It's time to go."

Nance hummed a little song. Penrod walked away from his brother and sat down a few yards away. He rolled a cigarette and smoked it, then rolled and smoked another one. He did not know what to do. He couldn't just leave his brother out in the middle of nowhere.

Penrod looked around the camp at the others. At that moment he saw them all, including himself, for what they really were. They were all filthy and nasty and they all needed a good long hot bath . . . some of them more than one.

"Pitiful," Penrod said, loud enough for all to hear. "We sure don't look like very much."

"You sure as hell don't." Falcon spoke, just a few yards away.

Heads turned, eyes wide in surprise that anyone could slip up on them that easily.

Falcon stood there, both hands filled with .44s. "Unbuckle your gunbelts and kick them away from you," Falcon ordered. "And if you want to die, just touch the butt of a gun and I'll start shooting and I won't stop until my guns are empty and all of you are on the ground."

Gunbelts quickly hit the ground.

"That's better," Falcon said. "Now then, what's wrong with Nance?"

"Somethin's gone bad in his head," Penrod replied. "He's real sick, MacCallister. We got to get him to a doctor."

Falcon looked at Nance. The man was slobbering down the front of his shirt and humming a little melody over and over. Falcon could smell the stink of him from where he stood. It was really rank. Nance had soiled himself, from the way he smelled, more than once.

"A doctor won't be able to do Nance any good," Falcon said. "Just commit your brother to an asylum, probably."

"Reckon where one of them is?" a Noonan cousin asked.

"I don't know," Falcon said. "I don't know what I'm going to do with you, either. I came back to kill you."

That produced a babble of excited voices. Penrod's voice finally overrode all the others. "We're done huntin' you, Mr. MacCallister. That was all Nance's idea anyway. Yeah, we went along with it, 'cause he was the boss. But he ain't nothin' no more. He's . . . goofy."

Falcon certainly couldn't argue that. Falcon looked at each member of the Noonan clan. They were a sorry-looking bunch, for a fact. All the fight was gone from them. They were finished; there was no doubt in Falcon's mind about that.

"All right, Falcon said. "Pack up your possibles and get Nance on a horse. There's bound to be some sort of asylum for the insane down at the capital. Take him down there. But hear me good, boys: Stay clear of Colorado. If I see any of you there, I'll kill you. I won't say a word to you; I'll just shoot you where you stand. You understand all that?"

They all did, and said so several times in very excited voices.

Falcon nodded his head. "Leave your six-guns where they are and ride out of here. Keep your rifles to hunt meat. Move! Get gone right now!"

The Noonan clan was gone in five minutes. Out of sight. Heading for the capital. Nance sat his saddle and hummed and slobbered and peed his underwear.

Falcon walked out from the camp to look at the hastily covered bodies of Rod Stegman and his kin. Coyotes had already been working on them during the night, pulling away the branches and small logs and moving the rocks to get at the bodies. Falcon looked up into the sky. Great black carrion birds were gathering, slowly circling in patient expectation of something to eat.

"Hell with it," Falcon muttered. "It's all over, far as I'm concerned. I'm going home."

Thirty-Four

Several weeks later, Falcon rode into MacCallister's Valley just about an hour before dawn. He topped the ridge and sat his saddle, looking down at the town his parents had founded so many years ago. It appeared to have grown even since he'd been gone. Falcon rode slowly into town, avoiding the main street, and up to the livery stable. There was no one in sight. The liveryman was probably having breakfast. Falcon stabled his horse and rubbed him down and was forking some hay for him when the stableman walked in.

"Well, Mr. MacCallister! Lord have mercy but it's been a while since we've seen you."

"Jake," Falcon greeted the older man. "You be careful around this horse. He'll hurt you."

"I can tell that just by lookin' at him. I'll warn Maxwell to stay clear of him."

"Do that. You seen my kids, Jake? I bet they've grown about a foot since I've been gone."

"Why . . . your children are in St. Louis, Mr. MacCallister. Attending a private school. Your sisters thought that was best for them some months back."

"I see," Falcon spoke the words slowly. He was speechless

for a moment. Then he cleared his throat. "Well, my sisters probably know best. I'll get me some breakfast and then be over at the Wild Rose."

"Yes, sir, Mr. MacCallister. I'll take good care of your horse."

Falcon slipped in the back door of the café to avoid seeing any townspeople . . . he just didn't feel up to that at the moment. The cook spotted him and Falcon held up a warning hand. The cook nodded his head in understanding. Falcon took his breakfast in the storeroom, eating alone, then walked the alley to his saloon, one of the finest and best furnished saloons in the entire state. He used his key to enter through the back door and made his way through the darkness to his office. He lit the lanterns and opened the windows, airing out the large room. Then he made a pot of coffee. While the coffee was brewing, he washed up and shaved, then changed clothes, choosing one of the suits he always kept in a closet in his office.

Falcon poured himself a huge mug of coffee and sat at his desk for a time, his thoughts busy.

"I don't belong here anymore," he muttered. "I don't know why that is, but I can feel it. It's all wrong for me somehow. The Valley has turned sour for me."

One of the swampers came in and was momentarily startled to find Falcon sitting in his office, at his desk, drinking coffee alone. Falcon told the cleanup man to pour himself a cup of coffee and then waved him to a chair.

"Tell me what's been happening since I've been gone," Falcon said.

"Well, sir, your brother, Jamie Ian, has gone to Denver for a time, something about bankin' business and statehood or somethin' like that there. Two of your sisters, Joleen and Mary Kathleen, have gone to San Francisco for something or another, I ain't real sure of the why-fors of that trip . . ."

The man drank his coffee and brought Falcon up to date on his family and the town. The more the man talked, the more Falcon realized that he just didn't fit in to Valley any longer. He was out of place. Something had happened to him during the time he'd been gone.

The town was the same. But Falcon had changed.

Long after the swamper had finished his coffee and begun cleaning up the saloon, Falcon sat in his office and drank coffee and entertained his thoughts.

He wasn't real sure what he should do, but he knew one thing for certain: He wasn't going to stay in town for any length of time.

He would see to some business, visit his brothers and sisters, and then drift. His mind was made up about that. No point in staying in a place where you don't feel you belong.

Falcon went out the back door and walked the backstreets to the livery stable. There, he saddled him a horse and rode up to his parents' grave site. It was clean and had a profusion of flowers planted all around. The MacCallister kids saw to that. The grandkids weren't so attentive, and probably the next generation after them might come up every year or so . . . if that often.

Perhaps that was the way it should be, Falcon thought. Time doesn't stand still; it's constantly moving, and people changing with it.

Falcon stood by the graves for several moments, then put his hat back on his head—a new hat that he'd bought in a town on the way back. On the way back home? No, he thought. *For some reason I can't explain—and perhaps never will be able to explain—this isn't home anymore. I have a business here, I have a large ranch here, I have lots of family here. But this just isn't home for me any longer.*

Falcon turned away from the graves and mounted up, riding out to his ranch. There, he talked to the foreman for about an hour, then rode back into town. He didn't worry about the ranch, for his older brother, Jamie Ian, would see to the paying of all bills and the payroll and so forth . . . just as he'd been doing for a year now.

He spent the rest of the day visiting with those brothers and sisters who were in town. The next day he bought supplies and picked out a packhorse from his own stock at the ranch. He'd used this horse before and knew it would trail well.

He'd told his brothers and sisters that he was going to hit the trail; they would see him again when they saw him.

The next morning, Falcon pulled out before dawn, heading south. He was going to check out New Mexico, he hadn't been there in many years.

As he put more distance between himself and the town, Falcon felt a load being lifted from him. He knew he wasn't cut out to stay in one place for very long. He was a wanderer. Maybe someday he'd settle down again—maybe. But the way he felt at the moment, he doubted it.

He'd seen a lot of country, but he wanted to see more. He wanted to see the Pacific Ocean again and he wanted to see the deserts. He wasn't looking for trouble, and he hoped he wouldn't run into any. He just wanted to wander for a time . . . maybe for a very long time.

He smiled as he thought of Big Bob Marsh and Jack Stump enforcing the law in the town of Gilman. There damn sure wouldn't be any trouble in that town as long as those two were wearing the badges and keeping order. And as wild and woolly as those two were, once they took that oath, they would be arrow-straight.

"All right, Hell, ol' hoss," Falcon said, pushing his hat back on his head. "Let's you and me go see what's over the next hill."